Marc knew what he was looking for. Had known it all along.

He needed someone who could handle the rigors of the North Country, who put common sense before fashion. When Marc got serious, he wanted someone at peace with the land, at home in his house.

A vision of Kayla's coat hanging next to his zipped flannel had him squaring his shoulders.

He couldn't deny the attraction. She invaded his thoughts despite his best efforts. With his father's impending death, Kayla Doherty, R.N., was a wonderful asset. But that was it, he told himself firmly.

Thoughts of Kayla's face came to mind. She was spunk and spice, tucked into one great package.

It was no good. They had nothing in common. She was free flight. He was tied to the land. She looked at the bright side of things, while he took careful measure.

There wasn't much to keep a pretty thing like Kayla happy in the North Country. No cool designer shops, no trendy malls.

His heart hitched. Would she need all that if she had the right man? A husband to love and cherish her all the rest of her days?

RUTH LOGAN HERNE

Born into poverty, Ruth puts great stock in one of her favorite Ben Franklinisms: "Having been poor is no shame. Being ashamed of it is." With God-given appreciation for the amazing opportunities abounding in our land, Ruth finds simple gifts in the everyday blessings of smudge-faced small children, bright flowers, fresh baked goods, good friends, family, puppies and higher education. She believes a good woman should never fear dirt, snakes or spiders, all of which like to infest her aged farmhouse, necessitating a good pair of tongs for extracting the snakes, a flat-bottomed shoe for the spiders and the dirt....

Simply put, she's learned that some things aren't worth fretting about! If you laugh in the face of dust and love to talk about God, men, romance, great shoes and wonderful food, feel free to contact Ruth through her Web site at www.ruthloganherne.com.

Winter's End
Ruth Logan Herne

Steeple Hill®

Published by Steeple Hill Books™

STEEPLE HILL BOOKS

Steeple
Hill®

Recycling programs
for this product may
not exist in your area.

ISBN-13: 978-0-373-87588-7

WINTER'S END

www.SteepleHill.com

Printed in U.S.A.

To every thing there is a season, and a time
to every purpose under the heaven.
—*Ecclesiastes* 3:1

This book is dedicated to the Visiting Nurse Service of Rochester, New York, for their loving hospice care of my mother, Mary Logan Herne.

And to M. E. Logan Herne, from whence my talent came.

This one's for you, Mom.

Acknowledgments:

Thank you to the Canton-Potsdam communities for sharing with a stranger, and a special nod to Canton-Potsdam Hospital for their care of my son, Seth. Their professionalism helped during a difficult time.

Sincere gratitude to Kathy Kennel for her guidance and equal thanks to Mary Connealy, dear friend and beef farmer, who advised proper terminology for Marc's endeavors. All mistakes are mine.

I'm also grateful to the Seekers, our amazing writing group that does whatever proves necessary to help ensure the writing success of each member. You gals rock.

Special thanks to Sandra, Tina, Glynna and Janet and to Alice Clary and OKRWA, whose "Finally a Bride" contest put this manuscript on Melissa Endlich's desk at Steeple Hill Books. Their contest got the ball rolling and I'm forever in their debt.

Thanks and love to my family for their never-ending support, belief and sacrifices. They've overlooked crowded shelves, messy bathrooms, refrigerator science projects and thick dust. Their joy when "The Call" came was heartfelt. I couldn't ask for a better gift from God.

And warm thanks to my beloved pastor, Father Frank Falletta. His counsel, advice and humor are a blessing.

And of course my heartfelt thanks to Melissa Endlich, my editor, who paid me the ultimate compliment when she said I made her cry. Her enthusiasm is positively contagious, and I am ever grateful for her strong vote of confidence.

Chapter One

He stood hard and unyielding, one arm stretched across the entry as if to block Kayla's approach. Light spilled from the angled door of the old farmhouse, warming the mold-hashed porch with a splash of gold, backlighting his rugged frame.

Disadvantaged, Kayla stopped, wind-driven snow chilling her legs despite her well-fitted Ann Taylor pants. *Note to self: If clients leave you in the snow, spend the bucks and buy some of those cute, girly, long underwear. Soon.*

The broad-shouldered man remained shadowed, while lamplight bathed her approach. Well. She'd seen this often enough. The word *hospice* scared people, especially at first. With a small nod, she extended her hand. "Kayla Doherty, Visiting Nurse Service."

Eyes tipped down, he didn't give way, just stood for long seconds, contemplating her hand. Then he moved back, allowing her to enter while ignoring her gesture.

Kayla stepped into coffee-scented air. She breathed deep, wishing she'd had time for a caffeine fix, but weather reports had spurred her to this farm before conditions worsened. Sniffing the air with appreciation, she stood in a sparse but clean entry. The kitchen lay ahead, while a stairway hugged the wall to her left. A throw rug took up one corner of the polished hardwood floor. Various footwear stood along the colorful weave. Reading the silent message, she placed her bargain-basement-priced short-boot Sudinis next to taller, hardier boots. Setting down her tote, she slipped into jeweled, open-toed clogs. She'd tricked-out the shoes herself, using a flashy array of sequins and beads. Her older female patients loved the effect. Fun shoes became an easy conversation starter, and often jogged memories of easier times. She hoped so.

"In January?"

The deep, masculine voice showed disbelief and…scorn? Sure sounded like it.

Kayla didn't try to examine the vibes as she eyed rugged work boots and their tall, rubber companions. Proper barn wear for a man of the fields, a person who faced the prolonged winters of St. Lawrence County, New York, on a personal level. She assumed a look of patience and straightened, facing a good-looking man about her age, his features dimmed by shadows of anger and death, a formidable combination. "They're comfortable for working with patients, Mr.…DeHollander?" She ended on an up-note, making the statement a question, hoping he'd introduce himself.

Um…no.

She'd heard of Marc DeHollander. Women loved to talk about men, and the gals comprising the medical community of greater Potsdam were no exception. The rumor mill labeled Marc total eye candy, with a great personality.

Well. One out of two ain't bad.

She'd dated one of Marc's friends several years back, but Marc had never crossed her path. This man was the right age, but the taciturn expression didn't fit the image. Imminent death had a way of changing a person. Kayla understood that. He'd probably lighten up as time went on.

He glared at the outside thermometer through semi-frosted glass. "Six degrees. Wind chill's at least twenty below. Who wears foolish shoes like that in the dead of winter?"

Kayla scratched her whole "lighten up" theory. Some clients were just downright ornery, regardless. Marc DeHollander's name just got tucked under the heading "resident jerk." She ignored his negativity and swept the small room a glance. "Warm enough in here."

"It's comfortable for Dad." Face taut, he headed into the kitchen. Kayla followed as he tugged the collar of a black turtleneck layered beneath a green plaid flannel. The inside temperature was a little much for his mode of dress.

Kayla understood. End-stage patients often suffered effects of temperature. Extremities chilled, causing discomfort. She glanced around the kitchen.

The room lay spare, like the entry, but neat other than some breakfast clutter. Old-style, glass-fronted cabinets marched in formation around the upper level, offset by wood-fronted, thicker partners below. The cupboards wore a soft shade of green, faded with time. A chipped but uncluttered laminate counter met a backsplash of ivory tile. The effect appeared old and utilitarian, but cared for.

A man's house.

Kayla glanced up at the disgruntled man nearby. A big guy, about six feet and one-eighty, she wondered if he meant to intimidate her. If so, he was doing a good job. She hoisted her work case, determined to make nice. "Would you like to talk first, or introduce me to your father?"

His facial shadows deepened. A muscle in his right cheek twitched. He worked his jaw, then grimaced. "Dad's through here."

Thank you, Mr. Congeniality. Kayla followed him through a dining room into a small bedroom beyond.

A hospital bed dominated the space. The patient opened his eyes as they approached. His look darted, confused. Sighing, he settled into the pillow.

Dreaming, Kayla decided. Normal sleep or drug-induced, she couldn't quite tell, but the startle-awake reflex was not unlike a newborn. Cradle to grave, full circle.

"Your nurse is here." The son's tone left no doubt she wasn't here by his grace.

Kayla bit back a smart remark and focused on the sick man. She approached the right side of his bed, cheerful. "Mr. DeHollander?"

He nodded. His eyes cleared somewhat. "Yes."

She broadened her smile. "I'm Kayla Doherty from Visiting Nurse Service. Dr. Pentrow requested our services. Did he explain that to you?"

The older man glanced Marc's way. "He told us, didn't he, Marc?"

Gone was the look of antagonism that greeted Kayla's arrival. Marc leaned down and brushed a thin lock from his father's brow, his big hands gentle against his father's pale skin. "He did. And a home health aide to help out."

"Having people come to the house could get expensive." The dying man sent a look of concern his son's way. The bottom line had obviously ruled his decision making a long time, a concept Kayla comprehended.

"Your insurance covers both, Mr. DeHollander."

"Does it?" His frown deepened, trying to reason things out.

"Have you had pills this morning?" Kayla inquired. She angled her head and waited for his response.

"Yes," Marc answered, but didn't meet her eye. "Around five-thirty. I gave him two of these." He reached across his father's bed to hand her a bottle.

"You started this yesterday?"

Mr. DeHollander frowned.

Marc nodded. "I picked it up around four when I went into town to get my sister," he explained. This time he looked at her. "Is it the right stuff?"

"Yes," she confirmed. "It's a hydrocodone and acetaminophen mix," she continued, including both men in her explanation. Successful hospice care meant developing a strong working relationship with the caregivers and the patient. At some point the patient would likely lose the ability to participate in his/her own care. A satisfying hospice experience blossomed from establishing good rapport all around.

Kayla was good at working both sides of the bed, and that made her an effective hospice nurse, a fact she'd realized during her first years in the North Country. One of her hospital patients had brought her to faith, to hope, and eventually to her present gig.

She raised the container. "Effective for moderate pain. Side effects generally ease after a few days."

"Side effects like…?" Marc's look sharpened. He glanced at his father, then back to her.

Kayla addressed her patient. "Sleepiness. Confusion. Dreams."

Her list relaxed Pete DeHollander's features. "All of the above."

Glad to have relieved his mind, Kayla offered a proposal. "Since you just started this, I'd like to see if the side effects level out. They usually do as the body acclimates. Can we try that, Mr. DeHollander?" She posed the question with a look of inquiry. "I don't want you to think this is an automatic trade-off. Less pain for a state of confusion. We have lots of things at our disposal. Your care will be based on what works for you. Adjustments in meds are common."

He contemplated her words, then looked at Marc. "I'm not thinking too clear," he admitted. He fiddled with the uppermost blanket, nervous. "What do you think?"

Kayla met Marc's eyes across the bed. She read the look in them. His expression offered resignation and little else. He'd do what he had to do, but it was plain he didn't like the choices. Whether his unease stemmed from the question or the situation, she had no idea. His gaze narrowed. "If we keep Dad on this medicine, the side effects might clear up?"

"Yes. If they don't, I'll call the doctor and we'll modify the meds. Our goal is to provide sufficient pain relief with minimal side effects."

"And it can be done?"

She scrunched her face and offered Marc a firm nod. "Absolutely." She hoisted her tote onto a side table. "I have an amazing bag of tricks, gentlemen."

The old man smiled. When he did, his gray-green eyes sparked with life. For just a moment, Kayla envisioned the man he'd been before his long battle with cancer.

Her throat tightened. She controlled the impulse to sympathize too much by dragging a chair alongside the bed. "You boys could at least ask a girl to sit down."

The old man looked affronted by his carelessness. "I don't know where our manners have gone," he exclaimed, surprised.

Marc's look hardened. He kept his eyes trained on Kayla, studying her. Fighting the rise of negative emotion, she addressed them both. "We should talk. I want you to know what to expect of me, what kind of care I'll be giving and what choices you have."

"Do those choices include a nurse who isn't afraid to get dirty and knows enough to wear sensible shoes midwinter?" Condescending, Marc swept her pert, polished nails and well-fitted blazer a look of disdain, his expression intimating she didn't have enough muscle to get the job done.

Ouch. The young farmer's cutting appraisal hit home. Striving to remember why peaceful conflict resolution was a *good* thing, Kayla faked a look of calm. She'd dealt with antagonistic families before. His anger wasn't all that unusual. Death managed to bring out the best in some people, but that wasn't a universal reaction.

She kept her voice confident, but didn't negate the hint of challenge in her reply. "We have a group of hospice nurses, male and female. We work individually, concentrating on specific cases. But—" she added, strengthening the note of reassurance "—someone is always on call so there's no lapse in service." She addressed her words to the older DeHollander. "If your nurse is off or away, you'll still have help regardless of the day or the hour."

"Makes sense," the older man agreed, his expression serious but accepting.

"Of course you can request a different nurse," Kayla continued. Her gaze encompassed father and son. "That's not a problem, because your nurse acts as your case coordinator, overseeing all aspects of your care." She turned and met Marc's eyes, unflinching. "Facing the loss of a loved one is difficult enough without personality clashes making it worse. Our job is to make things easier for you, Mr. DeHollander." She shook her head. "Not rougher."

Pete struggled more upright. "Why would we want someone

different?" He glanced from one to the other before his gaze settled on Marc. His voice lost the fog of confusion. "What's going on?"

Marc squared his shoulders, eyes narrowed. "Nothing, Dad. I just want to make sure your treatment is taken seriously, every step of the way."

Kayla stared him down. He didn't squirm. She lifted her left brow. "Laughter is the best medicine. Haven't you heard?" Deliberately slow, she winked at the older man. "It aids in pain reduction, increased glucose tolerance, emotional bonding and vascular function." She gave Pete a perky shrug and a smile. "All for the price of a belly laugh. Fairly cheap, I would say."

"The price is right, sure enough." Pete grinned back at her, restoring the twinkle in his eyes. The smile made him look more vibrant, more alive.

Marc's expression noted that. His look softened. He reached out a hand to his dad's head in a gesture of comfort. "I've got to take care of some things in the barn. My cell phone's on." He patted his side clip. "Call if you need anything."

"I will," Pete promised. "Sorry about that business last night."

Marc frowned. "You remember that?" At his father's look of surprise, he added, "You were pretty confused, Dad."

"I'm not dead yet," the older man retorted.

"But definitely incapacitated," Kayla inserted. She kept her tone helpful and amused.

Pete DeHollander joined the game with a look Kayla's way. "Under the weather."

"Down, but not out."

"Rounding third and heading for home."

"And the crowd goes wild." Kayla raised her arms and widened her smile.

Marc stood, glowering. "I'm glad you two find this so—" Face tight, he drew a sharp breath, his jaw rigid. "Whatever. Some of us have work to do."

He strode out, his footfall decisive against the wide-planked floor.

Kayla watched him go with regret. She'd hoped a little humor might lighten him up, but no. She'd only angered him. Obviously the tact and diplomacy she'd been praying for needed fine-tuning.

Fine tuning? Her conscience prodded. *How about major structural repairs? Run after him, Doherty. Maybe the guy's got a paper cut. You can apply a salt-water rinse followed by a splash of fresh lemon. Really make his day.* Kayla sucked a breath and sighed.

"He'll be fine."

She turned back to Pete. "You think?"

Pete nodded. "Had a rough night. Lost a cow and a calf. She got bred in the wrong season and Marc didn't pick up on it. A lot going on, you know?"

Oh, Kayla knew. Doctor visits, hospitalizations, surgeries, tests, meds. All time consuming. And scary.

"By the time Marc realized she needed a C-section, it was too late."

"They died?" Kayla opened her laptop and stood to record Pete's vital signs. "They both died?"

"It happens." He shrugged. "Not often with Marc's cattle, though. He's got a good eye for line and crossbreeding. Hybrid vigor. He's made a nice business of it."

"Has he?" Kayla tried to shroud the doubt in her voice. From the looks of the farm buildings, Marc could use a lesson in painting, and dead cows didn't sound all that successful. And two at once? How sad.

"Farming's like life," Pete spouted, drawing himself up so she could examine him. "Full circle. Birth, death and everything in between."

"I guess." Kayla thought of the choices available in this day and age. Why would anyone farm?

She had no idea. Extremes of weather, fluctuations of market, never-ending days of slogging through muck and mud, snow and slush. What normal person chose that over climate-controlled nine-to-five, paid vacations, full benefits and a 401(k)?

Huh. She'd just answered her own question.

In her brief interlude with Marc DeHollander, she recognized normalcy as a relative feature. The father had it in abundance. Warm. Kind. Sociable, despite his illness.

The son was fresh out.

Chapter Two

Marc finished loading the carcasses as his cell phone rang. He tugged off his gloves and fumbled the narrow instrument, his broad fingers awkward in the cold. "DeHollander."

"It's Stu," the truck driver reported. "I've finished at Brall's. I'm heading your way."

Marc worked his jaw, regretful. Last night's time glitch had cost him the life of a young cow and her calf, no small thing in the beef business. Even one as strong as his. "They're loaded. I'll wait for you at the end of the drive."

"I'll pull alongside," Stu replied. "Sorry you lost 'em."

"Me, too."

They both understood how disease could spread from one farm to another via contaminated wheels and equipment. Even soiled boots could track pathogens into a barn. Marc took no chances. He'd worked too long, too hard to get his beef operation up and running. As a result, his business had grown strong, a credit to his time and patience.

Marc kicked himself for not calling his veterinary friend out sooner. He hadn't notified Craig until it was too late, the calf trapped too long in the birth canal. A stupid mistake. Slipshod. And he was never careless with his business. That was why he turned a profit on both the feed store and his cattle production.

But Jess had mustered a bee in her bonnet over something

crucial to a fourteen-year-old girl, Dad was disoriented after his new medicine and Marc hadn't made it back to the barn in time to see something was dreadfully wrong.

He revved the engine and edged the tractor bucket off the ground. The animals jerked as the shovel lurched. The cow's hock shifted and hung, midair. Marc frowned but relaxed as the bulk of the body settled into the crook of the shovel. Sighing in resignation, he shoved the tractor into gear and headed up the drive.

Looking way too stylish for a harsh North Country winter, the slim, blonde nurse approached her car as the tractor rumbled toward her. She watched him navigate the big John Deere, her blue-eyed gaze sweeping the sad load, the hock protruding from the bucket's edge.

Her eyes narrowed. She stood still, despite the cold, the trendy pea coat no match for the frigid temperatures. The spunky jacket looked good on her, reminding Marc that appearances outweighed everything for girls like Kayla Doherty. Her face tightened at the sight of his loaded bucket. Disgust? Dismay? From his vantage point atop the enclosed tractor, Marc couldn't be sure.

He winced. Was this what he wanted for his father's care? His buddy's old girlfriend, with her insensible shoes, expensive clothes and saucy attitude? Oh, yeah, he remembered Craig dating her, bemoaning her panache and love of style. Definitely not North Country material. No way. No how. But here she was, pert and pretty in his driveway, cringing at the thought of death.

Why did they need a nurse, anyway? Why was his father so anxious to throw in the towel? Was he that tired of the fight, that worn?

Where there's life, there's hope.

The adage came straight from Pete's mouth, and Marc put stock in the saying. He'd brought some pretty sick animals back from near-death experiences. Maybe that's why it hurt so much to wrestle the reaper and lose as he had last night.

The idea of waging a similar battle for his father had been wrested from his hands, and Marc didn't like that. Dr. Pentrow tossed around terms like visiting nurses. End stage. Translation: Give it up. Party's over. Call the undertakers, have 'em ready a spot.

Shoulders tight, Marc continued along the drive, not pausing until he braked at the road's edge. As the nurse pulled next to him in her sporty red car, he averted his face. He didn't need her disapproval at the nature of his work. In a way, it wasn't much different than hers. You battled, you toiled and in the end, death came regardless.

But at least he had sense enough to wear proper footwear.

"Horses all set?"

Jess nodded as she shrugged out of her coat. She kicked off her boots, pegged the khaki-green jacket and headed for the kitchen.

"Jess." Marc angled a look to the entry floor.

Jess groaned, turned and righted the boots, exasperated. "Better?"

Marc hid a smile as he stirred a pot of simmering soup. "Much. How old do you have to be before you just do it?"

She laughed. "An indeterminate factor." Grinning at the shake of his head, she hugged him around the waist and slid a look to the foyer. "You'd probably have to care, first."

No joke there. Marc mock-scowled. "That much I understand. I've seen your room."

"I know where everything is," she claimed, grabbing a cookie from the counter. After the first bite, she snatched another. "Usually."

"Mmm-hmm," Marc rejoined, skeptical. Hadn't they been late for church because she couldn't locate her favorite pants?

It seemed peculiar to walk into the white clapboard building after so much time, then late, besides. They'd drawn looks as they proceeded to the front instead of sliding into the empty last pew. His fault for letting Jess pick the seat.

Dad had gone with Jess these last years while Marc busied himself with farmwork. Always something to do on a cattle holding, regardless of weather, and Sunday mornings were no exception. Neither were Wednesday evenings. Or Saturday potlucks. Busy times, all.

But their current situation altered things. Pete's weakness minimized his options, so Marc was pressed into a new fraternal duty. He'd accompanied Jess at Christmas and this past week, feeling hypocritical. Attendance at church wasn't high on his priority list.

But there was nothing he'd deny his father, even taking his adolescent sister to a service that meant little.

"Grace looks huge," Jess commented around bites. More through them, actually. "I can't wait to see the foal."

"Next month. Valentine's Day, I figure. Thereabouts."

"If it's a girl, we'll name her Sweetheart," Jess declared.

"Boys can't be sweethearts?"

"Please."

"Well, not at your age," he added, firming his voice.

That brought a glare. "I'm nearly fifteen."

"Six months," he corrected.

"Five-and-a-half," Jess shot back. "In a little over a year, I'll get my driver's permit. Then I can work toward my license."

Marc sent her a teasing look. "If your room's clean."

"Grr."

A third voice interrupted them. "Have you gotten so old you don't kiss your dad anymore?"

Jess crossed the room in a flash. "I didn't want to wake you." She grabbed her father into a gentle hug. "You were sound asleep when I got home."

"Pills." Pete's voice sharpened. He sounded disgusted.

"But you're up," she continued, "and dinner's almost ready."

Marc gave Jess extra points for her positive outlook. She always saw the bright side where their father's care was concerned. "I'll set another place at the table."

Marc gave his father a once-over. "You don't seem as foggy. Not like last night." He didn't add how scared he'd been, to see his father dazed and confused. Pete DeHollander had been a caricature of his true self. Not pretty.

Pete shook his head. "That part's better."

"Good."

The phone rang. Marc grabbed the receiver, one eye on the stove, the other on the sports section. The Division One hockey team of St. Lawrence University was pouring on the steam as their season progressed. Sweet. Hockey and North Country were synonymous. If you lived in a climate rife with snow and ice, you better find something to make winter palatable.

"Mr. DeHollander?"

"Yes?" Marc pulled his attention from the scores with effort.

"Kayla Doherty," the voice continued.

Marc bit back a groan. She still sounded perky, even this late. Was it a blonde thing? At the moment he wasn't sure. And really didn't care. As he turned to his father, she continued, "I wanted to follow up on the meds situation from this morning. Are the side effects still as strong or are you feeling more in control?"

"Wrong man." Offering no explanation, Marc handed the phone to his father, fighting the rise of disapproval. "Your nurse."

Pete's eyes narrowed. "Miss Doherty?" His features relaxed as he listened. No way could Marc miss the ease in tension that had been prevalent the past few days, as if the nurse held all the answers.

Yeah. Right.

"No, that's fine," Pete told her, a brow shifting up. "We do sound alike. Everyone says so." He glanced Marc's way, paused, then bobbed his head again, eyes crinkling. "Yes, much better, thank you. Tired, but not confused."

Marc listened, unabashed, as his father continued.

"I'd like that, too, Miss Doherty." A brief silence followed, then Pete shrugged assent, his look intent. "Kayla, then." His face relaxed, his eyes taking on a youthful gleam at whatever she was spewing, then he chuckled out loud. "I expect that *would* work with man or beast." He nodded once more before he firmed his voice. "That would be nice. Thursday's good." Pete said his goodbye and disconnected.

Marc's inner turmoil shifted upward. "What would work?"

"Hmm?" Pete turned Marc's way while Jess hung up the phone.

The younger man pushed down impatience. "You told her something would work with man or beast. An odd thing to say to a nurse, Dad."

Pete laughed again, a good sound, no matter what inspired the reaction. Or who. "She's feeding cookies to a neighbor's dog who offered to take a chunk out of her as she approached her apartment. Seems the owner's away and the gate latch is broken."

"Cookies?" Why did he *not* have a hard time picturing that? Marc humphed. "Who gives cookies to a dog?"

"It would work on me," Jess proclaimed. "I could live on cookies."

"Empty calories," stated Marc, his voice gruff. Somehow the picture of the leggy, blonde nurse thwarting a dog attack with cookies increased his ire. Too late he realized his tone and words might be misconstrued.

Jess's look confirmed his fear. Weight was an issue since puberty set in, and he'd just put his size twelve shoe in his big, stupid mouth. "I just meant—"

"I know what you meant." Her eyes clouded. She looked away. "I'll pass on supper, thanks."

"Jess, I—"

"I'll be upstairs. See you later, Daddy." She swiped a kiss to her father's cheek before charging from the room, her lower lip thrust out. Marc was pretty sure it trembled, too.

"Oh, man—"

"Marc, you've got to use a little sensitivity around her," Pete protested.

Marc shot him an incredulous look. "I didn't mean to hurt her feelings. My mind was on cows, how we strive to balance energy food versus nutritional needs to achieve a proper ratio of fat to lean. Good marbling."

His father eyed him, his features a blend of amazement and disbelief. "I don't think that explanation's going to do it for her," Pete chided. "Comparing her to a cow might make matters worse. If that's possible." He rubbed a hand across his jaw. "I'm still trying to figure it out myself."

"She's too sensitive," Marc returned.

"She's fourteen." Pete's tone stayed matter-of-fact. "That's how they are."

"And how am I supposed to know that?" Marc asked. He slid into the chair opposite his father. "My experience with adolescent girls is limited to what I gleaned seventeen years ago in eighth grade, and let me assure you, I was more caught up with the physiological than the psychological." He hoped his arched eyebrow clarified his declaration.

Oh, yeah. A grin tugged his father's mouth.

"So my training is zip," Marc went on. "Zilch. Nada." He raised his hands up, palms flat, displaying their emptiness. "Knowing that, you might want to discard any notion you have of dying, dial up Kaylie or Kylie or whatever her name is, and tell her you've decided to outlive us all because I can't raise Jess on my own and not make a complete mess of things."

His father met his gaze. His voice stayed level. "I can't change the inevitable, Marc. I would if I could, at least 'til my work's done. You know that."

That was part of the trouble. Marc *didn't* know that. He heard his father's words but couldn't believe them.

Pete's body was wearing out from choices the older DeHollander made long ago. A steady smoker, Pete's actions probably brought this cancer on, and Marc had no clue how to rationalize that. In Marc's mind, sucking poisons into your system was asking for trouble. Marc didn't understand the choice and he sure didn't like it.

Everyone else seemed okay with the eventuality of the prognosis. They used terms like natural. Understandable.

Their acceptance exacerbated Marc's anger. His father's cancer wasn't inevitable, but avoidable. Watching the fabric of his family torn by years of bad choices, Marc tried to deal with both sides of the issue and came up short.

Jess had come to terms with Pete's illness, on the surface at least. She seemed determined to make her father's last months stress-free. Quite a commitment for a hormone-stricken teen. A teen who shouldn't be left with no one but Marc to steady her path to adulthood. At fourteen, Jess needed an understanding mother and a thriving father. Through no fault of her own she had neither.

Resentment choked him. He knew his feelings were counter-productive, but had no clue how to change them. Mounting thoughts swelled, emotions he didn't dare show. Suppressing the urge to throw something, he stood to finish supper, his fingers tight, his shoulders tense, a rod of anger anchoring his steps.

In one day he'd managed to lose a pair of livestock, insult his father's nurse, ruin his sister's wobbly self-esteem and add weight to a dying man's pressures.

And it was only the dinner hour. If his streak continued, he might be able to instigate World War III by bedtime. Nuclear holocaust. Plagues of locusts.

As long as his luck held steady.

Chapter Three

A welcome blast of heat greeted Kayla as the pneumatic door of the VNS offices swung open.

Christy Merriton glanced up, dropped a questioning look to her leather-strapped wristwatch and compressed her lips. "What are you doing here?"

Kayla met the supervisor's frown with a half grin. "I, um, *work* here."

"Not at six-oh-five," Christy argued. "At six-oh-five you should be home making supper. Or on a date. Maybe curling up with a good book. Having a life."

"About that…" Kayla indicated her boss, then tapped her more feminine timepiece. "You're here."

"Mmm-hmm." Christy stood, stretched, then leaned down, her fingers tapping computer keys. The main drive shut down as the printer kicked in, the sound marking the end of a long day. "I have an excuse. Brianna gets picked up from basketball practice at six-thirty, so it didn't make sense for me to drive home and come all the way back. What's your story?"

"Supplies." Kayla raised her tote. "I saw the lights and figured I could restock. Save time tomorrow."

Christy looked unconvinced. "I'd have bought that line an hour ago. It's after six, Kayla." She studied the younger woman, then nodded toward the door. "Go home."

"Consider me gone." Kayla opened her case and moved to the supply cabinets. "Right after I load up."

Christy stepped to the printer and retrieved a fresh pile of assignment tickets. She handed a slim stack to Kayla. "Tomorrow's schedule."

"Awesome. Now I don't have to stop by at all. Thanks." She eyed the uppermost printout and tapped a wild rose pink nail against the second name, the glossed color reminding her of summer. Sun. Sand. Flowers. "This one came back from Arizona, and this one," her finger scaled down, "from Florida. Why would they do that?"

The simplicity of Christy's look underscored her meaning. "To die."

Her words rang true. Several of Kayla's recent patients had sought the softer climes of southern states after retirement, opting away from the snow and ice. But in those final months, when fate held the winning hand, many came home, wanting the familiarity of what they knew first. Family. Friends. Church.

Back outside, the storm pelted her with slanted snow, stinging cold. Shoulders hunched, she headed to her Grand Am, its warmth a respite.

She was a Thomas Kinkade girl caught in a David Morrow canvas. Winter lovers esteemed Morrow's work. His snow-filled landscapes offered haunting insight into the breathtaking reality of upper latitude cold. Thought-provoking. Windswept. Sometimes brutal. North Country, through and through.

Kayla preferred sprigged cottages and thatched roofs. Decorative grasses, grown in abundance. Sources of light, teeming with hope.

Winters at the forty-fifth latitude outlasted their welcome. She hadn't given that proper consideration when she'd made the move north after graduating from the nursing program in Syracuse. Her goal then: financial, financial, financial. The Potsdam community had offered to forgive student loans and extend her a nice paycheck in exchange for years of service. The proposal sounded good to a young woman who'd struggled to make ends meet for as long as she could remember.

But now her contract was nearly up. What next? She had no idea. She put the car in gear and aimed for Route 11, her headlights battling the snow.

Numerous options lay open to an experienced nurse. She'd spend the next few months exploring them. Because her afterwork life was fairly nonexistent, she'd have plenty of time.

That thought could have drawn a sigh, but she resisted the pity party. Focused, she gripped the wheel and peered through the snow, wondering how warm a person would be to be warm enough. Someday she'd find out firsthand.

Kayla wiggled her thermostat on Wednesday night, listening for the magic click that promised heat.

Nothing.

She thumped a corner of the radiator and paused, hopeful, glad she didn't chip her polish with the useless maneuver.

The upright, ivory-painted contraption maintained its silence, barely warm. The effect across the room proved negligible. Brittle weather stripping, designed to bind the storm window to the frame, was equally ineffective. The flow of chilled air across the ice-encrusted pane made her living room frosty.

The bedroom stayed warmer. The windows in that room actually sealed. And she had a comforter she'd bought two years ago, her one concession to comfort, down-filled, thick and cushy. She'd made a duvet cover for the layered blanket, one of her first sewing projects, and she'd been proud of the careful work. Of course the piece was comprised of straight lines, intersecting, and who couldn't sew a straight line with today's machines? Still, it became a job well done. A new skill learned.

She faced the living room, hating her choice. Skip the hour of television she'd promised herself, or drag the comforter to the couch and shroud herself in cumbersome down fluff, the only way she'd be warm enough to enjoy the show. Moving the dinosaur-era TV to the bedroom wasn't an option.

Grumbling, she trudged to the bedroom, dragged off the heavy throw, and retraced her steps. With care she arranged her nest and climbed in, hot chocolate steaming at her side.

She'd be toasty warm someday. She'd made herself that pledge nearly two decades back, a mere child, and now the woman stood on the verge of the goal. Warmth. Hearth. Home. And flowers in abundance, blooming here and there. The kind of life she'd wished for, longed for, prayed for. Normal, by most people's standards.

Close. So close.

Vi Twimbley's attic apartment wasn't the most reliable home, but the price was right. Every two weeks Kayla banked wages toward a place of her own. Her own little bungalow, well-lit, a cottage rigged out just for her. Flowers in the summer. Vines, creeping upward, covering craggy surfaces. Ornamental grasses waving in the breeze.

And maybe, just maybe, a cat.

Thursday's dawn gave Kayla a better look at the DeHollander home. Thin light shrouded the farm, making the rough exteriors look worse against the pristine snow. What could be a pretty porch offered woebegone protection from the biting wind under peeling paint. Kayla snugged her collar close as she climbed out and surveyed her surroundings.

A sign on the nearest barn proclaimed the wonders of scientifically blended dog food and medicated chicken feed. She pursed her lips as she scanned other outbuildings.

Barns. Sheds. Grain bins. A light in a distant barn drew her attention, its glow fighting through an upper window hazed with dirt. Her gaze locked on the dingy, light-enhanced glass as her thoughts tunneled back to cold, hungry, silent nights, fed by the unreachable square of light and the chill of her limbs.

Nope. Not going there. Not now. Not ever.

She set her jaw and withdrew her gear, pushing memories aside, then strode up the shoveled walkway.

"How're we doing today?" Kayla didn't wait for an answer when Pete opened the door himself. His tranquil features spoke for him. She smiled, knowing his reprieve might be short-lived, but grateful for his increased comfort. "Better, I'd say."

"Much." The older man swept the door wide. "Come in. It's cold out there."

"It is," Kayla agreed. The interior warmth enveloped her again. For an old house, this one held its heat well. Either that or the DeHollanders had massive heating bills. "That makes your entry twice as welcome."

He smiled back, pleasing her. With the host of medicinal combinations at her disposal, there was no reason Pete DeHollander should suffer. She appraised him as she peeled off her boots. "You've been up and around?"

"Yup. Feels good."

"I bet."

Pete hesitated, then shrugged. "Can't do much, though. Get tired easy."

"Understandable." Kayla slipped into her jeweled clogs and caught his glance as she straightened. "Yes, these are the shoes your son objects to."

"Pretty," Pete offered, his tone easy. "Your toes don't get cold?"

Kayla laughed. "Not here. I couldn't wear these at my place because my apartment's like an Arctic wasteland. I double my socks to avoid frostbite."

"Heat don't work?"

"That's debatable," Kayla answered. He turned toward the kitchen. She followed. "My landlady claims it works fine, but my place is on the third level of a three unit. The hot water rises through two other families before getting to me. By then, it's barely warm."

"She won't fix it?" Pete eyed her, surprised, as if wondering how such a thing could be. Huh. In Kayla's world of never-ending landlords, Vi Twimbley ranked pretty high, though that wasn't saying much.

"Says she can't fix what ain't broke," Kayla quoted verbatim. "She offered me the second floor apartment last year, but the rent is higher. I decided I'd deal with the cold and guard my cash flow."

"Smart girl." Pete sank into a kitchen chair. He sighed a hint of relief, his only concession to his grave condition. Kayla drew up the chair next to him and slid a small box his way. "From the Main Street Bakery."

"Them wafery things?" His smile made the effort to stop worthwhile.

"Yes." Kayla laughed at his description of Rita Harriman's tender French pastries. "Would you like coffee to go with them, Mr. D.?"

The use of his familiar nickname hiked his smile. "Yes, I would. Will you have a cup?"

"Absolutely." Sharing the hospitality of her client families bridged a gap that could hinder care. She rose and eyed the carafe. "I'll brew fresh, if that's all right?"

Pete laughed. "Yes. Those dregs are the remnants of Marc's early pot. He likes to get up and out once Jess catches the bus. And before, truth be known. You might want to make a full pot, though. No doubt he'll be up for some before long."

"Okay." Reaching into the nearest cupboard, Kayla withdrew a bag of fair trade coffee and a fresh filter. The bag snagged her interest. Pretty cool. A farmer supporting other farmers on an international scale. Marc gained a point in his favor. Then she recalled his Monday morning attitude.

Make that half a point.

"How old is Jess?" Kayla asked as she measured.

"Fourteen."

"Interesting age."

"It is that." Pete paused, then added, "But Jess isn't too bad. Does us proud in school and on the farm. Like Marc, she got her mama's brains."

"I think you're selling yourself short," Kayla argued while the coffeemaker sputtered. "You seem pretty quick on the uptake, Mr. D."

"Not like my wife." Silence followed the assertion. He drew a deep breath, his gaze on his hands. "There was a brilliance about her."

He missed her. Kayla understood loneliness, even in a room full of people. "How long were you married?"

"Seventeen years."

Kayla frowned. Pete read her expression. "You aren't from around here."

"No."

"Ari left about fifteen years back. Made for interesting talk."

Ouch. "A dubious honor."

"Yes."

"But Jess…"

"Was an infant. Rough time, all around."

"I guess."

"But we did all right," the older man testified. "Between Marc and me, we did okay by Jess."

Kayla laid a hand over his. "I'm sure you did. She's in school?"

"Freshman at the high school."

"Does she play any sports?" Kayla rose as she asked the question. The coffeemaker had gone silent. Feeling at home, she retrieved two hefty mugs.

"Jess rides and does horse shows," Pete explained. "Marc trucks her and Rooster around, using time he probably should spend here." Pete raised his gaze to the sprawling farmyards. "A farmer only gets so many good days and fine weekends, but Marc had Jess on a horse before she could walk. She rides like she was born to the saddle."

"That's very cool." Kayla weighed the time frame. Summers never had enough weekends to accommodate everything slated for good weather. Work, home repair, social functions. From Pete's depiction of Jess's pastime, Kayla caught a glimpse of the younger DeHollander's conflict. He was a one-man band, without the juggling monkey. Filing the information, she raised a thick-based cup into the air. "Guys' mugs. I love 'em."

"Nothing fancy."

"But they hold a solid cup of joe." Kayla flashed him a smile as she poured. "Smells good."

"You're not going to lecture me on the evils of caffeine?" Pete teased, pretending surprise. "What kind of nurse are you?"

"The kind that picks her battles," Kayla retorted. She crossed to the refrigerator and pulled out a plastic jug. "Besides, I'd have to point the same finger right back at myself. You buy milk?" She turned to face him. "When you've got all those cows?"

"Beef cattle."

The deep voice startled her. She turned. Marc's flat and un-friendly expression did little to enhance his gasp-out-loud good looks, and that seemed a crying shame. For a moment she wondered if God had been distracted by some urgent need when Marc DeHollander moved to the front of the "winning person-ality" line, then reminded herself that blaming God was unfair. Jerks generally achieved their status on their own, and most de-servedly. She arched a brow his way.

"Dairy cattle give milk," he continued, his stance rigid.

"They're mammals," she corrected. "They all give milk. Those of the female gender, that is."

His expression toughened another shade. "Not for commer-cial purposes."

"I see." She slid her gaze to the pot. "Would you like coffee, Mr. DeHollander?"

The formal name tightened the hard set of his eyes, but his lips twitched. Either he'd actually considered gracing her with a smile or he had some mild form of palsy.

Kayla put her money on the palsy.

"I'll get it." He moved through the room with the outdoor elegance of a man comfortable with himself. He'd left his boots at the door and his socks were a heathered blend of brown, ivory and gray. They looked warm. Kayla eyed them with a hint of envy, then glanced up. "Excuse me."

Marc didn't bring his cup to the table. He stood with his back to the sink, arms folded, waiting for the coffee to cool. He frowned, then glanced around. "Who? Me?"

Difficult man. Could you try being nice? Kayla nodded. "Your socks." She pointed down.

"Yes?"

He drew the word out deliberately, his voice tinged with dis-belief. She ignored the cool bite. "They look warm."

He paused too long, stretching his response to make her feel awkward. No way would she let him see his strategy worked. She held her ground and her tongue until he answered. "They are."

"Where did you get them?"

He swept her feet a glance. "Your toes cold?"

She fought back a retort and counted to five. Why were her sassy clogs such an issue? Couldn't he answer a simple question without being a jerk?

"I walk for exercise," she answered. She didn't mention she needed the socks to keep her feet warm at home. That would give him an opening to make some schlocky remark about her shoes. "Warm socks would be nice."

"Ostrander's."

"The bed and breakfast?" Marc DeHollander didn't seem like the B and B type.

"They have a wool shop beneath the house."

"Really?" Kayla pictured the farm's bucolic setting. Tourists spoke highly of the accommodations. "Thanks." She nodded. "I'll stop by."

"Better check the hours," Pete warned. Kayla turned his way. "During winter, the family might not be around as much."

"Good point. I'll call first. Were they expensive?" She turned back to Marc.

He looked as though he wasn't sure what to make of her or the discussion. "Quality has its price. They do the job."

And the award for warm and fuzzy personality goes to…anyone but you, Farmer Boy.

Kayla swallowed words she would have voiced short years past and nodded. "That's the important thing, isn't it?"

His eyes pierced, the gray-green color flint and flat. Long seconds ticked by before he switched his attention to his father, the move dismissive. "I'm picking Jess up from Nan's later. Anything you need from town?"

Pete patted the small package. "I had a hankering for some of them filled wafery things. Kayla got some for me."

"Wasn't that nice?" The edge in Marc's voice told Kayla she'd stepped on his toes again.

She bit back a groan. What was it with this guy? Wasn't anything easy? Did bringing his sick father a box of Napoleons constitute war?

Marc rolled his shoulders. With one long swig, he drained his cup and plunked it onto the scarred counter. "Anything special you'd like for supper, Dad? I can defrost the meat."

Pete mulled, then said, "Stew."

Marc smiled.

Whoa. Secret weapon, highly effective. Definitely part of his arsenal that should be kept sheathed, only to be revealed with a mandatory warning to all females within relative proximity. Kayla's heart beat a rat-a-tat-tat against her breastbone, a totally adolescent reaction. *Stop. Stay cool. Distant. Step away from the smile. Avert your eyes. Whatever it takes.*

The grin held a high-amp flash of teeth and a dimple that should have made him look soft, but didn't. Just the opposite. The man looked good. Self-assured. Confident and happy.

His father grinned in response. Kayla looked from one to the other, mystified. "Is there something I'm missing? A private joke?"

Marc shifted his weight. "Family stuff."

Her spine tightened. The rebuff was meant to keep her in her place. He'd drawn a line in the sand, a marker of domination.

She didn't need his marker. She knew her place. Always had. With an audible intake of breath, she reached into her laptop bag and withdrew papers. "Are you up to doing paperwork, Mr. D.?"

He nodded. "I'm okay."

"Good." She smiled at him and worked to focus on the more rudimentary aspects of her job. Sparring with Marc would get her nothing but aggravation. She didn't need that. With his father's terminal condition, Marc didn't either. The guy was spoiling for a fight, and she refused to give him the satisfaction. Maybe she could suggest a night at the gym, a bout with a punching bag. Did gyms still have punching bags?

She didn't know, but figured Marc might feel better after an evening-long session with one. Hours of repetitive thrashing could release his anger at a situation beyond his control. And beyond hers, for that matter. She'd been assigned to do a job, and had every intention of performing her task to the best of her ability.

With or without Marc DeHollander's approval.

Chapter Four

Marc pulled into Nan Bedlow's at 5:40 p.m. He'd spent the better part of the day moving rotational fencing, allowing the herd new winter grazing on old cornstalks. His shoulders ached and his back knew the strain of bending and shifting, but he'd finished the job.

The task wasn't rhythmic like when he partnered with his dad. Then, one would drive, one would stake and unspool the wire to the plastic insulators, and they'd leapfrog one another to keep the installation moving. They could encircle a cornfield in a few hours time.

Quick compared to today, anyway. Setting fence was a two-man job.

He'd hired help for the feed store so he could have more time with his father. Even with the midwinter slump in business, he couldn't be in the store, the barn and the house at the same time. Superman, he wasn't. But he couldn't justify paying two hands with the decreased work, so the store got the extra hands and Marc got the farm labor.

He smiled as Jess swung open the passenger door.

"Cold?"

Jess tugged off her gloves. "Oh, yeah." She placed her hands palms down over the dashboard vents. "Thanks for having the truck warm."

"It's all right. Good session today?" Jess worked Rooster several times a week. The saucy paint had been a relatively inexpensive purchase five years past. He'd proven to be a good horse, with instinctive showmanship. The gelding loved an audience.

That made him perfect for Jess's needs. Rooster defied the laws of gravity with his leans and Jess had no problem eyeing the arena's dirt floor with him. They made a team, with the show ribbons and acclaim to prove it.

Jess kept her eyes trained ahead. "Good enough."

Uh-oh. "But?"

"He needs to work."

Ah. January doldrums. Working horses didn't like being put to rest. They'd stabled Rooster with Nan so they wouldn't have to trailer him. Jess worked off his feed by helping Nan. It seemed a good plan, but Rooster was a "go" horse. Hanging out with the pampered babies of weekend riders wasn't his cup of tea. Marc understood that. "You're probably right."

"But trailering him here takes a lot of time."

"Not so much."

Jess started to object. Marc raised a hand. "We want to do what's best for him, right?"

"Yes, but you're doing everything on your own. That's hard."

She didn't add that the advanced state of their dad's cancer not only removed a capable set of hands, but added a pall to everyday life. They both recognized that. She continued, "I wish I didn't have to go to school. I'd rather stay home and work with you. Ride. Feed. Muck."

"Castrate."

Jess laughed. "That, too."

"You're a born rancher, kid. And when those calves start dropping, I'll put you to work."

"I know." Her voice was smug. "I'm a chip off the old block."

Marc tuned in more carefully. Something else was going on. Something unspoken. "Problems?"

"Nope."

She answered too fast. Marc mulled the possibilities. Jess was a good student. High honor roll, a favorite of teachers. He frowned as a thought occurred.

She rarely brought friends around. She'd meet up with other riders at the ring and sometimes hang out with them, but that was different.

School friends? None he could picture. Did she feel funny bringing them home with Dad sick? "Why not have some friends over this weekend? We can do a winter barbecue."

Jess's careful smile set off warning signals. "I've got to get ready for first semester finals and work Rooster, plus help you. And I'd rather spend time with Dad right now."

Marc couldn't argue. Time with Dad was growing short, although his father seemed more energized today. Still, the feeling he was missing something stuck with him. Resolving to figure it out, he turned into the drive.

The nurse's car sat in his spot. He frowned, parked and followed Jess in.

"You must be Jess." As he crossed the threshold, Marc saw the nurse offer her hand. "I'm Kayla Doherty, your dad's nurse."

"Nice to meet you." Jess's voice mirrored the sincerity of her smile. She grabbed the nurse's hand in a firm grip. "Dad says you're wonderful."

The nurse laughed. Jess's dimples deepened at the carefree reaction. Marc cleared his throat, drawing their attention. "The door, Jess."

"Oh. Sorry."

Jess stepped in farther so Marc could close the door. Turning, he caught the nurse's eye. "Is Dad okay?"

"He's fine," she replied. "He asked me to come by and meet Jess." She smiled Jess's way. "We hadn't met and your dad wants you comfortable around me. That way you can ask me questions, approach me about anything. If I don't have the answer, I'll find it for you."

"You came back to tell us that?" Marc stared, trying to read her angle. Women like her always had an angle. Part of the inborn metabolism that fed her need for stylish clothes and trendy shoes. Not to mention sassy nails.

"And for stew."

Marc fought a groan. She met his look and continued, "Your dad invited me."

"That's great." Jess's voice pitched up. Obviously her taste was less discriminate than his. She grabbed Kayla's hand, excited. "There's never another girl around here."

"Imagine that." The nurse leveled Marc a look that said nothing and everything.

Marc narrowed his eyes. Her gaze offered a challenge. Silent, he pushed his boots into the corner and strode into the kitchen as Jess exclaimed, "Great shoes. I love wedges, any time of year. Where'd you get them?"

The nurse's answer was lost to him as she and Jess headed toward the living room.

Great shoes, my—

Marc clamped the thought. With Jess growing up, it was normal for her to like girl things, right? Although tempted, he couldn't keep her in flannel forever. Girls didn't wear barn clothes to the prom. Or on dates. But he fought inner panic at the thought.

He didn't want Jess to be like their mother, more concerned with appearance than substance. He wanted her to be a woman of merit. Women like that didn't wear insensible shoes in January.

Responsibility tugged as he tended the stewpot. He didn't know anything about raising a girl. How would he talk to her about…stuff? Girl stuff? Boy stuff?

Laughter from the front room caught his attention. Didn't the nurse say she'd answer Jess's questions? Hadn't she just made that offer? Nurses were trained for that, right?

After all, Jess was raised on a ranch. She'd seen animals mating in a natural dance of life from the time she could walk. Truth be told, she could probably tell the nurse a thing or two. They'd raised dogs, cows and horses. Jess had been present at births and deaths and everything in between.

Even knowing that, he couldn't bring himself to talk to her about the facts of life. No way, no how.

He grimaced as he withdrew a loaf of Amish bread from the oven. To approach the nurse, he'd have to be nice to her. Ignore her foolish shoes and her Meg Ryan haircut. The saucy look. And the "notice me" fingernail polish. For a moment he wondered if she painted her toes to match, then pushed the thought aside.

He was a tough guy. A farmer and rancher. He could be nice to a woman who placed looking good above everything else if it meant help with Jess.

But it wouldn't be easy.

Chapter Five

"Great stew," Kayla announced, but didn't wait for Marc's customary gruff acknowledgment. "I've never had better."

Marc met her gaze, surprising her. "Thanks. Dad and I came up with this."

Pete laughed, his fork aloft. The sound inspired a quick smile from Jess. "After too many failures to count," he lamented, grinning. "Our early attempts were disasters. We'd have never made it in the restaurant business. Jess being little, we could always mash something up for her."

Jess groaned.

"But for us, we had a long spell where we grilled everything," Pete continued. The memory deepened his smile. "Steak, chicken, burgers, hot dogs, chops. I bought a propane grill so we wouldn't have to mess with charcoal in the dead of winter."

"Makes side dishes a challenge," Kayla offered.

Once again Marc surprised Kayla by looking right at her. "Frozen veggie casseroles you stick in the microwave." He arched a brow that would have done Pierce Brosnan proud. "And baked potatoes."

"Always baked potatoes," agreed Pete. "Peeling and mashing was too much work."

"Exactly." Marc exchanged another smile with his dad before turning back to her.

Kayla nodded in appreciation. The fact that he wasn't growling pushed her to make the look more sincere. "That sounds all right, though. A good meal, all in all."

"Every night."

She laughed out loud. "Seriously?"

Marc leaned her way. The green flecks in his gray eyes were joined by points of gold surrounding a jet-black pupil, a myriad of muted color, very Monet. He held her gaze. "Every single night for over a year." Then he flashed the smile she'd seen once before and she couldn't help but grin in return. Maybe he had a personality after all.

She was a smart girl and she'd been raised in an environment that made her examine other people's motives. That made her reasoning simple.

Marc DeHollander wanted something.

Kayla tamped down the feeling. She could be wrong. He may have had a change of heart in the quarter hour she chatted with Jess, sitting on the worn but comfy sofa. Maybe he'd come to realize she wasn't evil personified.

Not likely. Lifting her coffee, she let her eyes meet his.

Strength. Ambition. Focus. She read the attributes in his expression and couldn't find them lacking. They were good qualities. There was a potency about Marc DeHollander that lent itself to aspirations.

He was a goal-setter. Whether he had the gumption to reach those goals was another thing, but she sensed the determination from that one look.

So why the sudden change to nice? Was he trying to smooth things over for his dad's sake?

Possibly. He clearly loved his father.

Or maybe Jess's presence inspired him. Perhaps he shelved rude behavior in the presence of impressionable teens.

More likely.

Kayla set down her mug and appraised him.

He met her gaze with no animosity. Different, in a nice way.

But Kayla had learned to study the motives behind behavior rather than accept actions at face value. She knew better than to trust the surface. She liked the more relaxed demeanor he offered, but wouldn't be fooled by it.

As long as he put a lid on that "sit beside me" smile. The wattage alone was enough to ruin a girl's resolve. Luckily, Kayla's self-generated "I'm leaving in six months for places unknown" force field was firmly intact.

"Dinner was good." Kayla shrugged into her coat with careless ease. "I know you were surprised to find me here. Your father didn't mention he called me?"

Marc shook his head. "He was asleep this afternoon, and I ran errands before I picked up Jess." He watched as she positioned her scarf, long fingers snugging the ends beneath the coat. "You wear open-toed beach shoes in the house and bundle up to walk thirty feet to your car."

"They're not beach shoes," she argued. "They're comfy shoes, with quiet soles that don't disturb resting patients. And the car," she nodded toward the drive, "has been sitting for over two hours. It'll barely be warm by the time I get home."

"Your heater doesn't work?" Why did that bother him? A professional woman ought to have sense enough to service her car, shouldn't she?

"It's pokey," she replied, pulling on her gloves, "and I'm not patient enough to wait for it to warm up."

Because he did the same thing, he couldn't say much. Still the thought that her windows might not fully defrost gave him a nudge of unease. He pushed it aside and cleared his throat. "You've got cookies?"

Her hands paused. She frowned, puzzled, her bright blue eyes shading darker.

"In case the dog's out."

She flushed, but didn't lose her cool. "A good Scout is always prepared."

"You were a Scout?"

The flush tinged deeper. "Just an expression." Her voice toughened to a more pragmatic tone. "I was never in one place long enough to do things like scouting."

"A gypsy," he mused out loud. "Or an Army brat."

"Neither applies." Her closed expression said he'd get nothing more. She nodded toward the kitchen. "Thanks for giving me time with Jess. She's a great kid. Does your dad always beat her in Scrabble?"

Marc acknowledged Jess's losing groan with a wince. "Not always. The kid's got a hefty vocabulary. She's a reader," he added. "And a loner."

"Really? That's surprising."

"It's true enough," Marc rejoined. He stuck out a hand in what he hoped was a peace-making gesture. He didn't like the reasons that brought the stylish nurse to his house, but he needn't make her task tougher. "Thanks for coming."

She slipped a glove off and grasped his hand. "I was glad to do it, Mr. DeHollander."

Her skin felt soft between his work-roughened fingers. Nice. Warm. He dropped her hand with a minimum of finesse and stepped back. "Marc."

Her eyes sparkled at his gesture of peace. "Then feel free to call me Kayla," she told him, her voice low. She leaned forward as if sharing a secret. "Instead of 'that nurse.'"

Her sassy smile reminded Marc why women like Kayla should be avoided. High-maintenance women didn't belong in the North Country, much less on a farm.

There were good reasons why Marc avoided savvy women. His mother had been brilliant and beautiful. Arianna DeHollander reveled in the latest trends, a fashionista before the term became a buzz word.

Nope. No way would he repeat his father's mistakes. Pete married a woman too worldly to be tied to the ruggedness of northern New York. She'd never learned to love the rock-strewn land and the simplicity of the population. She was destined for bigger and better, and let everyone know it. That made her desertion less a surprise, but still devastating. Throw a five-month-old baby into the mix, and you had an interesting family dynamic. Two men and a baby, one guy short of a movie title.

They'd made it work, treasuring the baby to lessen the trauma of her mother's disappearance.

And Jess was just fine, Marc assured himself. A strong girl, an accelerated student, sure-seated on the back of a horse.

Marc pushed aside the signs he'd noted earlier. Her lack of friends, her singularity. Her anxiety over her appearance. Why hadn't he noticed that before? Was that normal for girls going through puberty?

He had no idea, but he was rethinking the notion of having Kayla talk with Jess. Jess was a commonsense kind of girl, unafraid to put her hand to work, unlike Miss I-Think-I-Chipped-My-Nail Doherty.

The nurse was smart. And sure of herself. She maintained her equilibrium when challenged, and he'd seen that firsthand because he'd been the challenger.

But she was beautiful and knew it. Saucy and unapologetic. Self-composed, a quality that seemed achieved rather than intrinsic.

But too concerned with her mode of dress, style of hair. She was Reese Witherspoon pixie-pretty, not Julia Roberts gorgeous, but either aspiration was beyond Jess's caring.

Wasn't it?

As he headed for the shower, Marc tucked Kayla's image aside. He'd be nice to her. That was the least he could do.

But that was as far as he'd go. He wouldn't ask her help with Jess. That would be too personal. Allowing that intimacy could ingrain her. Better that she do her job, he'd do his and they'd face whatever happened as it came.

He nodded, satisfied, then frowned as he grabbed the water knob. Were there fourteen faint freckles dotting the bridge of her nose, or fifteen? He pictured her face and did a mental scan.

Sixteen. Evenly spaced and divided, right to left.

Not that he cared.

Chapter Six

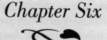

"How's your dad doing?" Craig Macklin watched as Marc latched the stall door enclosing the spry but very pregnant horse.

"Like you'd expect. Some good days. Some bad."

"Have they given you a time frame?"

Marc stared. "For?"

"His prognosis."

Marc swore under his breath. Why was it that everyone else accepted Pete's fate? Was his family last night's feature on the late-breaking news?

"This just in: End-stage lung cancer patient Pete DeHollander has a short time to live. Let's visit the family and see how they're doing.

"Excuse me, Miss, you're Jess DeHollander?"

"Yes." Jess nodded to the man with the mic while a cameraman jostled for position.

"Tell me, Miss DeHollander, how do you feel knowing your dad is at death's door?"

Jess's smile revealed the gentle spirit within, a hint of pathos strengthened by faith. "I feel blessed to have been his daughter all these years. He raised me when my mother abandoned me. He fed me, clothed me and saw to my education at the highly rated local school. And he gave me a horse."

Suddenly Rooster appeared, his head bobbing equine agree-

ment. Jess cradled the paint's neck and cuddled him, cheek to cheek, both facing the camera. "We'll miss Dad dearly, but he's going to a better place."

The reporter nodded, then turned Marc's way. "And you, sir? You're Marcus DeHollander, Pete's son and soon to be the sole proprietor of DeHollander Hereford Holdings and the DeHollander Feed and Grain. How do you feel about your father's impending demise? Will you be able to handle the work of two thriving businesses, raise your sister, keep a home and maintain the kind of social life a thirty-year-old man craves?"

Furious, Marc broke the imagined camera into a thousand pieces and strode briskly away.

"Marc? Where are you, buddy?"

Marc sucked a breath and tried to calm his feelings without much luck. "Your old girlfriend is working here."

Craig frowned. "My old— What are you talking about?"

"The nurse. The Doherty girl." As Craig's expression changed, Marc raised a brow. "Don't pretend you've forgotten now that you're married."

Craig laughed. "They won't let me forget. Sarah and Kayla are friends. Sarah taught Kayla to spin and knit."

Marc nearly choked. "Awkward at best."

Craig disagreed. "Naw. Kayla and I only dated a few times. It was never going anywhere. She and Sarah got friendly once Kayla joined our church and the rest is history. She even watches the baby now and then. When she's not working," he added.

Craig's words painted a picture for Marc, of Kayla and little McKenna Rose, a year old now. The image of the baby's dark curls pressed against Kayla's fair skin made his fingers tingle. He clenched his hands. "Still weird."

"Why?"

"Wives and old girlfriends are an odd mix, Macklin. Oil and water. Can't possibly work."

"It can if you know Sarah."

Marc frowned. "I know Sarah. What's that got to do with—"

Craig interrupted, laughing. "Housed in the lowest level of my well-mortgaged country home are three lambs that needed warming, a barn cat due to deliver and a nephew who is rapidly becoming a dedicated farmer like his aunt." When Marc looked confused, Craig punched his arm. "Sarah's good with strays. Kayla fits right in."

Marc pictured the feisty nurse. "Are we talking about the same woman?" He met Craig's eye and raised a hand shoulder level. "So high, short blond hair, big blue eyes, crazy shoes and an attitude that barrels into next week?"

Craig's brow shifted up in interest. "Sounds like the same girl to me. She's good at her job, Marc." He shook his head, his face out-turned. "That doesn't mean we're solid inside. You know that."

They'd reached the west-facing door of the barn. Slanted beams from the early setting sun shone through the glass upper. Marc worked his jaw before facing Craig. "Life's plenty full around here. Between Jess's schedule and Dad's illness keeping him up at night, the feed store, the cattle…" Marc shook his head. "I can't imagine squeezing one more thing in."

"Some things don't take space or time. They just make the rest easier to handle."

Craig was talking faith and fellowship. Marc refused to take the bait.

Wasn't it enough that he was taking Jess to services, standing by her side as their minister droned platitudes from a contradictory ancient book?

Nope. He'd count on good fortune and hard work. They'd held him together so far. He opened the door and stepped into the last rays of daylight. "I appreciate you coming by. It would break Jess's heart if anything happened to Grace. Or the foal," he added.

Craig clapped a hand to Marc's shoulder. "Glad to do it. And you haven't been over in a while. When can we expect you? Saturday?"

Marc exhaled, his breath a cloud of ivory steam. "It's tough, with Dad and all. I feel bad if I leave. And Sarah sounds busy enough."

"True on all counts. But you don't want your dad to feel guilty about you hanging around, either. And I'm not averse to helping Sarah in the kitchen." Marc's look inspired Craig's laugh. "Being nice in the kitchen brings rewards."

Marc hid a stab of envy.

Craig was different now that he was a husband and father. Calmer. More focused. Was that because of marriage or his strengthened faith? Marc refused to ask. He dipped his chin. "Dad mentioned that this morning, how he hates to have us tied up, waiting."

"Come over on Saturday," Craig urged. "Have supper, play with the baby."

A night away sounded good. Marc smiled. "Which one? The kittens, the lambs or the human?"

"All of the above." Craig's tone was half teasing, half lament. "That's what I get for marrying a sheep farmer. A personal petting zoo in the basement."

Marc laughed. "Not so bad, considering the sheep farmer."

Craig's smile deepened. "No argument there. We're good, then?"

Marc hesitated.

"It would give Jess a chance to have some private time with Pete."

He hadn't thought of that, but Craig made a good point. It wouldn't hurt for Jess to have Dad to herself for a while. And he wouldn't mind an interruption in the constant round of casseroles the good women of the church seemed bent on providing. Marc nodded. "What time and what can I bring?"

"Six, and don't bring a thing. Let Sarah spoil you. It'll make her day."

Marc surrendered, hands up, palms out. "I would love to be spoiled."

"Good." Craig climbed into his car and started the engine before opening the window. "Tell Jess everything's looking fine. She's done well."

Grace and her foal were the end result of a 4-H project. The paint mare had won several ribbons with Jess as a mount, but this was her first breeding. First-time mothers were unpredictable, and Marc wanted to avoid more trauma right now. Their father's illness was enough for Jess to handle. Having her big brother smooth the barn path was the least he could do.

"Kayla? How's your time frame?"

Kayla groaned. "Why do I suddenly wish I'd taken a different route out of this place?"

Christy smiled. "Ask the busy person…"

"Or the last one out the door," Kayla mused. "Whattya got?"

Christy's expression sobered. "A new intake in Gouverneur at one-thirty."

"Tricky to be in Norfolk at two if you're in Gouverneur at half-past one." Gouverneur and Norfolk were at opposite points of St. Lawrence County.

"Mmm-hmm."

"If I do the two o'clock at Maeve Morris's, you're okay with the intake in the southern sector?"

"Forever in your debt," Christy declared. She held up a candy bar like the grand prize of a church raffle. "Would chocolate settle the issue?"

"From your private stash in the dark gray filing cabinet marked 'No unauthorized entry'?"

Christy handed over the bar. "So much for private. Anyway, if you take Maeve, I'll be clear for this. Who else do you have this afternoon?"

"Mr. DeHollander, so it works out since he's up that way," Kayla told her. "I'll see if I can back him off an hour. That will give me time with Maeve, then off to the beef farm, then back home to Potsdam. Keeps me in the northern quadrant for the afternoon."

"And we live in the largest geographic county in New York State because…?"

"We love piling miles on our cars while we travel inhospitable backcountry roads for hours on end." Kayla returned Christy's chagrined smile and shrugged. "My answer's simple. They pay me and forgave my student loans. Sweet deal, all around. What's your excuse?"

Christy winked. "Fell in love with a guy who thought the North Country was a great place to raise a family. I decided he was right."

Kayla leaned in. "Fifty states, Chris. I'm gonna go way out on a limb and wager there are other great places to raise kids."

Christy shrugged. "I'm sure there are. Heaven knows we get sick of winter up here about two-and-a-half months before it officially ends—"

"In June," Kayla spouted.

There was no denying that. May nights got downright cold. Kayla tried not to picture her chilly living room, the comforter that was a mainstay on the couch for simple warmth. Christy grinned, noting, "Good snuggling weather."

"Since I'm single, I'll take your word on that." Kayla rolled her eyes, hefted her workbag and headed for the door.

Chris's voice followed her. "Romance hits when you least expect it, kiddo. You wanna hear God laugh? Tell Him your plans."

Biting her tongue, Kayla waved as she bumped her way out the door.

Romance. Hello? Haven't had a date in too many months to count. Definitely a downside to dealing with a primarily geriatric crowd.

At the hospital she'd been surrounded by people her age. Well, okay, surrounded was generous. Canton-Potsdam Hospital was small, but well-run. A tidy operation, all told. The busyness there, nestled in Potsdam's center, had provided her with the occasional flirtatious moment.

Hospice? Not so much. She laughed at the differences as she climbed into her car. The car had chilled back to deep-freeze status, but the heater sprang to life easily this time. Kayla shot a look heavenward. "Thank You. And ignore what Christy said, okay? I'm not looking for anything up here. I've got a date with destiny coming up, and the one thing I can guarantee is that winters will be short or nonexistent. I give my word on it."

She waited for the promised laugh and didn't hear it. *Good.* She and God were on the same page. Before exiting the lot, she dialed the DeHollanders.

No answer. Wishing she'd gotten hold of someone, she left a message on Pete's machine, explaining she'd be late, then headed to her first call of the day.

"Where have you been?" Marc's harsh tone had Kayla taking a step back. His shoulders blocked the kitchen light. In shadow, she had a hard time assessing his expression until he turned. The darkened countenance became an easy read then.

"Seeing patients." Shrugging off her coat, she tried to size up the situation but fell short. Marc's face showed anger and fear, heavy on the former. "I got your voice mail."

"But didn't answer it." His tone was ragged. Accusing.

"I just got it," Kayla corrected herself. She kicked off her boots and faced him. "Let's see what's going on."

"Your shoes."

"I was hurrying when I got your message. I must have left them at the Morrises'." Sliding her glance to the kitchen, she dipped her chin. "Where's your dad?"

"Where do you think?"

Kayla bit her lower lip hard enough to pierce it. The guy was obviously worried and scared. She'd cut him some slack for the moment. Next time he met her at the door and acted like a first-class jerk? She'd let him have it, both barrels, no holds barred.

Okay, probably not, but that didn't mean she wouldn't *want* to. Moving to Pete's side, she laid a cool palm against his skin. "Fever."

"Yes. High."

Kayla nodded as she retrieved her thermometer. "What are his other symptoms?"

Marc frowned. "He's not making much sense. Confused. Almost a little—" his breath hitched as though he hated to say the word "—crazy."

Kayla met his gaze, sympathetic. Sometimes she forgot that family members might come into hospice with no nursing skills, especially in a house without a woman. She checked Pete's pulse and blood pressure, then eyed the thermometer. "103.6."

"I told you it was high."

"Probably an infection," she explained. "Has he been emptying his urostomy bag daily?"

Marc's blank look was all the answer she needed. "You have no idea, right?"

"It's not dinner table conversation," he retorted.

"It will be." Drawing back the sheet, she puckered her lips. "I think we're dealing with a UTI."

"In English, please."

"A urinary tract infection. It's not uncommon. I'll let the doctor know. He'll probably phone in a prescription for an antibiotic. Amoxicillin's a common treatment for this. Your dad has no allergies to antibiotics, does he?"

"I've answered that question a dozen times in the past three months, but, no. He doesn't."

Kayla retrieved her phone. "What about his bag care? Has anyone trained you on how to empty the urine bag?"

Marc's face paled under the late-day growth of beard. "Why should they?"

She drew a short breath and counted to five, then decided she might want to go the full nine yards and make it ten.

Ah, yes. Ten was better. Fighting a scowl, she looked up at him. "Your dad needs help with it. This is a small crisis overall, but keeping the site clean and irrigated is important. The bag needs to be emptied daily and we'll change it every week or so. I'll do that part," she added. "Has your dad done total care of his bag since his surgery a few years back?"

"Yes. Dad would be mortified to have me..." His voice faded as he contemplated the situation.

Kayla returned his look of angst with one of compassion. "But he's sick now. He's going to need your help." With a flash of insight, she nodded her head to the window. The big barn rose beyond the glass, its walls dark umber in the late-day light. "You've dressed animal wounds, haven't you?"

"Of course."

She shrugged. "Same thing. An easy but firm touch, clean and antiseptic. I'll show you how."

He didn't look thrilled by that pronouncement. "Now?"

"No." Turning back, she smoothed a gentle hand across Pete's brow. "Let's cool him off, get the antibiotics in him and go from there. We want him comfortable, and he isn't."

She drew off Pete's extra blanket. Marc moved forward. "Would cool rags help?"

"To sponge him?"

"Yes. My mom did that when I was a kid and Dad did it with Jess."

"Of course." Kayla nodded encouragement. "Bring cool water and a washcloth. That way you can chill the cloth off as it heats up."

Marc looked relieved to have something concrete to do. "All right."

As he strode away, Kayla pressed her eyes closed. *I'm too harsh, Lord. I've grown tough because I do this every day. I forget that for some people the simplest forms of care are mountains to be scaled. School me in my faults so I don't get caught up in his. Give me patience. Compassion. Mercy.*

"Are you all right?"

Kayla jerked. "Fine. Just saying a prayer."

"Sorry. Didn't mean to intrude."

"It's okay. Pete and I have prayed together. Did you want to join me?"

"No."

No doubt there. Marc laid the well-wrung rag above his father's eyes. "Is that right?"

Kayla eyed the cloth. "It's fine." Settling into the adjacent chair, she waited for the doctor to return her call. "You'll want to flip it soon. It'll heat up fast."

"I'll say." Frowning, Marc redipped the cloth, then wrung it out. "He's burning up."

Kayla reached for Pete's hand. "You haven't given him aspirin or acetaminophen for the fever?"

"Not yet. I thought of it, but I don't know what things cause reactions. Drug interaction." He lifted a shoulder, frustrated. "I assumed it would be okay, but then I couldn't get the doctor, you were late and I wasn't sure what to do." After a hefty pause, he glanced her way. "I panicked."

"You did." She refused to cut him any slack while she administered Tylenol. "But this won't be the only crisis he throws your way and you'll get better at assessing them."

"I don't want to."

Kayla thought hard before phrasing her next question. Marc's answer could mean a complete reevaluation of Pete's care. Not all families were meant to provide hospice. "You don't want to be responsible for his hospice care or you don't want to get better at crises?"

"The answer is C. All of the above." A frown darkened his face as Marc reapplied the cloth. "I don't want him to die."

Not much choice there. Swallowing a sigh, Kayla worked to keep her expression placid. "We all die. It's as natural as birth, just not as celebrated."

Marc's shoulders stiffened. "People don't have to die this young. They make choices that invite cancer."

Obviously the source of Pete's cancer was a spot of contention. "Your dad smoked."

"Nearly two packs a day."

Kayla cringed. "I'm sorry."

"Me, too."

She had no platitudes for him. She understood his anger all too well. Hadn't her mother made choices that ended in her death at the hands of a madman? Oh, yeah, she understood Marc's disappointment. Sympathized with it. His dad played the odds and lost, but at least he'd had his love for thirty years. Kayla would have given anything for that.

The room stayed quiet until the doorbell broke the silence. Kayla stood. "I'll get it."

Marc looked grateful. A definite improvement. "Thanks."

Kayla returned with Dr. Pentrow.

Marc stood. "A house call?" His voice thickened with uncertainty.

Dr. Pentrow walked to his side and clapped him on the back, man-to-man. "I had to drive this way so I swung by the pharmacy, picked up the prescription and figured I'd drop it by. How's our patient doing?" He swept his look from Marc to Kayla.

"Uncomfortable," Kayla answered. "Looks like a UTI. We'll have to train someone with his bag care. I think he's grown too frail to handle it."

The doctor nodded. "Marc can do that. He's doctored almost as many animals as the local vets, right, Marc?"

To Kayla's surprise, Marc agreed readily. "If someone shows me how, I can take care of it."

Sure. Minutes ago he was crying about not wanting to handle care at all, now he was Clara Barton in Levi's. Please. She shot him her arched-eyebrow look, the one meant to make him feel like a chauvinistic jerk.

His jaw tightened.

Good. The days of bowing and scraping to doctors while nurses were treated like poorly paid servants disappeared long ago. Marc DeHollander might have every right to be upset by his father's situation, but he had no right to single her out for his rising angst.

"Have you got an IV setup?"

Kayla pulled her attention back to the doctor. "I'll order one. They'll have it here within the hour."

"Good. We'll do IV antibiotics to get them right into his system." He turned slightly to include Marc in the conversation. "That should clear it up fairly quickly, Marc. Then Kayla can show you how to drain the bag. It doesn't take long, but the stoma site needs to be kept clean. You can handle that, right?"

"Of course."

Kayla groaned inside. She shot him another look, but he kept his eyes trained on his father. Good thing. The "knight in shining armor" act was hard to stomach from a guy who'd been nice to her exactly once. She phoned in the order for the IV and agreed to wait until it arrived. She shared a brief exchange with the doctor before Marc showed him out. Kayla sat, drew Pete's hand between her own and mulled her situation.

Fun, she thought, rueful. Sixty minutes of Marc DeHollander

treating her like a plague carrier. Talk about a good time. Maybe she could slide hot pepper slivers under her fingernails and magnify the thrill. A solid form shadowed the bedroom door.

"Doc says thank you for staying."

Kayla refused to look Marc's way. She didn't trust herself to speak properly. Better to say nothing at all until she calmed down. Temper tantrums and end-stage home care were at distinct odds. She drew a breath to calm the rise of feelings, then another, deep, cleansing.

Better. Much better. She might just let Marc live after all.

"Are you okay here while I go to the barn?"

Kayla kept her attention on Pete. "Yup."

"If you need me, here's my cell number." Marc moved forward and slid a piece of paper across the bed. "I'll come right in."

Kayla kept her gaze angled away. "We'll be fine. Do what you gotta do."

His hand tensed. After long seconds, the fingers relaxed. He pushed away, then strode out the door, his footsteps determined.

She needed a temper check. Couldn't someone invent a device that interrupted her "zap 'em now" responses? Electric shock might work. She'd think a bad thought, then *Wham! Zap! Zowie!* Instant electric penance. Pavlovian-style reparation. Even she might learn to guard her temper if shocked a time or two. It worked on dogs, right? Invisible fencing, nursing-style.

She smiled at the thought, then drew a breath. "Heal this infection, Father. Give Pete comfort and peace. Let these last days and weeks be filled with love, not pain. Guide his way, send him legions of angels to shelter and protect him.

"And, while you're at it? Soften my thoughts, Lord, guard my tongue where the son is concerned. I sense his worry and distrust, but instead of reacting with compassion, I want to smack him. Point out all he has and make him grateful for it."

She'd have given anything for a parent like Pete. Anything. Someone to love her, watch over her, praise her. She pressed Pete's hand lightly. Marc DeHollander had no idea how blessed he was.

He'd enjoyed thirty years of unconditional love. A lifetime. Kayla reapplied the cool rag Marc garnered. The faded gold cotton gave off a hint of October spice as she pressed out excess water. A nice smell. Homey and comforting. Her nose twitched in appreciation.

If she ever had children, they'd know her love. She wouldn't smother them with it. Oh, no. She was experienced enough to see that a houseful of bratty kids was no fun. But they'd know their mother's love firsthand. The cookies, the stories, trips to the park. Sunday evening ice-cream cones and Saturday mornings at the zoo.

She'd be a good mother someday. Strong and true.

With a great shoe collection, of course.

Chapter Seven

He owed the nurse an apology.

Marc mulled that with no small reluctance the next afternoon. He checked Grace, just weeks shy of her confinement. She looked fine. Cattle lowed beyond the propped barn door. A brutal west wind had the first-bred heifers huddling beneath the overhang, their combined breath a vaporous cloud.

Dad seemed better today. The fever was down and his reactions were more cognizant. When he mentioned Kayla's message the previous morning, Marc bit back words of self-reproach.

He'd assumed she'd blown them off, coming late with no regard to their time frame. Realizing she'd changed her appointment because another patient needed her had him eating crow. Try as he might, he couldn't find a way to make this her fault.

Marc glanced at his watch. She'd promised to be here to show him bag care. He winced, then squared his shoulders, remembering that Pete had diapered him long years back. He owed him, period. He'd raised Marc on a working farm, showing the young boy the intricacies of coaxing a living from the rugged terrain. When Marc returned from college and started the beef herd, his father had staked him financially. He'd believed in the younger man's foresight and work ethic. The least Marc could do was take good care of him now.

But apologizing to the nurse? Marc remembered her expression when he'd agreed with Doc Pentrow. He winced once more. A diplomat he wasn't, and he'd put his foot in it if her cool, clipped tones were any indication.

The sound of her engine drew his attention. Heaving a sigh, Marc headed for the door. Might as well get it over with.

As he exited the barn, she stood framed by the frozen pond beyond her, its surface dipping west from the road's far shoulder. Come spring the melted pond would teem with life. Swans, geese, ducks. Pigeons that gathered atop the fowl house, scavenging dropped grain. Today the pond lay stark, a sheet of pale gray breaking the winter white while deepening its austerity.

Seeing him, she waited. The wind buffeted her short coat. She snugged it closer and Marc motioned to the door. "Come inside. You're cold."

Her expression unreadable, she moved to the porch ahead of him. Reaching beside her, Marc pushed the door open, then stepped in behind her.

"I wanted to—"

"I'd like to—"

They paused simultaneously. Marc rubbed a hand across the nape of his neck while Kayla pursed her lips. She looked down while she toed off her boots. "You first."

"Ladies first."

She huffed and looked anything but happy. He moved a half step back, expecting a full frontal. She surprised him.

"I wanted to apologize for being tough on you yesterday," she began. Shaking her head, she pulled her gaze his way. "You're new at this, your dad is gravely ill and I know you're trying. It takes time to get used to nursing an ill person, and I should have cut you some slack." She bit her lower lip, pensive, her eyes troubled.

Something clicked in Marc, warm and flowing. He had the urge to reach out and smooth her furrowed brow. Tuck the longer strands of pixie hair back, behind her ears. Maybe let his hand linger, just a moment.

Shoving his hands into his pockets, Marc acknowledged her words with a shrug. "I was a jerk."

She arched her left brow.

He glanced away, then brought his eyes back to hers. "I thought you blew us off. Just didn't bother showing up on time."

"But I called," she began.

Marc waved a hand. "I know that now. Dad remembered your call today, but he'd deleted the message. By mid-afternoon he was too sick to tell me and I—"

"Blew a gasket? Went over the top? Flew out of control?"

"What happened to playing nice?"

She clamped her lips together, frowning. "If I could learn to close my mouth, I'd avoid a lot of trouble."

Watching the transformation from troubled to tart, Marc realized he liked the animated version better. Spry. Sprightly. A hint of her sparkle returned, but it was like replacing a hundred-watt bulb with a forty. Just didn't cut it.

Annoyed by his thoughts, he stepped back, then looked down. "You're short today."

Her look was priceless as she tried to read him and failed. She didn't try to hide her sigh of resignation. "You generally see me with shoes. I haven't had a chance to pick them up yet, so I'm disadvantaged."

"One pair of shoes?" Why did that bother him? What did he care if she had no shoes at all?

She shook her head as she tugged her coat from one shoulder. Easy, he reached out to help her, his hand brushing the curve of her neck.

Kayla went deer-in-the-headlights still. For an instant Marc hovered there, feeling her warmth along the curve of his arm. Reaching farther, he hooked the coat label. She exhaled before following his motion with her scarf. Resolute, she turned to face him. "I have other shoes," she admitted. Two spots of color brightened her ivory cheeks. "Too many, probably. But those are my nursing shoes."

"I've noticed." He kept his voice dry as he appraised her feet. The socks looked thin. He remembered her inquiry about his wool pair from Ostrander's. "A real fashion statement."

That put her back up. She faced him, head on, her eyes

flashing. "Listen, Mr. Flannel-Goes-with-Everything, I'm here to do a job. My shoes aren't your concern."

Her indignation almost made him laugh. He worked to control the twitch in his jaw and angled his head. "I'm not concerned about your shoes, but the welfare of your feet. If you get sick, my father has to deal with someone else and that wouldn't be good. Like it or not, keeping you healthy has taken on measured importance."

She stared at him, uncertain. Huffing, she shrugged by him. "I'm fine. Hale and hearty. Let's go see your dad."

"Right behind you."

He'd riled her on purpose. Why? Because he'd rather see her flash and sizzle than repentant? Because she was cute when agitated and her blue eyes sparked flash fires of heat?

No. Not exactly. There was something else, something deeper that pulled at him when she looked penitent. A sense of old baggage, well-hidden.

Well, who didn't have a history? No one he knew. From the looks of Kayla Doherty, it couldn't have been too bad. Maybe she got cut from the cheerleading squad, or was first runner-up instead of prom queen. Appearances said Kayla was a girl born to life's successes. Having a mother of similar fate, Marc knew the shallowness of the facade and had no intention of letting the spunky nurse imbed herself. The three remaining DeHollanders had learned to circle the wagons to protect their family. They shared a Three Musketeers mentality: All for one, one for all.

He watched as she greeted his father, her voice cheerful, her manner soothing. Something stirred in Marc again, a little stronger this time. Firm, he pushed it down. He was here to learn how to help his father for whatever time was left, and had to deal with the nurse to do it. So be it. Other than that, she was on her own. Totally.

"Was Kayla at the house today?" Jess's voice danced when Marc picked her up at Nan's. Marc stifled a groan. Was he the only one who saw through the nurse's veneer?

"Yes. Why?"

Jess settled her gear into the confines of the truck cab. "No reason. I just liked her. When is she coming again?"

"Monday afternoon." Marc hesitated, not wanting to offer, then waded in. "Did you want to see her?"

"Sure. It's nice to have a girl around."

"What about your friends?" Marc asked again, his curiosity deepening.

Jess's expression stayed carefully calm. "Kayla's older. She doesn't act stupid."

Marc thought hard. There was a message in those words, but he wasn't sure how to sort it out. Was Jess looking for a mother figure or were the girls in school acting cliquish? He had no idea.

"I can have her stay on Monday," Marc conceded. "Would you like that?"

"See if she'll stay for supper again," Jess implored. She turned his way. "It was fun having her there."

Like fingernails on slate. "She might not be able to, Jess. She needs time off, like everyone else."

"I think she will," Jess decided. "She told me she'd make herself available if I had questions."

"Do you?" Marc glanced away from the road to eye his younger sister.

Jess shrugged. "I just like to talk to her."

Great. Just what he needed, Jess bonding with the woman. She'd lose Dad and her nursing friend all at once and he'd be left to pick up the pieces. He decided a change of subject was in order. "How was Rooster?"

"Better." Her voice perked up. "Nan's been riding him since we decided to keep him there. She saw he was getting anxious and wanted to get rid of some sass."

"Nan's a good woman," Marc declared. "Sensible. A woman who knows what kind of shoes to wear in winter."

Jess stared, confused. "Her shoes?"

A flush invaded Marc's neck. "Never mind."

"She had her Oak Trees on, anyway, the antique leather ones."

"Good for riding and working in the barn." Marc tried his best not to look stupid. Well. More stupid.

"Right." Jess eyed him, perplexed. He gripped the wheel tighter.

"Got homework?"

She still looked puzzled, but relaxed her shoulders. "Yes. I might need some help researching sub-Saharan Africa."

The computer was a great invention when you lived in the boonies. Marc nodded. "That shouldn't be too hard. Do you need a trip to the library?"

"Not yet. I can do preliminary stuff on the Web, then read the recommended books."

She hadn't discovered Cliffs Notes yet. Good. "If the local libraries don't have what you need, we can order books online. What's your time frame?"

"Plenty," she assured him. "This is our second-semester project, so it's not due until May. First draft is due before Easter."

"Easter's early this year," Marc warned.

"That's so weird," Jess mused. "Why don't they just set a date? Would it really matter?"

Marc turned onto Route 11. "They've talked about it."

"Really?"

He nodded. "It comes up regularly. You've got the variances of ancient calendars at work, and there's a respect issue involved."

"How so?" She eyed him, her brow furrowed. Religious topics weren't usually on his priority list. Her look of surprise highlighted that.

"Christ was crucified at Passover time."

"Yes."

"Because Passover changes with the first full moon of spring, Easter follows suit. Since the calendars don't match, the dates for Easter don't always match."

Her eyes narrowed. "How do you know all this? I know it's not because you're paying attention during services."

He bristled. "I'm there, aren't I?"

"You're there because Dad asked you to take me," she reminded him. "Not because you want to be. Give me a break. I'm not stupid."

"Jess, I…" What could he say? The idea that one unseen force held their destiny seemed quaint and misinformed.

Sure, he'd bought the idea when he was a kid. Then reason invaded in the form of adult reality, and Marc understood that no one, no God, had the kind of power churches accredited him with. He faced Jess once the truck was parked. "I like going with you, Jess."

Jess met his gaze. "You like helping me. If that means going to church, you do it. But you don't like it, Marc."

Coming around the front, Marc slid an arm around her. "Be patient, huh? I'm new at some of this."

Jess faced him. "Will we make it, Marc? You and me, once Dad's gone?"

Fear shadowed her eyes. Marc tugged her close, feeling as lost and alone as the fourteen-year-old he held. "Of course we will. We've got each other, Jess." He pushed back and smiled down at her. "We'll always have each other."

"Is it enough?"

Sometimes he wished she weren't so smart. He knew what she was asking, and had no answers. He hugged her again and planted a kiss on her hair. "We'll make it enough. We're tough, we're tight. We're DeHollanders, remember?"

She forced a half smile.

"You smell like a horse. Might want to shower before you bust in on Dad. His nose is sensitive."

"Okay."

Would they be all right? Marc pondered the question as Jess hurried upstairs.

I've no idea, Jess, but I'll do my best.

They'd figure it out. The thought of coming into the house, day after day, without his father's presence, chilled him. Not just the responsibility of Jess and the cattle. The feed store, quiet midwinter, but churning from March through Christmas.

The loss of a man so dear and defining. Could they survive that and remain a unit? Jess was growing up, she'd be off to college, then what? Marriage? Career?

I don't know, Jess. I shouldn't make promises I can't keep, but I'll try, little sister. I'll try my best to do right by you, no matter what happens. We're family, bound by blood. Nothing can break those ties.

    I love you, kid.

Chapter Eight

"I've got two words to say to you, Kayla."

Kayla looked up from the supply closet. "Yes?"

J. T. Donnelson grinned. "Hubba hubba."

Kayla frowned. "That's not a word, J.T., much less two." She hoisted her tote. "And if it were, I'd still have no idea what you meant."

"Come on, girl," J.T. implored. J.T. had taken up hospice care because she hated the confines of hospital hierarchy. Roaming the countryside worked well for her and she was great with patients. "You're hip to hip with Marc DeHollander two days a week. The guy is significant eye candy."

A burr formed between Kayla's shoulder blades. "That family's hit a rough road, and Marc's carrying the brunt. He's got a lot on his plate."

She didn't add that he thought her a witless blonde. Some things were best kept private.

J.T. shook her head. "He's had a full plate for a long time." She raised her brows in sympathy. "He wasn't like this when he was young." Seeing Kayla's look, she continued, "We had classes together in high school. Marc was cool. A real heartthrob. Once his mother took off, he got an attitude."

Curiosity got the best of Kayla. "Why'd she leave?"

"Didn't like the farm. My mother always said there was

something different about her. That you never knew what to expect. She was beautiful. And had great clothes. Mom used to say she'd be happy with half the clothes Arianna DeHollander gave away each year."

"Really?" Kayla tried to imagine Pete with a woman like that. Picturing what life must have been like with an infant and an angry teen, her sympathy doubled. "It's hard on kids when a parent leaves. Tough on the remaining parent, too."

"Oh, yeah." J.T. eased away from the wall. "But Marc and Mr. D. have done a great job with Jess. She looks like her mom."

"I figured as much," Kayla replied as they approached the exit. "She doesn't resemble her brother and he's the spitting image of Pete."

"And speaking of that brother," J.T. intoned, "give him my regards, will you? Tell him I'm free Saturday night. And Sunday night. Friday, too, from the looks of things."

Kayla laughed. "I'll tell him no such thing. I don't think he knows if he's coming or going half the time. I'm sure he'll be spending Saturday night with his father."

Craig and Sarah Macklin's doorbell chimed Saturday night precisely at six.

"I'll get it," Kayla called up the stairs. Craig was offering veterinary advice online and Sarah was changing a shirt that had been burped on. Kayla scooped up McKenna and padded to the door in her socks.

Marc looked as surprised as Kayla felt, but he recovered faster. Sweeping her a look, he stepped in and shut the door against the frigid night. "Someone sick?"

Kayla clutched McKenna tighter. "No. I came·for supper."

"Ah." Marc shrugged off his leather bomber jacket and hung it on a rack of pegs. The ever-present flannel had been replaced by a simple turtleneck in loden green. The soft country shade did wonderful things to his eyes. Why did that seem unfair? "Me, too."

The night had disaster written all over it. Kayla jerked one shoulder. "I can come another time."

She turned. A firm hand caught her shoulder. Marc stepped

in front of her, his hands reaching for the baby. "We've eaten together before. No one suffered irreparable harm if I remember correctly."

"Still." She met his gaze. "You deserve a quiet evening with your friends. I'm sure Craig and Sarah had no idea that…" Her voice trailed off.

"That I give you a hard time because I want the best possible care for my father?"

Something inside Kayla snapped. "That you give me a hard time because you have a truckload of misplaced anger and should spend the better part of a week, no, make that a month," she expounded, "with a punching bag, sorting things out."

She clapped a quick hand of regret over her mouth. Well, that little tirade should do wonders to clear the air. Nice going, Doherty.

He stared, long and hard. She squared her shoulders and stared right back until a muscle in his cheek jumped. A sheen of hard-won respect softened his expression. He scrubbed a hand across his jaw and nodded. "Probably wouldn't hurt."

"Shall I call the gym, set up a time?"

His Derek Jeter eyes darkened with amusement. The difference was she *liked* Derek Jeter, the always-a-class-act shortstop for the New York Yankees.

"No, thanks. I've actually got one in the barn. High school leftover."

Marc shifted the baby. In turn, McKenna patted his cheek with chubby hands. He smiled at the little girl, then dropped his gaze to Kayla. "So. What do you think of Division One hockey? St. Lawrence?"

"I think the coach should duct tape Norwen's mouth."

She surprised him. His eyes narrowed. He switched McKenna to his left arm and walked into the great room. "Because?"

"The kid's trouble," Kayla defended her position. "He shoots off his mouth and brings the team down. I'd cool his heels on the bench until he develops a better public attitude. Or bump him."

"Coach says he's had a tough life," Marc offered. He sank to the floor and grabbed a waddling plastic toy puppy for McKenna. Grinning, he watched as the baby toddled after the toy, her arms outstretched.

"That's no excuse for being a jerk."

He sent her a cool look. "You figure he should suck it up, turn the other cheek?"

"Yup."

"Simplistic."

She refused to look annoyed. That would give him too much power. "Straightforward."

"Perhaps." He turned his attention back to the baby. "Or patronizing."

Kayla sucked a breath. Her heart signaled an upsurge of adrenalin. Marc didn't seem to notice.

"Not everyone gets handed a gilded life and a happy childhood," he advised, his tone nonchalant. He gave her Ann Taylor ballet-neck rose silk sweater a sharp look. "Or designer labels."

Kayla bit her tongue. Let him think what he would. He had no clue how she'd worked to be where she was today. The foster homes where she never quite belonged. Hustling tables in a sports bar through college, cranking the books until she fell asleep on top of them in a bug-infested basement apartment requiring bars on the windows.

Nope, he had no idea and she had no intention of setting him straight. Marc didn't have to know that working girls could afford Ann Taylor if they waited for half-price online sales. If she could pull off the look of being normal, more power to her. That he thought her uncaring dented her spirit, but nothing that couldn't be filled with…something. Something that wasn't Marc DeHollander and his casually cold demeanor.

"Marc, you're here." Sarah Macklin hurried down the stairs and gave Marc a welcoming hug. "How are you? How's your dad? It's been way too long," she scolded, smiling. She looped her arm through his. "And you know Kayla. Craig said she was working with your father, so I knew we'd make a nice group tonight."

Marc never missed a beat. He sent Kayla an even look over Sarah's head. "And you were right." Stepping back, he motioned to McKenna, who was enthralled with the intricacies of trying on Kayla's much-too-large shoes. "I can't get over how big she is. And independent."

"Yes." Sarah beamed. "Her coloring may be mine, but there's a lot of Macklin in that child. She can charm her way into anything. And obviously has great taste in shoes already."

"A trait from her father," announced Craig as he came down the stairs. "The charming part. Not the shoe thing. I'm sure that's Kayla's doing. Marc. Hey." He reached out a hand to Marc, then turned Kayla's way. "It's nice you guys know each other so we could have you over together. Between work, lambs and the baby, we don't get to do this often enough."

"Me, neither," replied Marc. "It's nice."

Kayla had been just about to beg off the evening and go home. Craig's words stopped her. He and Sarah had been good to her these past two years. It had seemed odd at first, being Sarah's friend, since Kayla had dated Craig a few summers back. But a kinship had formed between the two young women that moved beyond petty jealousies and developed into an abiding friendship. There hadn't been too many of those in Kayla's life. Her fault, she knew. Ties meant heartache when they had to be broken, and hers were always severed.

"Kayla? Where are you?"

She turned, surprised. "Hmm? Sorry. Lost in my thoughts."

"I was asking how you like your steak," Craig explained. "I'm grilling while you girls finish in here, since you'll be moving south before barbecue season really takes hold."

"How masterful." Kayla gave him a full-fledged grin she bestowed on Marc, as well. "Pete assures me that Marc is a top-notch griller. Right?" She turned the full benefit of her smile Marc's way.

Eyes tight, he did a Clint Eastwood jaw twitch, then turned to Craig. "I'll stand in the cold with you, Doc."

"Eight degrees and falling, I hear." Kayla kept her voice cheerful as she nodded to Marc. "Did you bring a flannel?"

His eyes sparked. His nostrils flared. Then he relaxed into a full, megawatt smile that had her heart hitching. "You got me."

As Kayla quirked her jaw in victory, Marc added, "But paybacks can be tough. And totally unexpected."

"I'll take my chances," she told him as she headed to the kitchen. "We'll be in the nice, warm house if you boys need anything."

"Right."

Kayla felt his gaze as she moved across the carpeted room. Sarah called to Craig, "Honey, there's an extra flannel in the closet for Marc." She sent Kayla a knowing look. "L.L.Bean sells flannels, you know."

Kayla laughed. "Great."

"So does Lands' End."

"Not to mention every Salvation Army thrift store," Kayla rejoined. She flashed a grin to Sarah. "Actually, Calvin Klein and Eddie Bauer both carried flannels last fall."

"Well, then." Sarah grinned. "I'll feel quite stylish as I tend the sheep."

"*Très chic,*" Kayla agreed. "What am I helping with?"

"Mostly keeping McKenna out from underfoot," Sarah replied. She swept the spacious kitchen a glance. "I did a potato casserole with enough carbs to last us a month, and green beans with garlic and slivered almonds. And rolls, of course, straight from Main Street Bakery."

"Best around," declared Kayla. She scooped up McKenna and gave the baby Eskimo kisses. "Has this little bundle eaten yet, or is she eating with us?"

Sarah grimaced. "I don't think our single friends are ready for what McKenna does to food. It isn't pretty."

Kayla blew bubbles at the baby and laughed when the toddler tapped her mouth to break them. "So?"

"I've got mashed up stew if you're brave enough to feed her."

"Oh, I'm pretty tough," Kayla answered. She snugged the baby into the high chair and located the stew. "It looks strangely like dog food."

Sarah laughed. "It does, but it's stew. Although McKenna's eaten her share of kibble, and it doesn't seem to do any harm."

"Ugh." Kayla eyed the mop-haired baby. "Stay out of the dog dish, kid."

"That's like telling the snow not to fall," replied Sarah as she brought the last things to the table. "She likes to float things in Lady's water bowl. Or dump it."

"Sarah." Kayla laughed up at her. "How do you handle it all and not go crazy? I mean, you've got to be tired when you come back from the barns."

Sarah's smile softened. "She's a new generation, Kayla. A new hope."

"Opening strains of intergalactic movie theme music have taken hold of my brain," Kayla exclaimed. *"Long ago, in a galaxy far, far away…"*

Sarah's smile deepened but her eyes looked thoughtful. "You know what life was like for me. My family. The history here."

Kayla nodded. Sarah's father and two brothers had dragged their family name through the mud. Sarah bore the brunt of that shame a long while. McKenna protested the pause in her food supply with a squawk of indignation. Both women grinned.

"McKenna's a symbol of what's been put to rest," Sarah added. "The past is buried."

"Can you bury it, Sarah? Really?" Kayla didn't mean to sound desperate. No one knew what she'd seen, what she'd done as a child. There was no reason for them to know. None whatsoever.

Sarah touched her shoulder. "You know you can. We give it to God and move along, trusting in His goodness and forgiveness."

Emotion crept up Kayla's throat. Her jaw tightened. Her eyes filled. She bit her lower lip to keep the tears at bay. "Maybe some things aren't forgivable."

"As far as the east is from the west, He has removed our transgressions from us," Sarah quoted. Her voice stayed soft and even. "Maybe it's not God's forgiveness causing the problem. Maybe you haven't forgiven yourself."

Kayla's hand paused, the spoon inches from the baby's mouth. McKenna chirped. Kayla sighed and fed the hungry girl a hearty spoonful. "Forgiveness isn't easy."

"No."

A thick core lay within Kayla's soul, a hard center that refused to budge despite heart-felt prayers. Wasn't God supposed to soften those rough spots, ease the harshness that dwelled within her?

Hadn't happened. Kayla pushed the feelings aside. It was a maneuver she'd gotten good at over the years. The world saw what she wanted them to see, a cool, classy chick with quick wit and fashion panache.

Sarah saw through that facade. Always had. Maybe because underneath, they weren't all that different. Beneath the surface, they both carried scars. Wounds.

The door to the deck opened with a blast of chilled air. "We've got meat, ladies."

Sarah gave Kayla's shoulder a quick squeeze before she moved to welcome the men. Her maneuver gave Kayla time to catch her breath. Firm, Kayla pushed aside the influx of feelings. It wasn't the time or place for airing old linens. It might never be the time or the place if just thinking of the past dragged her into it so fully.

She drew her lower lip between her teeth and pressed down hard. Then, saucy smile in place, she finished feeding the baby. She'd eat, she'd smile, she'd chat back and forth like nothing was wrong in Kayla's world. It was an act she'd perfected over years of practice. No one did it better.

Marc felt the change as soon as he stepped into the room. His eyes went to Kayla. Her back was to him as she fed the dark-haired child, but her profile was wrong. All wrong.

The pert jaw had slackened. Her forehead furrowed. She blinked several times, and he had to fight the urge to go to her, wrap his arms around her and soothe the anxieties away.

She drew him and he hated that fact. She called to his instincts, and he couldn't control his internal reaction to those summons.

But he had full control of what the outer world saw. He might have to deal with the inner turmoil of an attraction to a woman too like his mother for safe being, but no one else need know. He squared his shoulders and strode to the table. "Need help?"

Her profile smoothed. When she turned, her smiling gaze was cool. Unperturbed. "I can handle it, Farmer Boy."

"Farmer Boy?" Sarah laughed as she brought the potato casserole to the table. The scent of cheese and onions filled the air. "Almanzo Wilder. He was from Malone, right?"

Kayla nodded. "Not too far from our farmer here."

Marc's chest loosened. If she was trading barbs, she was doing better. Guilt pricked him. Had he hurt her feelings before they cooked the steaks? Had she taken his brusque act too much to heart?

He scrubbed a hand across the nape of his neck as she mopped up McKenna's cheeks. Reaching out, he took the cloth from her. "I'll clean her up. You go wash your hands."

His hand lay over hers, his palm rough against the skin of soft knuckles. For a moment he kept her hand there, resting against his own before he nudged her aside. "Go ahead. I've got this."

She glanced up.

His pulse chugged to a stop. His chest tightened. The pain behind the smile stabbed his awareness. Sorrow. Despair. His heart reached out to the vulnerability he read and he fought to push it down.

She stepped away and the connection was broken. By evening's end, he was sure he'd been the victim of an overactive imagination. Kayla Doherty was easily the most self-assured, annoying woman he'd ever met. Tough and sassy, with a flair for looking good. Just the kind of woman he'd sworn off.

He might be a lot like his father. Their similarities ran more than skin deep. Marc recognized that. But he took a lesson by what his father endured for loving the wrong woman.

No one would have that chance with Marc. Better to choose sane and sensible than obey a rush of indiscriminate hormones. He refused to be at any woman's mercy. Calm and cool would be the order of the day when Marc was ready for a steady woman in his life. Someone who loved the land, appreciated the farm and knew how to cover her feet in the dead of winter.

"It won't start." Marc couldn't hide his chagrin as he rocked back on his heels in the Macklin's entryway later that night.

"Mine started right up, but yours chugged and died. I tried to jump it, but got nothing."

"No." Kayla's look reflected his discomfort. "I have AAA," she offered. She moved toward the phone. "I'll call them."

"You don't have to do that," Craig argued. He stood and stretched. "I can take you home and we'll look at the car tomorrow. How old's your battery?"

Kayla shrugged. "Almost five years."

Marc exchanged looks with Craig. "And the starter?"

"Fairly new," she answered. "I replaced that last year."

Craig tugged Sarah to her feet and gave her a quick kiss. "I'll take Kayla home and be back shortly."

"I'll take her."

Kayla turned, her chin up, her look defiant. Obviously, she didn't want to be indebted to him. Or maybe she didn't want to be stuck alone in a truck cab with him. Oh well.

Craig looked grateful. "You don't mind?"

"Potsdam, right?" At Kayla's nod, Marc shrugged. "No sense both of us heading out. My truck's ready to go and I head right through there anyway."

"Thanks."

Sarah eyed Kayla. "You're okay with this?"

"Of course."

Marc read the look that said she wasn't, but that was too bad. He could be nice for the fifteen-minute trip. Either that or maintain complete silence. He nodded to himself. Quiet might be a better strategy, if the nurse actually understood the meaning of the word. From what he'd witnessed to date, Kayla didn't do silence all that well.

He waited while she eased into short, unlined boots and wondered what she did when they got more than an inch of snow. Freeze, probably. It didn't seem to matter as long as she looked good. That kind of girl could drive a man crazy trying to take care of her, right up until she left him.

"Ready?" He looked her way, patently ignoring that she always managed to put together a tidy little package.

She nodded. "Yes, thank you," then swung toward Sarah. "I'll be happy to watch the baby next Thursday night. I'm free and you guys could take care of the stuff you want to order for the basement."

Sarah and Craig exchanged looks. "Sounds good," Craig replied. "I'm not on call and we really need to get things organized if I'm going to work on it this spring."

"I should be off the road by five," Kayla told them. "Is six good with you?"

"Perfect," Sarah declared. She leaned into Craig's arm and smiled up at him. "This is our new version of a night out. Picking out paint and carpeting colors from DIY home stores."

"When McKenna shops with us, there's no such thing as browsing." Craig grinned at his wife.

"Too true." Sarah squeezed Kayla's hand. "We'll see you Thursday, then. Plan on eating here, okay?"

"Sounds good."

They stepped into the cold of an early February night. Marc put a hand to her elbow. At her questioning gaze, he nodded to the concrete. "Slippery."

"Oh." She paused, then "Um…thank you."

Because he was already holding her arm, it made sense for him to open her side of the truck. Help her up. He watched to make sure she gathered her scarf in before he swung the door shut. As he climbed in his side, she thanked him again.

He acknowledged that with a gruff nod. "It's all right. Are you right in Potsdam?"

"Garden Street."

He shoved the truck into gear. "Towards Market?"

"The other end. I have the attic apartment in one of Vi Twimbley's houses."

Marc knew Mrs. Twimbley. She was tight with a buck and then some. Her apartments were affordable, but that was because she refused to do anything with them. Upgrades went against her credo. Typical college-town flats with none of the amenities a girl like Kayla would demand. He headed away from Pierrepont, working his jaw.

By the time they saw the lights of Potsdam, he was wishing he hadn't pledged a vow of silence. The ride along snow-frosted, winding roads under a waning half moon should have been relaxed.

It wasn't. Maybe if he'd spoken up initially they could have chatted about something, but he hadn't and it seemed silly to start a conversation now. Ridiculous, actually.

"A left here, then a right onto Garden."

He nodded. He knew the streets of the village like the back of his hand.

"This one, on the left."

"With no lights."

She puffed out a breath of air. "The outside lights haven't worked since before Christmas. I replaced the bulbs, but nothing happened."

How safe was that? he wondered. He climbed down from the truck. Kayla looked surprised to see him as he rounded the front bumper. "I'm fine, really. You don't have to—"

"It's dark as pitch. I'm walking you in."

She chewed her lip, then shrugged. "It's not like people lie in wait in zero-degree temperatures, Marc. Not if they have another option."

"Which door is yours?"

She nodded toward a tall, wooden staircase in the back.

"Outside stairway?"

"Mmm-hmm."

She was killing him. It didn't add up. This was cheap even by Twimbley standards. "I'll walk you up."

"You're being silly." She swung to face him. The moon hung to the south, out of view. The little light they had spilled from a neighbor's window. "No one is going to leap out of the frigid shadows and get me, Farmer Boy. And if they did, what would you care?"

She was right. Why would he care? What would it matter? One more careless girl walking into danger with no thought to her own safety.

He reached for the door handle as she plied the key. "My father needs you in one piece."

"We've got tons of staff. I'm replaceable."

He laid one finger against her mouth and tried not to think of how soft her lips felt against his callused skin. "You're not."

"Really?" Did his touch inspire that single, whispered word, the small, sharp intake of breath?

Or the bone-chilling cold? Most likely the cold.

Then she smiled.

It was a real smile, down to her toes. The kind she shared with his father and the Macklins. With Jess. Deep inside he longed to inspire that smile more often. He jerked his head to the narrow wooden stairs. "Up. I'll follow you. Then I'll relock the bottom door when I go back down."

She moved ahead of him, picking her way along ice-glazed steps. "I salted this morning," she said, apologetic. "It seems to have worn off."

"Just be careful." He tried not to focus on the narrow heels of her boots, how they skittered as she planted her foot, or how unbelievably good she looked from behind.

Once secure on the small landing outside the third-story entrance, she turned his way. "Staircase and fire escape in one fell swoop. A package deal."

He didn't dare say what he thought. How the tall, turning, narrow wooden stairway shouldn't be construed as legal or safe. It was probably grandfathered from some old statute. He was sure it wouldn't meet new building code standards, no way, no how.

But she was safe and sound. He nodded. "Make sure you salt these again first thing tomorrow."

She fit her key into the lock. "I will."

"Do you have to go out in the morning?"

She looked up, surprised. "It's Sunday."

Ah, yes. Obligatory church attendance. Right. And she had no car. He hesitated, but no way was he about to invite her to accompany Jess and him to a service he attended in name only. "Walking distance?"

Her eyes said it wasn't, but she gave him the nod he wanted. That made him feel cheesy. "Yes."

"See you Monday, then."

"All right."

She pushed the door open with barely a shove. Great. A door that sealed offered resistance. Not this one. "Thanks for bringing me home."

He paused but refused to look up. "No problem."

"Good night."

He gave a careless wave she couldn't see and continued downward, crunching the rugged soles of his boots against the layer of ice.

She lived in a downscaled apartment that was probably half the price of others in the immediate college area. A three-story walk-up in a drafty old house that could use caulk and weather stripping. Probably insulation, too.

But it was no business of his where she lived or what she did.

The thought of her not being able to attend her church niggled him. Glancing up, squares of yellow light poured across the gabled roof beneath her windows, brightening the snow-covered shingles. A silhouette passed the criss-crossed panes, paused for long seconds, then moved on.

She almost looked out. For him? Why would she do that?

But she didn't, Marc reassured himself as he climbed into the driver's seat. She walked on, just like she should. For an all-too-brief moment, he wished she'd tugged back the curtain to see him. Wave to him.

Sleep deprivation, he decided as the truck roared to life. *There's absolutely no other reason I'd be wishing for a ditzy blonde to wave goodbye to me at zero degrees Fahrenheit with a wind-chill factor I don't even want to think about. I need sleep and I need it bad.*

But he scanned her windows one more time, just in case, before he pulled away and headed across Leroy Street toward Route 11.

Chapter Nine

The ring of the doorbell interrupted Kayla's coffee. She frowned and read the clock. Who would be there before 8:00 a.m.?

She faced a chilly quandary. She could either buzz the person up unseen, or brave the cold to check him/her out.

Safety won. Stepping onto the narrow landing, she peered over the half wall. Surprise mixed with something else as familiar gray-green eyes gazed up from beneath a drawn brow. "Marc?"

He looked disturbed. What else was new? "I've got your keys. Let me up."

"My keys?" She stepped back and punched the button to release the lower lock. His footsteps echoed on the turning staircase. Once at the top, he faced her, gruff.

"You have to walk outside to see who's ringing your doorbell?"

Oh, man. "Yes."

His frown deepened, but instead of talking he handed her the keys she'd left at Macklins'. "Here."

"What will I do with them?" she asked, confused. "The car's at Sarah and Craig's."

"Not anymore."

Kayla frowned. "Then it's…?"

"Parked out front. Wal-Mart opened at seven so I grabbed you a new battery and installed it in Craig's garage. You're all set. You'll be able to go to church now."

He hadn't bought her fib the night before.

Her throat tightened at the unexpected kindness. The early Sunday hour compounded the sacrifice. "You got up early to do that for me?"

He kept his face inscrutable. "I'm always up early. How were you going to work tomorrow with the car at Craig's?"

"I figured I'd get it fixed today."

"At any one of the service shops conducting Sunday hours."

"Hmm." She made a face, weighing his words. "Didn't think of that."

"Luckily, I did." He nodded to her keys. "Without a car, you can't work."

She didn't tell him the nursing service kept a minivan for just that purpose. While her starter was being replaced she'd borrowed a supervisor's car. When your business involved life and death, a broken car wasn't enough to keep you off the road. Marc didn't know that. She smiled up at him. "Thank you, Marc. That's a huge help. How much do I owe you?"

His eyes regarded her, then swept the apartment. "Consider it candy."

"What?"

He stepped in farther.

Kayla waved a hand. "Come in, why don't you?"

He was checking things out before the words were out of her mouth. She widened her eyes. "I'm still trying to figure out the candy thing."

He scowled at her thermostat. "Some families give their nurses a box of candy. Gift certificates to fancy restaurants. We give batteries." Looking perturbed, he eyed the temperature control again, then swung her way. "It's cold in here."

"It'll warm up once the heat comes on."

He crossed to the antique radiator. Determined, he placed his hand atop the heavy, painted metal. "Not likely."

Kayla shrugged, unwilling to say more.

He met her gaze. His mouth opened but then clamped shut. His nostrils flared slightly as he nodded toward the tiny kitchen. "Do I smell coffee?"

"Yes." Dismayed by her rudeness, she moved that way. This guy had gone the distance to fix her car and deliver it to her. She hadn't even offered him a cup of coffee for his trouble. "Come on in. It's warmer in here."

His look took in the flickering votive on the countertop. "Candlelit breakfast?"

She smiled as she filled his mug. "I like how it smells, the mix of spices. Homey. Warm."

His brow lifted and she cringed, wishing she'd picked a different adjective. He added milk and sugar to his cup, took a long sip and nodded. "You make good coffee."

"Thanks."

"And your place is nice."

"Thanks again."

"You been here long?"

"Almost five years."

"And how long has the heat been broken?"

"About…" She stopped, chagrined. Sucking a breath, she reminded him, "It's not broken. It just doesn't pump well to the living room."

"You've mentioned this to Vi?"

Kayla couldn't count the number of times. "It's under control."

"Hmm." Tipping his cup, he finished his coffee in record time and set the broad-handled mug on the counter. "Nice cup."

Kayla tried to read something into that and couldn't. "Thanks. I'm a little surprised that you're noticing my coffee mugs, though."

He headed for the door and stood, gloves tapping against his thigh. "Most girls have cups that match their dishes. Skinny handles. Too wide at the top. I like a solid mug that holds the heat."

"Me, too."

She followed him to the door and put a hand to his sleeve. "Thanks again."

"You're welcome, but we're not done yet."

"No?"

"No." His hand came up, palm cupped, as if he wanted to touch her, cradle her cheek, but then fell back to his side. "Grab your boots and coat."

Boots and coat? "Because?"

He leaned forward until his face was close. Very close. Warm, coffee-scented breath bathed her skin, putting her in mind of lazy mornings and Sunday papers. "It's a long walk back to Craig's and I have to have Jess to church by ten."

"A long— Oh. Of course."

Duh, Kayla. How did you think the guy was going to get back to his truck? She nodded and stepped away from those gray-green eyes, the warm, spiced scent of his aftershave. "I wasn't thinking."

"There's a surprise."

She started to scowl, but that would only heighten his amusement. Her mouth tugged up in a smile instead. "I'll get my coat and be right there."

"Take a minute," he advised. He swung open the door. He glared at how easily it tugged free, but when he turned, his expression was easy. "I'll salt the steps before you fall and break your neck."

"Okay."

He shut the door as he stepped outside, then hoisted the thirty-pound bag with a man's ease. Deliberate, he sprinkled gray-white crystals over the iced decking.

Kayla hurried to the closet and pulled out her coat, then pushed her feet into her boots. By the time she was dressed, Marc had disappeared. She stepped onto the ice and felt the reassuring traction of salt beneath her boots.

For a quick moment she reveled in the feeling of someone caring for her, doing a nice thing with no payback required.

Pete's illness sobered her moment of fantasy. Marc DeHollander was rescuing her out of a sense of regard for his father's health. She'd be silly to think otherwise. For just a moment, though, it had been nice to be silly.

* * *

It didn't add up.

She lived in a cheap, chilled apartment but wore trend-setting clothes. Her television was a seventies throwback. Thrift store furniture. A few pillows and throws warmed the appearance, but not much. As if she was waiting to move out. Pack it in.

Marc shrugged as he waited. The spartan apartment only added weight to his assessment. Kayla Doherty wouldn't stay in the North Country. Everything about her said "moving on."

That was okay by him. He knew better than to think a girl like Kayla would find happiness in the rugged climate of the Adirondack region. Better she follow her dream, whatever it was. As long as she took good care of his father, Marc could care less.

Hearing her footsteps, he squared his shoulders. She stepped out, swung the door shut and waved her keys. "Come on, Farmer Boy, let's get you back to your truck. I didn't mean to hold you up."

He fell into step beside her, then grabbed her arm when she slipped on a patch of ice-glazed snow. "Does anybody own a shovel, or do you all just walk on the snow and pack it down?"

She scrunched up her face, guilty.

She used that expression often. He tried to remember when he started thinking it was cute, imagining a little girl with Kayla's features. A tiny version of Kayla with a pointy chin and huge, round eyes, who would follow him around the farm like Jess had.

Yeah. Round eyes. Pointy chin. Like the aliens in Independence Day.

Imagining that kept him rational. Rational was good. No way did he want to deal with the broken heart Kayla Doherty was sure to hand out. She smiled up at him as he opened the door for her. His breath hitched, watching her, eyeing her mouth.

His internal warning system brought Marc back to earth. Marc had developed a safety net to save him from his own stupidity.

He stepped back and ground his jaw before moving to the

opposite side of the car. A girl like Kayla wasn't meant to hang around too long. Marc had no intention of being in the path of total destruction.

"Jess. How are you?"

"Kayla!" Jess flung her coat and boots as she charged into the house late Monday. "I'm so glad you're here."

"Your dad said you wanted to see me." Kayla smiled, then offered Jess's outfit a nod of approval. "I like the way that sweater sets off the shirt. Cute. Solid."

"Seriously?" Jess sparkled and Kayla flung an arm around her shoulders.

"Girlfriends don't lie about something that important. Our mantra? It's totally about the look. How's school?"

Marc pushed through the door. Anger swept aside what might have been a welcoming gaze. Kayla swallowed hard, unable to remember what she'd just asked Jess.

Luckily, Jess didn't notice. "School's fine." She saw Marc eye her jacket and boots. She picked up her coat and pegged it while Kayla set her boots in place. Marc shook his head, bemused, then stopped, sniffed and turned, puzzled. "What's cooking?"

"Lasagna. And garlic bread. With mozzarella and parmesan."

"I love lasagna," declared Jess. She grinned at Kayla. "So do Marc and Dad. How did you know?"

Kayla crossed to the stove and stirred the extra sauce. "I didn't, but since I like lasagna, I figured it would be a nice way to thank your brother for fixing my car yesterday."

"You fixed her car?" Jess turned. "When? I was with you all day."

"First thing in the morning," Kayla replied when it became apparent that Marc had no intention of joining the conversation. He avoided her gaze by staring into his coffee cup.

"Really?" Jess drew out the word. At Kayla's look of warning, Jess nodded, woman-to-woman. "Well," she added, matter-of-factly, "that was nice of you, Marc. I'm going to spend some time with Dad until supper's ready. Think he'll join us?"

Kayla hesitated. "I wouldn't count on it. He's pretty tired. You go see him, see what you think. You guys could always eat in there. You've got tray tables in the living room."

Jess brightened. "That's a good idea."

As she turned to leave, Marc called her name. Jess swung back. "Yeah?"

He waved in her general direction. "That looks nice." When Jess looked confused, he continued, "That sweater thing. I like it."

She stared, then dropped her gaze to sweep the outfit Kayla complimented earlier. "Thanks, I think. Are you all right?"

"Fine."

"Okay, then." She slid a look of surprise to Kayla, then grinned at her brother. "I'm going to see Dad, now. Thanks for noticing my clothes, Marc. Those consciousness-raising classes are really paying off."

She ducked the towel Marc pitched at her and disappeared.

Marc watched her go before shifting his attention to Kayla. His eyes dimmed. "You didn't have to do this."

She nodded, determined to ignore the note of displeasure. "I know." She reached into the cupboard and withdrew three plates. "I wanted you to know I was grateful for your help. And I needed to see Jess. Your dad said she'd been pestering him about when I'd be back, so I decided to cover both bases with one pan of lasagna." She smiled. "Pretty frugal, actually."

"Like your apartment?"

His tone was casual. Kayla hedged. She wasn't good at talking about herself, why she did what she did, proving to herself she could stand the cold, no matter what. "It's affordable, if not perfect. I'm saving for my own place and I hate to throw away money on higher rent."

"That's fine, but your living space should be warm. And safe."

"I can handle the cold."

She could. She knew that from experience. She hated the chill, the discomfort, but refused to let it win. No matter what, she would emerge triumphant, old fears vanquished. She slanted him a look. "Anyway, spring will be here soon."

Marc laughed, skeptical. "It's February. Spring's a long way off."

"Not so far."

Her optimism made him groan. He poured another cup of coffee and moved closer, his voice low. "Dad's slipping."

No evading this. "Yes."

Marc swore under his breath. His face changed. Seeing his distress, she wanted to help him, but there was little she could do. Death loomed inevitable. If accepted, the passing from mortal life to immortality with God wasn't such a hard road. Treated like an enemy, death proved a formidable foe, ever victorious. She didn't want Marc to see it that way, but didn't know how to ease his frustration.

She'd seen the gentle side of him, how careful he was to brace his father in strong hands when helping the older man out of bed. The hours he spent reading to Pete, talking with him, arguing hockey stats and football greats when he should have been tending cattle. There wouldn't be much more male back-and-forth. Kayla knew that would be a bitter pill for Marc. It would be him and Jess against the world, orphaned together. But they had each other, and a father who'd loved them since birth. They were way ahead of her on that score.

Marc eyed the plates. "You're not staying?"

She shook her head. "I left some at home. You guys need time together, without outsiders. As things progress, you'll have people in and out." She didn't get more specific than that. She knew he understood. "It's good to have family time now."

He stepped forward and reached into the cupboard, withdrawing a fourth plate. "Please stay."

Kayla stared, then blinked. "I—"

He moved close. So close. She could count the tiny flecks of gold in his gray-green eyes, their muted tones the color of thin, wisped clouds in a summer sunset. "For Jess."

Of course. How foolish she was. For just a moment she thought… *Crazy, girl, just plain crazy.*

His hand brushed hers as she accepted the plate. Just a brush of the knuckles, but enough to send her heart racing, wishing he'd clasp her fingers. Smile down at her. Touch her cheek with his work-worn hands.

She *was* crazy. Crazy as a loon. She'd be leaving the North Country soon, her loans paid, her commitment fulfilled. She wanted sunshine and light, flora and fauna. A Kinkade bungalow, minus the thatched roof.

Something Anna said came back to her. "I always wanted what I couldn't have and never realized I had everything I wanted until I threw it all away."

Anna. Her initial hospice patient taught Kayla about life and loss, love and fear. When she lost her long battle with HIV-related ailments, Kayla stood by the unmarked grave and cried. She cried for the mother she'd lost and the children Anna abandoned. She cried for all young souls bereft of mothers.

Her freshman year professor had rambled about it in Psych 101, making the link between abandonment and lack of conscience formation. The emptiness brought by parental desertion. Holes that could never be filled.

But the professor forgot about God. The strength that came with belief in a higher power.

Maybe Kayla should advise him to restructure his lesson plan. There *was* a hole-filling substance, a transcending grace. She'd found it as she tended an indigent woman, seeking peace at death's door.

So why did she continue punishing herself? Living cold in an attic apartment. What was she trying to prove?

She knew the answer. It was a no-brainer. She made her choices to prove that she was in charge. She had control.

Nodding Marc's way, she set out four plates and arranged the silverware in case Pete wanted to make it to the table. "I'll stay," she told Marc, without looking up. "For Jess."

Chapter Ten

"Mr. D.?" Kayla popped her head through the bedroom door Thursday afternoon.

"I'm awake."

"Good." She smiled as she crossed the room. "How are you doing?"

His face looked tired, but his eyes held sparkle. "All right. How about you?"

"Hmm." She mock-scowled. "You really want to know?"

"I asked, didn't I?"

"Oh. Well. You're feisty." She made a face as she dropped into the chair, ticking off her fingers. "I slipped down the bottom three stairs of my outdoor stairway and landed on my butt, so maybe that will teach me to shovel and salt more often like your son advised. I got a parking ticket in Canton because people are coming into town for the big game and I had to squeeze close to someone's driveway. They called the sheriff, so that little fine is gonna chip away at the old checking account. I was going to stop and grab you a few treats from Main Street Bakery, but I got caught at Miss Mary's and Miss Martha's, and there's no way you can get away from them without a good, long chat." Kayla paused, then held out her hands. "And I broke a nail."

Pete hooted. "Poor thing."

She grinned, then smoothed a hand across his forehead. "How are you really feeling?"

His expression sobered. "I've been better."

"I thought as much. Your respiration's up and your eyes aren't as relaxed. Same meds as Monday? No changes?"

"Everything's the same. Except me."

"You're not in pain?"

He shook his head. "Not really. Not much, anyway. I get tired of being in this bed, but I'm too winded to get out much. Marc takes good care of me," he added, as if defending him.

She made a sympathetic noise. "I know that. They both love you, Mr. D."

His hand worried the blanket's edge. "I don't know how to say goodbye." After long seconds of staring, he blinked. "No mother, no father. What have Ari and I done to these kids?"

Kayla posed her next question carefully. "Would she come, if asked?"

Pete shook his head. "No. Her coming would only confuse matters." He heaved a sigh. His left hand moved, restless. "Marc is so angry with her that he still can't see straight, and Jess never knew her. They'd be complete strangers. No," he frowned before meeting her gaze, "it wouldn't be in anyone's best interest now."

"Have you forgiven her?" Kayla clasped his hand. Skin that had once been vigorous felt waxen beneath her fingers.

Pete nodded. "A long time ago. Ari wasn't like the rest of us. I saw it," he confessed, his eyes dark. "I saw the difference and married her anyway. Thought that since she loved me, it would be all right. That I could make things better."

"You couldn't."

"She had pills that helped." His gaze moved to something unseen. His lips thinned. "They kept her focused. But they made her feel caged. She felt trapped in her own skin. She'd stop taking them and fly off on a tangent. She was exciting without them, but…"

"Unpredictable?"

"You can say that again. When she was off 'em, I never knew what to expect. Then she found out she was pregnant with Jess and nearly came undone. It was all I could do to keep her under control until Jess was born." Pain shadowed the older man's eyes. "One time I found her in the hay loft. She wanted to fly away, she said, and she perched in the bale loading door with her hands up high. I didn't know what to do," Pete confessed. His fingers picked at the satin binding. "If I climbed up, she might jump. If I stood outside, I had no chance of getting to her."

"Where was Marc?"

"Sleeping, thank God. Her rough times were hard on him. He never knew what to expect. Don't get me wrong," Pete added, his voice thinning. "She wasn't a bad mother in the beginning. She just couldn't stand to take those pills month after month. Year after year."

"She didn't jump."

"No." Pete narrowed his gaze. "She stood there awhile, shrieking and singing, all wild and crazed. Then she stopped, smiled down at me and held out a hand. 'Come get me, Pete.'"

"Really?"

He nodded. "I said, 'Are you okay if I come up the ladder?' and she answered, 'I'm right here waiting for you, Pete. I'm not going anywhere without you.'"

"But she did, once Jess was born."

Pete's face clouded. "If only she realized I didn't care like she did. I understood her like no one else could. I loved her."

Kayla gave him a blank look. "You lost me."

Her words straightened his shoulders. "Just an old man's ramblings." His appearance said it was time to change the subject. Squeezing his hand, Kayla stood to check his vitals. She jerked her head toward the kitchen. "We have a birthday to celebrate."

Pete nodded, mute, while she checked his temperature. Once she'd removed the probe, he smiled. "We sure do."

"I didn't realize," she explained. "Or I'd have grabbed something for Jess. The box on the table with the big, pink bow was a giveaway," she continued.

Pete grinned. "Jess was born in June."

"Then…" A commotion drew Kayla's attention.

* * *

Jess walked in balancing a chocolate cake, the top lit with way too many candles for her. Marc followed. Singing "Happy Birthday" in really bad harmony, they said her name instead of Jess's.

"How did you know?" She put a hand to her throat, fighting emotion, her voice a whisper.

"Talk later. Blow out the candles before we explode." Marc's look encompassed his father's oxygen.

Kayla smiled at his typical candor, drew a huge breath, then blew.

"You got them!" Jess beamed, her dark eyes bright.

Kayla feigned shortness of breath. "How many of those babies did you put on?" she demanded. "I'm not that old, am I?"

"Twenty-nine," retorted Marc. "One more year and you join the statistical nightmare of looking for a mate past the age of—"

"I get it, thanks." Kayla noted the amusement in his eyes. "Luckily I've never been a big fan of statistics. When God's ready for me to find the right man, he'll just plunk him down in front of me and say, 'Here he is, Kayla, all yours. Do what you can with him.'"

"That easy, huh?" Marc rolled his eyes as he helped Jess remove candles. "Simplistic."

"I'm a simple girl, Farmer Boy."

He swept her designer cowl-neck sweater and lined trousers a look of doubt. "Right."

"You like chocolate, don't you, Kayla?" Jess asked.

"Can't imagine life without it." Kayla ruffled the teen's hair. "But you still didn't tell me how you knew my birthday was this weekend."

"Sarah and Craig mentioned it on Sunday," Marc replied.

"They did, huh? Since I'm watching the baby tonight, I'll be sure to thank them. Or throttle them."

Jess grabbed her around the waist. "We have two kinds of ice cream. Sit and let us wait on you."

"But—"

"No buts," Jess commanded. "This is our gig. You finish up

with Dad while we get things ready. Chocolate caramel crunch or fudge swirl?"

"The first one," declared Kayla. She turned to Pete. "How about you, Mr. D.? Which kind would you like?"

"I'm a fudge swirl guy," he admitted.

Jess planted a gentle kiss to his cheek. "Exactly why we got it. Back in a minute."

When Marc and Jess had taken the cake into the kitchen, Pete turned to Kayla. "What I was saying before? About Ari? It's not common knowledge."

"You mean—"

"All of it." Pete's face showed the strain of trying too hard.

Kayla eased her palm across his forehead. "Consider it confidential."

"Thank you."

Marc and Jess helped take things to the car nearly an hour later. Marc glanced at his watch. "You've got plenty of time to get to Craig and Sarah's if you don't go home first."

Kayla agreed. "You're right. Listen, guys, I want to thank you again for these presents. You didn't have to do this."

Marc hoisted the box that contained a safety-conscious space heater and tucked it into the backseat of her car. "I think we did. I've been in your apartment, remember? If it makes you nervous, don't leave it on overnight. Just use it in the evening so you can relax in your living room."

Heat suffused her cheeks. He sounded almost concerned, but she knew better. "I love the socks."

The heater had been a combined gift from the family. Marc had made a trip to Ostrander's and bought her four pairs of thick wool socks like his, but smaller.

He shrugged. "I was tired of seeing your toes through your old ones."

"They were wearing thin," she acknowledged.

"Thin?" Marc stared. "I can read the sports section through them. Chuck 'em."

"I will." On impulse she reached a hand to his beard-roughened jaw. "Thank you."

He blinked long and slow, his gaze tracing her face, her eyes. Resting there. Then he backed up and nodded to his watch. "Better go."

"Right." She slid into the car, set a plate of extra cake on the seat to her right and smiled up at both of them. "Call me if you have any problems," she told them through her open window. "Otherwise, I'll see you Monday."

"All right."

"Bye, Kayla! Happy birthday!"

She waved, then hit the button to close the window before she headed out of the graveled drive.

Monday. *Too long.*

Marc pushed thoughts of Kayla aside while he trucked water to the cows. Calving would commence soon and he needed to concentrate his efforts. Lessen the distractions. He didn't care to have a repeat performance of January's bad birthing.

He threw another sack of cracked corn onto the growing pile in the feed store and tried to bury himself in manual labor. When the steady process left too much thinking time, he cranked a country station. Maybe music would push thoughts of Kayla out of his mind. Give him some peace.

That's not the peace you're looking for, son.

Marc buried that thought. He knew what he was looking for, had known it all along. He wanted the family dynamics that eluded his dad. Not a wife who couldn't handle the rigors of the North Country, who put fashion before common sense. When Marc got serious, he wanted someone at peace with the land, at home in his house.

A vision of Kayla's coat hooked next to his zipped flannel had him squaring his shoulders.

He couldn't deny the attraction. She invaded his thoughts despite his best efforts. With his father's impending death, Kayla Doherty, R.N., was a wonderful asset. But that was it, he told himself firmly as the radio station slid into Brad Paisley's "I Thought I Loved You Then."

Thoughts of Kayla's face came to mind. She was spunk and spice, nipped and tucked into one great package.

Marc sat on the feed stack, his head in his hands. It was no good thinking along these lines. They had nothing in common. She was free flight. He was tied to the land. She looked at the bright side of things, while he took careful measure. She had an innocent faith in God that showed in everything except her temper.

He grinned. Obviously, her flash and sizzle were works in progress.

He liked that about her. She was willing to work to better herself. That made the cold attic apartment out of sync with the rest of the girl. Why would she punish herself for seven months of the year when she had the option to move or insist on a better heating system?

He had no idea. What he did know was that the curvy nurse had every intention of leaving once her commitment was fulfilled.

He reattached a pallet of pig feed. There wasn't much to keep a pretty thing like Kayla happy in the North Country. No cool designer shops, no trendy malls.

His heart hitched. Would she need all that if she had the right man? A husband to love and cherish her all the rest of her days?

Thoughts of his mother crashed in. The love of clothes, for looking just so, being the envy of all. If it was out there and fashionable, Arianna DeHollander had bought it. Spark and sizzle, smoke and mirrors.

Then she was gone.

Try as he might, Marc couldn't separate the two. He didn't want a trophy wife. He wanted warmth and substance, worth and longevity.

Marc eyed the day, cold and clear, the sun sharp. Reflected rays bounced from fresh snow cover, blinding and bright. He glared at the sky, unsmogged, unhazed, the air crisp and clean. "Don't think You can con me with wayward thoughts. I've got a plan and intend to stick to it. I don't need a hook to heaven, a flighty girl or the host of problems that come with either. Leave me alone."

He heard no answering rumble of thunder. Saw no burning bush. Marc glanced around, glad no one bore witness to his obvious mental breakdown. Shouting at the heavens for God to stop sending him covert messages? What next?

The song ended and the DJ came on, effusive. "That went out by request to Laura in Canton from her husband Gary. He says, 'Happy anniversary, honey.'"

Marc smacked a hand to the back of his neck. Some nice guy dedicates a love song to his wife, and he construes it as a message from God. *Right. Good going, DeHollander. Find me an omniscient being who ignores the pleas of children. Who allows the evils surrounding us. War. Anger. Dissent. It doesn't jive. No loving God would sit back and watch it unfold. Would he?*

He turned off the radio with more vigor than necessary and headed to the barn. Grace's confinement was days away. He didn't want to face Jess if anything happened to the mare or her foal, but he'd been breeding animals long enough to understand the inherent dangers. Life didn't always turn out as you planned, but he'd spare Jess what he could.

Marc tugged off his left glove and grabbed up the ringing cell phone later that day. "DeHollander."

A feminine sigh came back to him, soft. Evocative. A tickle of delight made him grip the phone tighter. "That's no way to answer a phone, Farmer Boy."

"It's a business phone." Marc fought a grin at the sound of Kayla's voice, wondering if the upsurge in his heart rate was a healthy sign or implied imminent cardiac arrest. Then he wondered which might be worse.

"Why not 'DeHollander Feed Store' or 'DeHollander Hereford Holdings'?" she continued. "Something more cordial than barking 'DeHollander' into the mouthpiece."

"Was there a reason for this call?" Annoying, even when cute. Why was that?

"Yes," she answered. He heard a slight tapping in the background. "I'm holding two tickets to tonight's hockey game. I wondered if you and Jess might like to go."

St. Lawrence versus Cornell, a man-to-man ice battle. Marc breathed deep. Any Division One hockey fan would want a seat, no question. Still, he didn't hesitate. "We'd better stay with Dad."

"I'll stay with him," Kayla declared. "I'm sorry, I should have said that up front. I'll hang out with Mr. D., play cards, watch a movie, whatever. You guys will only be gone a few hours and he and I can chat that long without trying."

That was certainly true. His quiet father became a spirited debater with Kayla. Marc contemplated her offer. "How'd you get tickets?"

Admission for this contest had gone instantly. Marc hadn't even tried, knowing he shouldn't leave his father.

"A grateful family gave them to me this morning," she replied.

"You should go, then."

She laughed. "I thought of that, but there's no one to use the second ticket. Then I remembered how you liked hockey and thought it might be a good time to spend with Jess."

It would. He'd been concerned about her lack of friends, the few times she ventured out. Had he sheltered her too much in his quest to keep her as unlike their mother as possible? Probably, but he didn't know any other way to ensure a good outcome. "It would be fun. You sure you don't mind giving up your Friday night? Putting away your party shoes?"

Kayla laughed. "Not too many parties hereabouts, unless you're part of the college crowd. Spare me that, please. I'll come by around six, okay?"

"It's very okay. Thanks, Kayla."

He thought he heard a smile in her voice because he'd used her given name. "You're welcome, Marc."

Chapter Eleven

The night lay thick as Kayla wound her way along familiar roads. Celestial torches marked a star-soaked sky. Stars in the northern latitudes blazed brighter, longer. Was it the cleaner air? Less light pollution? Kayla had no idea, but she appreciated the brilliance, the way heaven tipped closer at night.

It was a big land, sometimes cruel. Just last week an old woman was found frozen in the snow. She'd fallen retrieving her morning mail and remained unfound for nearly a day.

North Country cold could be unforgiving, but it was no match for Kayla. She'd been cold before and she'd survived.

The shiver that thought inspired had nothing to do with the temperature.

She remembered Anna's hand as she reached out from the hospital bed, watching Kayla, her eyes dark with concern. "Whatever it is, let it go. Give it to God. Don't hold on to the anger. Your mother wouldn't want that."

Her mother? Kayla choked back bile at the thought.

Anna knew nothing of Kayla's mother, nothing of the locked room at the top of the stairs. The frightening sounds below.

Anna covered Kayla's hand. She was nearing her last days and still she ministered to Kayla, not the other way around. "Can you forgive her?"

Kayla shook her head, throat tight. "I don't know how."

Anna smiled. "He'll show you. He forgave those who murdered His only son. He'll show you the way, sweet Kayla."

It hadn't happened yet. Kayla hadn't a clue how to forgive those early atrocities. She'd shoved them away, determined to overcome her shoddy beginnings. She was cool and capable, sharp and smart. Kayla Doherty knew who she was and where she was going. Nothing got in her way.

Mostly because she refused to look back.

"We're never really free until we lose those bonds," Anna explained.

Easy to say… "Has *your* family forgiven you?"

Anna's eyes shadowed. Sorrow painted her features. "No. They won't. I hurt them. All of them."

Kayla grasped her hand. Unsure what to say, she squeezed the other woman's fingers. "I'm sure they've gotten over it."

"Kids don't." Anna stared out the window before shifting her gaze. "Not on their own. They need God's help, the help of a parent who won't let them down." She paused again. Her lips pursed in self-recrimination. "I was never that kind of mother."

Kayla had to ask. "With all that's happened to you, how can you still believe in God?"

Anna's face softened. "He was there all the while, child. I just ignored Him."

"Still…"

"No." Anna sank back, tired. Kayla felt guilty for making her talk, but longed for her gentle wisdom. "There was help for me. I disregarded it. There was a family who loved me. I resisted their help. There was a time and a place for me to make my mark and I walked away from it. I don't excuse my mistakes," she told Kayla, grim. "But God forgives even sinners like me. How much more easily will He open His arms to you?"

Her words nicked Kayla's armor. "If He knew…"

"He knows. He sees. He understands." Anna graced Kayla's

cheek with a touch. "Nothing you've done is beyond His for-giveness. He wants you, heart and soul."

"You make it sound simple." Kayla knew better. Nothing worth having was easy. She'd lived that truth long enough to respect its depth.

The dying woman smiled. "I wish I'd known how simple it was. Everything could have been different." She grimaced then, her face contorting.

"Are you in pain? Can I get you anything?"

Anna shook her head, but reached for Kayla's fingers. "Just sit with me. For a little while."

Kayla nodded and sat quiet while the older woman sank into sleep.

Anna's words piqued and dismayed Kayla. How easily the dying woman believed in a bountiful God, despite her wretched life. Kayla frowned at the inconsistencies, then recalled Anna's confession. "I chose to ignore it."

Was it that easy to stray? By simply ignoring the choices?

One of her foster mothers was a churchgoer. Kayla went to services with her. She'd loved the smells of the old church, the antique lighting, the warm intones of the prayers. She'd felt safe there. Normal.

But her foster father was transferred to Colorado and Kayla was left for others to tend. Still, she never forgot the feeling of safety she'd felt in that old, stone church.

Anna's death sparked no funeral. Kayla attended the indigent woman's burial in a county plot. She voiced her own prayers at the graveside, wondering if God cared that a guilt-laden nurse prayed for the soul of a dead bag lady in an unmarked corner of a windswept cemetery.

And now… Kayla jerked out of her memories as she approached the DeHollander drive.

Now she was a full-fledged member of Holy Trinity. She was part of a family, a church family. They'd opened their arms to her. Of course they didn't know who she really was, or what she'd come from, but every now and again she wondered if they'd care. She hoped not.

* * *

"You're sure you don't mind not going?" Marc had already asked twice, but he felt the need to press. It was St. Lawrence versus Cornell, after all.

"Ask me again and I'll keep the tickets," Kayla growled. She hoisted her book. "If your dad sleeps, I've got this. It's nice to relax where it's warm and cozy."

He shot her an exasperated look. "Did you try your space heater yet?"

"No." She sighed. "I was only home for minutes last night before I went to bed and I'm here tonight. Tomorrow. I promise."

"Good." What did he care? Why did he worry about her? What was it to him if her toes froze into one solid block? He glanced down. "You're wearing the socks."

"They're great." She wiggled her toes for effect. "You can't even see my toenail polish through them."

A solid relief. What Marc didn't need was a sneak peek at Kayla's perky toes, probably tipped the same saucy red gracing her fingernails tonight. He shook his head. "Wool socks and sandals."

"Clogs," she corrected.

Jess came down the stairs, bundled against the chill of the indoor ice arena.

"Open-toed clogs," Kayla continued. "Not sandals. Sandals are for summer."

"So are—" He stopped and shook his head in resignation. Things were peaceful at the moment. Best to keep his silence. He zipped his jacket and reached for the door. "Ready, Jess?"

"Yes." She threw her arms around Kayla. "Thank you for doing this."

Kayla hugged her back. "Glad to. If your dad's in one of his talkative moods, I get to dig up dirt on you two." She winked as she let Jess go.

"I can fill you in on stuff about Marc," declared the teen. "Lists of girlfriends, crazy parties…"

"Ancient history, Jess." Why did he feel funny having Kayla know he wasn't always the solid citizen he laid claim to today? Everyone did stupid things as a kid, right? Somehow, her opinion mattered. Her respect. He tugged Jess's sleeve. "Let's go. I don't want to miss face-off."

"All right." Jess turned, then swung back. "Marc has his phone. You've got his number?"

"In my pocket and taped by the wall phone. I shouldn't need it, though."

Jess squared her shoulders. "I just wanted to be sure."

"I'll call if anything happens."

Kayla's matter-of-fact tone offered reassurance. Marc laid a hand on Jess's shoulder. "Thanks, Kayla."

She met his gaze. It took effort to hold himself back, not reach out to her. Give her a quick kiss goodbye. "You're welcome, Marc."

"You haven't been much company tonight," Kayla chided Pete as he stirred nearly two hours later. "Sleeping the night away."

Pete blinked. "A night call? Am I dying?"

She grinned. "Eventually. But that's not why I'm here. Marc and Jess went to the hockey game, remember?"

"Now I do." Pete gave her a tired smile. "Things come and go in my recent memory. I remember things from long ago like they were yesterday, but the stuff now?" He shrugged. "Not so much."

"Meds can interfere with short-term memory," Kayla told him. "Makes it tricky sometimes."

"What was your name again?"

Kayla appraised him, then saw the glimmer in his eye. "Very funny. Are you comfortable, Mr. D.? Can I get you anything?"

"I'm all right." He struggled to pull himself more upright. Kayla helped him.

"Better?"

"Yes." He smiled, but the look behind the smile stayed tired despite copious amounts of sleep. "It was nice of you to give them the tickets."

"So now you remember."

He nodded.

Kayla tucked her book away. "Would you like to beat me at Scrabble?"

"Aren't you any good?"

"Oh, I'm good, but it's not nice to beat patients on borrowed time."

"I won't be buying green bananas, that's for sure," he shot back. He scanned the shelf across from his bed and pointed. "Scrabble's right there if you think you're tough enough to take me on. And no holding back because I'm sick," he added.

"Please. I'll win fair and square and brag about it wherever I go."

"Talk's cheap. Get the box."

Thirty minutes later Kayla eyed him, assessing. "Pyx is not a word."

"It is."

Kayla shook her head. "No way I'm buying that. And for a triple word score besides? Uh-uh."

"Dictionary's right here." His voice went expectant, anticipating victory.

"Hmm." Kayla surveyed the board before sizing up her competition. Well-practiced, his expression told her nothing. "Pyx, huh? You look too sure of yourself and it's not worth losing my turn. I'll play my tiles."

He grinned, triumphant. When they finished the game, she faced him, eyes narrowed. "Gloating's an unattractive trait, Mr. D. It was only seven points."

He beamed. "A win's a win."

Kayla sighed. "Too true. So tell me. Is pyx a word or should I have challenged you? "

"It's the box that holds Eucharistic wafers."

"Not exactly common usage."

"Common enough in a church," he argued as he laid away the game. "Ari always went to church when she was young. She fell away as she got older. I've often wondered if that was my fault."

"Why?" Kayla set the box in its customary spot and turned, curious.

"I didn't go back then," Pete explained. "I was always working and I left it to her to see to Marc's upbringing. I got careless, then she got careless, then she was gone and I was left with an angry son and a baby daughter."

"You did things differently with Jess."

"Oh, yes." He nodded, solemn. "I wasn't going to mess up again. I thought I gave Marc so much by teaching him to farm, to love the land. He's got a great hand with animals. But I left out the most important component and then it was too late. He was angry at his mother and had no faith to fall back on."

"It's never too late, Mr. D." Kayla knew that firsthand.

"What time is it?"

"Nearly ten."

"Can you do something for me?"

She moved to the side of the bed. "Of course."

"I need you to go upstairs, into the middle bedroom."

"A clandestine mission. My favorite."

That drew a smile. "In the tall dresser, third drawer from the top, beneath the stack of pants, there's a picture. I want you to bring it down."

His respirations rose. Kayla smoothed a hand across his covers, gave his fingers a light squeeze and nodded. "I'll be right back."

At the top of the stairs she paused. Walking forward, she stepped through the center door and switched on the light.

The woman's touch was evident, if old. Floral-striped wallpaper half covered three walls. A stenciled border marked the wall's upper edge. Kayla moved to the dresser. Sliding open the third drawer, she worked her hand beneath sturdy jeans. Her fingers met metal. Carefully, she withdrew the frame and held it up.

Four people looked back at her. A man, a woman, a much younger Marc and a baby, perched on the woman's hip. Kayla ran her fingers over the family portrait. For that moment they looked happy. Pete's arm draped his wife's shoulders, his smile benevolent. Marc looked ruggedly handsome, even as a teen.

Jess was adorable, her chipmunk cheeks round and full, her mouth open in a toothless grin.

And Ari, Pete's wife. Kayla studied the woman who'd left it all behind. Dark hair tumbled over narrow shoulders, a riot of curls. A crisp white sleeveless blouse, whose pin-tucked lines screamed quality, nipped into front-pleated pants that echoed the conclusion. She smiled into the camera, bright, vibrant, healthy and happy. The picture-perfect wife and mother.

As Kayla reached to switch off the light, the photo shifted.

She paused, staring down. Her fingers clenched.

It can't be.

Kayla's heart stutter-stepped as she reexamined the image, studying the blue-stoned ring on Ari's fourth finger, right hand.

Kayla sank onto the bed, thoughts churning. Once more she tilted the picture. Once more she reached the same conclusion. This very ring now sat in a velvet box on her dresser, a gift from Anna.

But how? Why?

Christy's words flooded back. *They come home to die.*

Is that what Anna did? She came back to die near her family? But she hadn't contacted them or asked about them. And her name, Anna?

Arianna. She remembered Pete saying that the first time they'd discussed her. The sound half lament, half love.

Arianna DeHollander was Anna Hernandez, Kayla's faith mentor.

Kayla gripped the frame. What should she do? What could she say? Should she tell Pete that Ari was dead, had died a short ride away, unaccompanied by anyone but her nurse? That she lay in a pauper's grave nearby?

She had no idea what choice to make. The woman who blessed her with faith and love broke a trio of hearts in this house.

Kayla swallowed hard. No way could she make this right in her own head, much less convey it to the family that lived and loved in this quaint old farmhouse.

She drew a deep breath and approached the stairs. *Father,*

help me. I don't know what to do with this information. I don't want to add sorrow to pain, but I can't imagine keeping this to myself.

At the bottom of the stairs, she turned the photo, double checking.

Anna. Arianna. One and the same. Without the ring she wouldn't have recognized it. Thirteen years of living hard had altered the woman's appearance. Anna's worn, heartfelt smile was nothing like Ari's camera-ready expression. Anna's face held eyes beleaguered by a decade of drugs and hard knocks.

Ari was sharp, a Latin vision of beauty and poise, camera-savvy from top to bottom.

The door opened with a blast of cold air. "We won!" Jess threw chilled arms around Kayla's middle and hugged. "Four-three, with the Saints scoring their fourth goal in the closing minutes. You should have come."

"Then one of you would have stayed home," Kayla reminded her. There was no way to hide the picture in her hands. Jess eyed it, her expression guarded.

"Where did you get that?"

"Your father's dresser."

"Why?"

"He asked me to."

Jess stared at the woman who looked like an older version of herself, her face awash in emotion, then she squared her shoulders in acceptance. "I'll let you take it to him while I get rid of some layers. I checked on Grace. Marc's checking the cattle."

Kayla wavered, then moved to the bedroom. Jess was right. Pete wanted the picture for his own comfort. When she stepped to the side of the bed, his eyes opened.

"Took you long enough."

"I got sidetracked," Kayla told him. She paused. "Jess is home."

Pete's eyes flickered, uncertain. He glanced at the picture she held, then toughened his gaze. "Can you set that on the night-stand so I can see it?"

Kayla did, then perched on the side of the bed, unsure what to say.

"We were happy once."

"You seem happy now, Mr. D." She kept her voice gentle.

"But it's not the same as being together. A family."

"You've done well. Marc is strong and successful, Jess is warm and loving."

He brought his gaze around. "Marc is distrustful of life and love and Jess has no woman to confide in. There's a lack in these walls and I've known it a long time."

"You did your best."

"Did I?" He examined the picture. "Maybe I did, maybe I didn't."

Kayla's heart hammered. Should she tell him what she knew, how Anna regretted her choices? That she died alone, a vagrant whose history read like a big-city Jane Doe?

Jess's arrival spared her decision.

"What a game! Give me the remote, they'll show highlights on the news. Cooper was amazing in the attack zone, and Dobson played the boards like he was born to it."

Pete grinned up at her. "Hockey and horses. You should have been a boy."

"But I clean up nice." Jess twinkled down at him. Her eyes strayed to the picture, but she kept her silence. Whatever feelings Jess had for the woman who'd abandoned her were hidden for the moment.

Kayla stood. "Since you guys are back, I'll head out." She stretched and yawned. "It's been a long day."

"Thanks, Kayla."

Marc's voice gave her a start. She turned, half frowning, half smiling. "I thought you were in the barn."

"Everything's fine there."

Kayla gave Mr. D. a smile and Jess a hug. "See you Monday."

She ducked through the doorway so she wouldn't block the TV. As she rounded the kitchen, Marc caught her arm. "What's wrong?"

She hesitated, eyes down. "Nothing. Just tired."

He studied her, his look sharp. "No."

"It's been a long day, Farmer Boy."

"Testy," he mused. "But only with me. Why is that?"

She had no energy to spar with him. Her nerves lay too near the surface, and things that should have never involved this family now linked her to them.

Rule one of nursing: When you're tired, sleep. Kayla needed to rest and wake refreshed to reexamine the problem. Right now she rode on emotion alone. Not good.

"I'm not testy. Well, maybe a little, but just from being tired." She lifted her gaze to his. "I'm a morning person."

He eyed her. The hand on her arm gentled. "Are you okay to drive? I could take you."

Her heart thumped at his look, his words. She glanced down, then realized she should warn him about the picture. "Your father asked me to bring down a family picture. From upstairs."

Marc frowned, confused.

"With your mother."

He swore, then shook his head in realization. "Sorry. I just…" He scrubbed a hand across his face, then shrugged, his expression softening. "Whatever he needs is fine. Were you afraid I'd be angry?"

"I can understand you don't love reminders."

He straightened. "Jess is vulnerable right now. She has no mother and her father is dying. I'm okay."

Uh-huh. Kayla worked her jaw before turning to her boots. "Right."

"What's that supposed to mean?"

She shook her head, looking down. "Just agreeing with you, Marc."

"In that tone?"

"Yup." She straightened and retrieved her jacket.

"More like capitulating." Marc adjusted the left shoulder, then angled the sleeve to ease her arm into it. He kept his hands there, fingers clutched in the navy wool, looking down at her, those gray-green eyes thoughtful.

"Semantics."

"Perhaps." He tugged her closer. "Let's see what you make of this, Kayla."

His mouth covered hers with gentle pressure, the kiss warm and alive. He smelled of crisp air and wood stove, hay and Old Spice. It was the most delicious combination of scents she'd ever known. Masculine and rugged. She leaned into the kiss, hands flat against his chest, reveling in the feel of him, hard muscle balancing her softer curves. She felt safe. Warm. Cherished.

Three feelings she'd never experienced simultaneously. Talk about a head rush.

He ended the kiss and stepped back, studying her. His eyes narrowed and he frowned. "I'm not sorry I did that."

"No?"

"Not in the least. And it was way better than I imagined, by the way."

Gazing into sea-green eyes, Kayla free fell into a canopied forest of hopes and dreams. "You've thought about kissing me?" It took work to tamp down the note of hope. From his gentle look of amusement, she wasn't fully successful.

"Haven't thought of much else, and it's driving me crazy."

"Marc—"

"Shh." A thick finger paused her words. His eyes never wavered, never left hers. "If you're sorry about it, tell me tomorrow. Or next week. Let me enjoy this for a little while, okay?"

Okay? Did he want to know how okay it was? How his touch unnerved her, warmed her, melted her despite the frigid night? He drew her in and pressed a second kiss to her mouth, ending way too soon. "Thanks again for the tickets."

"Hey, listen, the tickets were a random thing," Kayla protested. "You didn't have to… I mean…" Her voice trailed. She didn't want him to think she was looking for payback.

He closed the space between them. "I didn't kiss you because you shared the tickets. I kissed you because I wanted to know what it would feel like to hold you." His palm touched the curve of her cheek. Then he grazed her lips one last time, a whisper of a kiss.

Oh, man. His words softened her heart.

"Now you better go or you're liable to get kissed again."

Like that would be a hardship. Kayla pressed a finger to her lips, his kiss warming her. "Okay."

He smiled at the single word and opened the door behind her. When she got to her car, she turned.

He stood framed in the doorway, lamplight spilling around him, much as he'd been the first morning they met. But this time his stance was relaxed and confidant, his profile serene. He waved. "Good night, Kayla."

With the thirty-odd feet of space between them, she had more sense of control. Distance proved an amazing equalizer. "Night, Marc."

Chapter Twelve

She was leaving in a few months. What was he thinking?

Marc beat himself up the next morning. Kayla wasn't anything he'd planned for, nothing like the girl he imagined, yet there she was, creeping into his heart, filling spaces left empty too long.

Marc wasn't stupid. He saw why he shouldn't fall in love with Kayla Doherty as plain as the mammoth pet food sign to his left. Mental, big-block letters explained why Kayla was wrong for him.

But this attraction refused to abate. He felt helpless in its grip. He thought of her, he planned for her, he imagined a life with her.

He'd pushed it aside for weeks, controlling himself with no small effort, only to kiss her the night before. Get a taste of the woman unafraid to go toe-to-toe with him when necessary.

He loved that about her.

The thought made him grin as he forklifted a pallet of rabbit food. Spring feed brought the promise of rebirth. Baby lambs, bunnies, cats, dogs and chicks prevailed as the days stretched longer.

The idea of baby animals made him almost giddy. He passed a hand across his face before pinching the bridge of his nose. *Slow down,* he ordered himself. *Step back and assess the situation.*

He'd tried to do that all morning.

No luck. The look on her face haunted him. Her expression had been vulnerable after that kiss. Needy.

Kayla wasn't needy. She was streetwise and book-smart, an intimidating combination.

Marc refused to be intimidated. Intrigued? Oh, yeah. Interested? Most assuredly, despite the hundred reasons he shouldn't be. Kayla was slated to leave shortly. She bore no resemblance to the kind of woman he intended to fall in love with, and a strong likeness to what he'd chosen to avoid. He didn't want or need a snazzy dresser, a woman on a first-name basis with designer tags, or one who didn't have sense enough to don sturdy shoes when the mercury plummeted.

Before you knew it, she'd have Jess following in her footsteps, messing up what Pete and Marc had invested to keep the younger girl grounded.

He should avoid her. Too much danger lay there, too many pitfalls. What kind of a fool walked into a bad situation, eyes open and let it get out of hand?

The worst kind, he reminded himself. He glared at the silent stacks of packaged feed. The future held nothing for them. He knew that. She wasn't a girl to give up her dreams and tie herself down to a North Country farmer.

Kayla had big league written all over her, from the name-brand sunglasses to the squared-off toes of her designer boots, and he was a girl-next-door kind of guy.

That was as it should be. He'd leave it at that. He might not like the choice, but he'd make it, nonetheless.

Arianna DeHollander and Anna Hernandez were one and the same.

The thought plagued Kayla Saturday morning.

How could it be? What were the odds? Kayla shook herself, focusing. Slim odds or not, facts didn't lie. Kayla's faith mentor, the woman who'd led her to redeeming love was the same woman who ran roughshod over Pete, Marc and Jess. She had no idea how to reconcile that.

He kissed me.

Kayla touched her mouth, remembering. The contact sent a quiver as she recalled Marc's kiss.

Why?

There was the question. The guy hadn't exactly been ambivalent in his feelings. His strong disregard for her was evidenced from the beginning, and now…

Now, what?

Now nothing, she assured herself. She had plans looming. Big plans. As much as she loved her job, she was a finger's width from her goal, the chance to let the sun bathe her skin more often. At one time in her life she'd had noticeable freckles. Five years in the North Country and they'd all but disappeared.

The wind howled outside, weighting her arguments, but the memory of Marc's mouth, his strength, refused to fade. The thoughts warmed her from within. She flushed, remembering, then gave herself a mental shake.

Schoolgirl nonsense. Resolved, Kayla downsized the emotion and grabbed a workout DVD. When all else failed, get sweaty. Not a bad credo.

Firm step back, Marc reminded himself on Monday. He eased the truck into a feed store spot opposite Kayla's car and figured he should probably kill time unloading supplies before heading to the house.

Chicken.

Yup. Jess was home early for a change. Because she was inside with Kayla, they'd be fine without him. For a while, at least.

He finished as Kayla stepped out of the house. She spotted him, then headed his way, purposeful.

Uh-oh.

Nowhere to run, no place to hide. He watched her approach from his vantage point on the raised dock, then swung down to meet her.

She jumped into the conversation with no preliminaries. "Jess is working on a school project and asked for my help. Would it be all right if we spend an evening together?"

"You and Jess?" *Duh, DeHollander. What did you think she meant? Were you expecting her to fall at your feet after that kiss, proclaiming her everlasting love?* Because Jess's schoolwork wasn't the expected topic of conversation, Marc's thoughts scrambled.

Kayla nodded briskly. "Yes. Her project includes research on AIDS in sub-Saharan Africa and since I've worked on that, I've got info to add. Would Wednesday be all right?"

Marc switched to big brother mode. "She rides on Wednesdays and her mare's due to foal. What about Friday?" He paused a quick moment, then realized his presumption. "Unless you have a date."

The shake of her head reassured him, but her words didn't. "If I'm with Jess on Friday, that'll still leave me Saturday. Okay." She started to nod, then stopped. "I forgot. Sarah and I are shopping on Friday. Craig's off and we're heading to Syracuse for some girl time." She pursed her mouth. "Sunday?"

"Afternoon or evening?"

"Probably both. Bring her by around one. We'll work through supper and you can grab her that evening, okay?"

"Okay." Marc nodded toward the house. "And Dad? He seemed all right?"

Concern shadowed her features. "His appetite is waning."

Marc waited.

"His pain is increased, as well. I called Dr. Pentrow. I expect he'll order a patch."

"A patch?" Marc frowned.

"A medicated patch," Kayla explained. She held his look. "It's a helpful tool for controlling pain without interruption when you near the end."

Near the end. The words resounded in Marc's brain.

He swallowed hard, then looked away. He shifted his jaw, his neck tight. "It'll keep him pain-free?"

"If it doesn't, we'll find something that does." Kayla glanced beyond him, then swept the truck and store a quick look. "You might want to take advantage of your slow time to spend more time with him."

Marc read the unspoken admonition. Pete DeHollander was on his last days and Marc was tending things that could be put on hold or delegated to someone else.

Kayla turned. Marc fell into step beside her. "Look, I know what you're thinking…"

"That's a trick." She pivoted to face him. "Usually you don't give me credit for having a thought process."

"That's not true." Marc shoved his hands into his pockets. "Not exactly, anyhow." He looked anywhere but at her. "I like spending time with Dad, but there's a farm to manage. The calves are almost ready to drop. The horse is about to foal. There's a business to run. Jess to care for."

Kayla watched him, unmoving.

Marc rubbed his jaw. He wasn't sure how to rationalize his feelings, but he wanted her to understand. "I hate sitting in there, waiting for him to die." He shook his head. "It's not natural."

"It's very natural," she corrected. "Life goes full circle. Your father sees this as going home to God."

"If he hadn't smoked for thirty-eight years, he might not be going home quite so soon," Marc returned.

Kayla shrugged. "You could get trampled by a bull tomorrow, or crash your truck taking a curve on ice."

Marc winced. She hit home. He tended to drive with his foot too heavy, always hurrying.

"Your father believes his days are numbered by God's calendar, not ours."

"And you accept that?" Marc stared at her. "Even though you know his smoking led to his initial cancer and now this." He waved a hand to the house. "Lying in there, waiting to die, because he wouldn't give it up? He's compromised his health for a habit he wouldn't break."

Kayla paused before responding. A trio of crows cawed above, sniping a caustic tune. Kayla's glance shifted up. She sighed, then tightened her mouth and shook her head. "I believe in God's plan, Marc, even though I'm new at this whole faith thing. I can't quote you chapter and verse to prove my points like some long-term theological student." She shrugged. "I believe because I choose to believe. It makes sense to me. And addictive habits are tough to break," she noted.

Her frown deepened as she scrabbled a loose stone with her boot. She glanced up at him, then away, her expression accepting. "I can't give you whys and wherefores, but I can look at your father's life and see it's been good. He taught you everything he knew. Kept you under his wing. It couldn't have been easy, doing that alone."

"He piled mistake on mistake," Marc retorted. He moved away, then swung back. "He married the wrong woman, then did nothing to rectify the problem."

"So he should have chucked her? Knowing she was sick?"

"Not sick. Selfish. Self-absorbed. Self-centered. Take your pick."

His words riled her. The sky-blue eyes snapped, then softened with effort. "You should talk to him while there's still time. Ask him about your mom. Let him confide in you."

"Like he's done with you." Marc fixed his gaze on her. "You come in here for the last chapter of a thirty-year story and think you have all the answers. But you don't. Not even close."

She didn't back down. Meeting his eye, she slid her look toward the house. "Talk to him before it's too late. You don't want to run out of time."

He actually thought he liked her directness? Her no-nonsense approach and her spunky attitude?

At the moment it ranked dead last on his list of criteria. He backed away from the car. "Will Dr. Pentrow call about the patch?"

Pensive, she tugged her lower lip between her teeth. "You should hear from him or the pharmacy within the hour. If not, call the service. They'll jump on it."

He read between the lines. *Don't bother me, it's my night off.* He nodded. "Okay."

She hesitated. Her look said there was more she wanted to say.

She didn't. Face tight, she eased down the driveway without a backward glance.

The yard grew lonely as her car faded into the twilight. Colder, somehow.

Marc shrugged off the feeling and strode to the house, determined to get through the coming days the best way he knew. Hard labor and minimal downtime always worked in the past.

Fatalism made sense to Marc. What happened, happened, but he refused to let fate rule him. Personal self-control and good planning held him in good stead so far.

Discounting the foolish things he'd done as a kid, Marc appreciated his maturity. He had a plan laid out. He'd achieved renowned status as a premier breeder of prize-winning Herefords and developed a crossbreeding program that commanded blue ribbons and high prices for his prime beef. He was schooled in animal husbandry and the debit and credit lines of a successful enterprise. He kept his costs minimal, but wasn't afraid to spend money to augment future prospects.

He stopped at the door.

Pete DeHollander demonstrated those traits to his young son. It was Pete who'd prodded him into taking one step more, Pete who urged patience when Marc didn't understand his mother's ever-changing moods.

Marc massaged the nape of his neck. He loved his father, but rationalizing the disease that could have been prevented, the mother not cut out to be a mother and the fact he was about to be left alone with Jess angered him.

He needed to move beyond the fury, but hadn't a clue how to accomplish that. It seemed like anger had been a part of him forever.

Not forever, son.

Hand out, Marc faltered.

No, he hadn't been mad forever. Just since the fall of his sophomore year, when he found his father and Jess both crying, the howling baby clutched in Pete's hands, tears wetting his father's cheeks, his chin.

He'd never seen Pete cry before and hadn't seen it since. The sight shook him. Marc glimpsed the truth of what Pete had done for long, hard years. He'd worked to provide a sense of normalcy to a relationship that was anything but.

Rock-solid, Pete set the tone for a young boy's life, his dreams. He was the first line of defense against a world of change. Marc had always been able to count on his father's love, his strength.

Pete's strength ebbed that autumn afternoon and never came back fully. From that day forward, Pete seemed different. Humbled.

Blessed are the humble, for theirs is the kingdom of heaven.

Humility or weakness? At the moment, Marc was unsure where one left off and the other began. With a firm twist of his hand he opened the door and let himself into the house that seemed emptier every day.

"Jess?"

Jess emerged from Pete's room, her expression questioning. "What's up?"

"Got someone I'd like you to meet," Marc told her. He tossed her a barn coat. "Grab your boots."

"Someone to…" Jess's frown deepened, then cleared. "Grace foaled?"

"Hurry up. You're slow."

"Did she, Marc? Why didn't you call me? I wanted to see the foal get born."

Marc snorted. "She managed to deliver in the one half hour I didn't check on her. Seems Grace enjoys her privacy."

"So what is it? What does it look like?"

Marc swung the door open. "Let's go see."

"Marc!" Jess ran ahead, her voice floating back to him on the northeast wind. "Is it a paint or not?"

Marc grinned. The sire was believed to be a tobiano, although he only had a dozen foals to his credit. Grace bore tobiano markings, but her heredity was more "Heinz 57," a little of this, a little of that.

Marc hurried to see Jess's reaction.

"It's a girl!" Even in her excitement, Jess kept her voice soft. "Oh, Grace, I'm so proud of you. She's a beauty, just like her mother."

"How about that color?" Marc nudged Jess's shoulder and nodded toward the red and white filly. "Pretty sweet?"

"Incredible," breathed Jess. "Absolutely the most beautiful little horse I've ever seen."

"Spoken like a proud mother," Marc teased. He ruffled her hair. "Can you check them hourly tonight? Wake me if anything seems wrong?"

"I sure will." Part of her 4-H project was to oversee the animals herself. She tipped a glance to Marc. "Can I miss school tomorrow?"

"Nothing I didn't do during busy times. And your grades put mine to shame."

Jess flashed him a grin. "You did all right for yourself, Mr. B.A. in Business."

"Eventually I got a clue."

"Can I go in? Do you think it would disturb them?" Her look of longing took Marc back to his early years of farming. The wonder of birth, of seasons recycled. Life moving on.

"There's some soiled straw that needs removing, but other than that I'd leave them be. Bonding time. Don't want to disturb that."

"You're right." Jess nodded. "We'll give them time."

"You remember the feed regimen for a lactating horse?"

Jess grinned. "I've had it memorized for eleven months."

Marc stepped back. "Then it's all yours, kid."

He kept a careful eye on Jess's progress into the stall. New mothers could turn anxious or defensive.

Not Grace. She eyed her babe like a woman in love and paid no heed to Jess's gentle ministrations.

"Done."

"Nice."

Marc slung an arm around Jess's shoulders. "How does it feel?"

Jess laughed. "Like I should hand out cigars. How weird are we, Marc?"

"Very." He squeezed her shoulder and headed for the house. "I've got to wash up and see Dad. Do you want to tell him about the foal? Sweetheart, wasn't it?" he asked from the door.

"Not Sweetheart," Jess decided. "Not now that I've seen her." She eyed Grace a moment, then turned Marc's way. "She'll be Glory."

"Glory?"

"Yes." Jess nodded. "The beginnings of my breeding program. Grace and Glory."

The names stopped Marc's progress. His throat tightened at the look on Jess's face, her belief in all things holy.

Her strength tweaked a memory of a boy who believed in God, in heaven and hell. Gifts of the Spirit. For a moment he couldn't say anything, then he took a step back, approving. "Nice combination, Jess."

A smile lit her face, her eyes on the mother-foal duo. "Yes. It is."

Chapter Thirteen

❧

"I needed this." Sarah sank back against the café booth and smiled at Kayla. "A girls' night out. No diapers, no drool."

Kayla laughed. "Me, too. For different reasons."

Sarah slid her glance to Kayla's bag once they'd ordered coffees. "Obviously. No one with a baby wears cashmere." She eyed her own small bag, then corrected herself. "Except when it's on the clearance rack with an additional twenty-percent-off coupon."

"And I think Craig will approve not only the bargain price, but also the fit of those sweaters. And as we both know," opening the menu, Kayla sighed dramatically, "winter will come again."

"Inevitably." Sarah eyed the choices, then laughed, rueful. "I'm so predictable. I read the menu, then order the grilled chicken salad with peppercorn ranch dressing." She closed her menu. "Why waste time?"

"Sounds good," Kayla agreed. "With the cappuccino, of course. Since I'm being sensible about food, if not my wardrobe."

"Your clothes are fine," Sarah argued. She made a face. "Just different from what you'd wear as a mother."

Sarah's statement brought Arianna DeHollander to mind. Her image didn't jive with North Country farm lore. Kayla leaned forward, curious. "Did you know Marc's mother?"

"No. Marc's older and we didn't hang in the same circles in high school. I got to know him in college." Sarah paused while they ordered, then turned back to Kayla. "Marc's got some pretty strong feelings about the whole thing."

Talk about an understatement.

"Craig knew her," Sarah continued. "He and Marc have been best buds since they were kids."

"Does Craig talk about her?"

"He would if I asked, but I think it's been an unspoken rule between him and Marc since she left. Why all the questions?"

Should she tell her? Sarah had become her closest friend and the temptation was sweet. Kayla would love to unburden herself, but she'd promised secrecy to Pete. Of course, he didn't know about her relationship with Arianna, but she respected the man as a person and a patient.

She'd made a promise. She had to keep it. She sighed and grimaced. "There just seems to be a lot of baggage there. I don't know how to help that."

"Why should you?" Simple words, straight and direct. Pure Sarah.

Kayla squirmed.

"Aha."

"No 'aha,'" Kayla protested, but her voice betrayed her.

"Let's see." Sarah appraised her. "You look trapped and frustrated. Generally that means there's a man involved, and since I know there haven't been any prospects *after* working hours, the only one in proximity is Marc DeHollander."

"Sarah."

"Uh-huh."

"It's nothing."

"Mmm-hmm." Sarah sipped her water.

"He's grumpy, short-sighted, moody and downright antagonistic."

Sarah pretended to swoon. "Be still my heart."

"Seriously…"

"Oh, I'm serious." Sarah laughed. "I'm familiar with the symptoms."

"Of?"

"Love."

"You're being ridiculous."

"Mmm-hmm."

"Stop that. Now."

"Okay." Sarah's grin told her it was anything but over. "Not that we didn't wonder when he showed up at seven-fifteen on a brutally cold Sunday morning to fix your car."

Kayla gulped.

"And he looks at you as if he wants to shelter you. Take care of you."

"He does not."

Sarah's smile grew. She raised her brows. "He does. You don't notice because you're too busy dodging his words, but Craig and I caught it. And my husband's not too quick with these things."

Restless, Kayla fingered her napkin, eyes down. "He kissed me."

"Really?" Sarah hunched closer. "Do tell."

Kayla twisted the napkin with more vigor. "There's nothing to tell. He regrets it and hasn't mentioned it. I think he's avoiding me because of it."

"That brings back memories." Sarah unfolded her napkin as the waitress dropped off their cappuccinos. The scent of rich cream and butter toffee filled the air. "I avoided Craig after the first time he kissed me."

"Why?"

Sarah shrugged. "I didn't think I was good enough for him. He was a Macklin. I was a Slocum."

"You're not like your brothers."

"Maybe not, but I was pretty discouraged after that storm knocked me into that sugar maple, face first. Something about a broken face and loose teeth does that to a girl. Especially since Craig had recently dated you." Sarah shot Kayla a wry look.

Kayla's cheeks heated. "We were never serious."

"I know that now." Sarah squeezed Kayla's hand. "But my self-esteem was low. I got defensive."

"You?" Kayla stared, disbelieving. "You're the most self-assured woman I know."

"Which is why we get along." Sarah arched one brow. "We hide our secrets well."

Kayla's spine prickled as thoughts of her mother's death invaded the moment. "I'm not sure what you mean."

Sarah regarded her, calm. "You are, but you're not ready to share. And that's okay." She paused as the food was delivered, then continued, "If you ever want to talk, I'm here."

If only she could. Kayla breathed deep, eyes downcast. Where would she start? Ancient history? Recent dilemmas? The fact that the two twined together confused her more. Sarah gave her arm a slight jab. "Eat. True confessions can wait. I'm tired of your waistline being two inches smaller than mine."

That made Kayla smile. "You just had a baby," she reminded her friend.

"And expect to have another in about six and a half months."

"Really?" Kayla hopped out of her seat and hugged her friend. "That's amazing. So that explains the decaf." She nodded to Sarah's cup.

"Absolutely." Sarah grinned. "McKenna will have a playmate come August."

"I don't know how you do it." Kayla fussed as she slid back into her seat. "With the farm, McKenna, the animals, the sheep, Craig's job pulling him out at all hours. When do you sleep?"

"Here and there." Sarah smiled at the truth in her remark. "It's doable. We don't sweat the small stuff. Life sends enough big challenges. Why make yourself crazy over what you can't change?"

"The Serenity Prayer."

"Yes."

Kayla studied the spear of chicken on her fork, then shrugged. "I'm not sure how to get to that point. If I ever will."

"Let go and let God."

"Easy to say."

"Much harder to do," Sarah agreed. "I won't argue that. We independent types have a harder time letting go. It takes humility to hand over the reins."

Kayla cringed. Did being humble weaken one's resolve, erode one's strength? She wasn't sure how it couldn't. Weren't humility and strength polar opposites?

"Enough discussion," Sarah declared as she cut her salad. "I'm eating for two and taking full advantage of it."

Kayla agreed. "And I'm going to celebrate how good you'll look in that red sweater by Christmastime, so you might want to rethink the whole dessert thing tonight."

"I just might. It was long weeks before I was back in regular clothes after McKenna, and I entertained mean thoughts about anyone who wore pre-pregnancy jeans after delivery. It's just not natural."

"Absolutely not." Kayla added a note of righteous indignation for emphasis. She raised her mug in a toast to motherhood. "Elastic waistbands, all the way!"

Sarah eyed Kayla, bemused. "The only elastic waistbands you own are on your pyjamas," she chastised.

"And my workout sweats," Kayla added. "But I love 'em."

"Uh-huh." Sarah glanced down to her thickening middle with a sigh of acceptance. "Me, too."

Marc moved to the entry as soon as Kayla turned into the drive. He swung open the door, then reached to ease her coat from her arms.

"Thank you." She shot him a look both puzzled and amused. Classic Kayla. "How's your dad?"

"Tired." Marc frowned. "He sleeps a lot."

"That can be a blessing," Kayla offered. She started toward the kitchen, but Marc stalled her with a firm hand to her shoulder.

"I've thought about what you said."

Kayla's look could have scorched his socks. "Which time?"

His jaw twitched. He gave her a wry smile. "Good point. The last time. About talking to Dad."

"Oh. That."

"I won't mention our conversation to him," Marc continued. He kept his hand on her shoulder, their gazes locked. "But you're right. If I'm going to be good for Jess, I need to know what's gone on."

"And get beyond your anger."

"You don't mess around with your shots." He didn't harden his look. He gave her shoulder a gentle squeeze, then released it.

She trained a no-nonsense look on him, a little bossy and very cute. Maybe even endearing. Maybe. "Jess deserves the big brother she's always loved. Without the giant chip on his shoulder."

Marc flexed the shoulders in question. "Easier said than done."

"Depends how bad you want it." Kayla stepped toward the kitchen, but once more he stilled her with a hand.

"Have coffee with me. Dad's asleep and I could use a good scolding."

She wheeled about. "You know, you—"

He grinned and watched for her reaction.

Positively stellar. Her breath paused, her eyes widened, her lips parted, then softened into a smile. One hand came to her throat, uncertain, fingers shaky. Eventually she drew a breath. "You wouldn't get scolded so often if you didn't deserve it so much."

He nudged her through the oak-trimmed arch. "I think I like being yelled at, actually. Or at least accept it."

She leaned against the counter while he poured coffee and retrieved the milk. He took the mugs and the milk to the table and drew out a chair. "Sit with me."

"I should check your father."

"I just did. Sound asleep." He slid his glance to the offered chair. "I promise to behave."

She flushed. "Listen, about that—"

"Yes?" He leaned forward. Up close, the pale freckles were more discernible, and the dark rim of blue made her light irises brighter. Noting that, he could imagine a child, their child, with dark, curly hair and vivid blue eyes.

She's leaving, Marc's inner voice warned.

For just a moment he weighed the counsel. He'd done it this long, surely he could manage a few more weeks.

Then she blinked, watching him, thick lashes hovering against peaches-and-cream skin.

The blink undid him. The tiny flash of uncertainty offered a glimpse of the vulnerable Kayla, the little girl trapped inside. Decisive, he leaned forward and kissed her, his arm snugging her waist, drawing her in, her curves a sweet reprieve from grit-hard farm muscle.

Yeah, she's leaving, he acknowledged the twinge that wouldn't let him be. *But she's here now.*

Kayla stepped back, trying to calm her cardiovascular system. It wasn't easy with Marc this close, those eyes warm and amused.

"Marc, I'm working." She spread her hands in a gesture of appeal. "This isn't right."

He closed the distance, the dark turtleneck outlining thick, broad shoulders, muscled arms. "It feels right."

She swallowed hard and shifted her gaze. "I don't kiss people casually."

"Me, neither."

She shot him a look. He held her gaze. "It's true enough, believe it or not."

For some reason, she did. Despite his rugged good looks and his air of independence, she didn't see Marc as a player.

Just angry, morose, grumpy, short-sighted and faithless. Reality hit. She took another step back. "We've got no place to go with this. We don't share the same faith or ideals and I'm leaving soon."

"By choice."

"Yes."

"So stay."

Her heart jack-hammered.

He moved forward, swallowing her space. "There's no rule that says you have to go. Stay a while. Give us some time."

"I don't understand." Oh, but she did. She saw what he was asking, what his eyes were saying and she was tempted until truth struck. How could she risk her heart to a man who shrugged off God? Would he brush her off when things got tough? How would she handle that?

She *wouldn't* handle it. Kayla recognized the thinness of her tough-girl image. Letting Marc in smacked of danger. Kayla had spent eighteen years making sure she was in charge. After her run of foster homes, Kayla worked to maintain her independence as a protective wall.

No one got through that wall.

Marc grasped her upper arms. "Look at me. Please."

She glanced up. The warmth in his eyes gave her unexpected pleasure. He flashed her a smile, gentle. Sweet. "Think about it."

"I can't." Her shaky voice betrayed her indecision.

He angled his head and read her hesitation. "You can. We've got months yet."

"I plan ahead, Marc. I've sent out applications, set wheels in motion."

His look stayed calm, but his jaw tightened. "I won't beg, Kayla, but I'm not afraid to ask, either." He finished his coffee in a chain of swallows. "Bring your coffee along. We should check Dad."

She stared at his retreating back. He turned, humor lighting his eyes, a glimpse of what lay behind the wall of anger. Seeing that, she followed him, trying not to think about what just transpired.

Kayla had plans. Not one of them included life on a farm resembling Antarctica seven months of the year.

She wanted waving grasses and twining vines. Cozy gardens, a bucolic setting for a porch swing, perfect for a summer evening's read. Dahlias and roses, brown-eyed Susans, mauve-rose coneflowers.

Today's snow struck the west windows with tiny bounces, miniature hailstones mixed among the flakes. The steady ping…ping…ping sounded austere.

Kayla had had enough of that by the time she was eleven years old. At twenty-nine, it was long since time to move on.

Chapter Fourteen

"You have to tell him." Christy met Kayla's gaze. "Or transfer your assignment."

That wasn't about to happen. "I can't."

"Because?"

"They mean a lot to me."

"You're too involved in this family, Kayla, through no fault of your own. You need to back away."

"Pete's slipping," Kayla argued. "To throw someone else into the mix wouldn't be right. Yeah, I'm involved. I probably should have removed myself when I learned who Anna was, but I didn't. Now it's too late."

"It's not." Christy moved to the coffeepot and filled her mug. "Want some?"

"No, thanks." Kayla refused to think of how cozy she felt having coffee with Marc. She needed to move beyond the emotional and deal with the professional aspects of her dilemma. "I need to stay on this case, Christy. We could be talking days, two weeks at the most. It would be unfair to Pete to change things, and running from the problem doesn't help."

"Then be honest with Mr. DeHollander about your relationship with his deceased wife." Christy brushed off Kayla's surprise. "I can't see what harm that would do. She died peacefully. That's all he needs to know."

"He'll ask more."

"Cite medical confidentiality." Christy tapped a finger, unhappy. "I'll be glad when this is done. I should pull you right now…" Her voice trailed. She frowned again.

"But you won't because it would make things harder on the family."

"My nurses don't need to bear everyone's burdens." She scowled. "Our job is tough enough. But I think the benefits to the patient outweigh the detriment to you."

"I agree." Kayla stood and turned.

"Kayla."

"Yes?"

"The son? The one who didn't like you, didn't trust you? The one who was angry at his father for smoking and causing irreparable harm?"

"Yes?"

"He's doing better? Not as confrontational?"

Kayla remembered the feel of his hand at her waist, his mouth on hers. The look in his eye that offered more than she dared take. "Um, no. He's much better, thanks."

Christy nodded. "It just takes time, doesn't it?"

"Yes." Kayla cleared her throat. "Time."

"All right, then." Sipping her coffee, Christy nodded. "Keep me informed, okay?"

"Of course."

She wasn't lying. Marc wasn't a problem, he was an opportunity, one she didn't dare consider.

Kayla stepped outside. Not so cold today. The sun shone brighter and the sky held breaks in the clouds, a pattern of blue and white, a promise of warmer days.

She'd been in the North Country long enough to understand the shift. The weather would break soon. It would turn cold and wet as opposed to bitter cold and snowy, like that was some sort of reprieve.

She sighed as she stowed her gear. The higher sun felt good. The wind that ruffled her feathered hair was brisk, not bone-chilling.

For a brief moment she wondered if winter would seem as long in the arms of someone you loved.

Of course it would.

She'd gotten a response from a service just south of D.C. Her résumé had been well-received and they'd offered her a position.

She refused to think of Marc's request. He was under a lot of pressure. His father's death loomed. It wasn't unheard of for two people to bond in times of hardship.

Soon she would be out of his home, no longer part of the routine. A sense of normalcy would return to DeHollander Hereford Holdings. Eventually he'd find a nice girl to settle down with. A brood of kids would dash in and out of the old house, toys scattered everywhere. She pictured cookies on the counter and supper in the oven.

The smell of roasting meat mingled with the scent of chocolate, providing a homey feeling. Glancing right, she realized she was passing the Greek restaurant as they prepared noonday specials.

Decisive, she edged thoughts of Marc away, but didn't try to fool herself it was far enough.

"How're we doing, Mr. D.?" Kayla inquired, keeping her voice soft. His pallor had increased. His respirations weren't as deep. They increased in strength and number as he struggled to wakefulness.

"Kayla."

She leaned forward. "I'm here. What's the progress report?"

"Rounding third."

She nodded and squeezed his hand. "I'd have to agree. How do you feel?"

He scowled. "Not ready."

The succinct words surprised Kayla. "Why not?"

His frown deepened. He tried to speak, then licked his lips. Kayla eased the dryness with a smidge of ointment to his mouth. "Don't hurry. We've got all day."

"One of us does."

His dry humor made Kayla smile. She patted his hand and met his eye. "Can I help?"

"No."

"You're sure?"

Pete shook his head. "Something I should have done and didn't."

"Your wife?" Saying the words, Kayla knew she needed to reveal her relationship with Arianna.

Pete glared at the wall. Kayla drew a breath and plunged in. "Mr. D.? I've got something to tell you."

"What's that?"

Kayla hesitated, then sat. "It's convoluted. The short of it is, I knew your wife. I took care of her when she passed away."

Pete's shoulders jerked. His head snapped forward. "What?"

"You have to stay calm if you want me to explain this." Kayla used her no-nonsense voice. It worked. Pete settled back. Long seconds later, he nodded.

Kayla faltered, then began. "Nearly three years ago I had a patient who meant a great deal to me."

Pete watched her, his gaze sharp.

"Her name was Anna Hernandez."

He frowned, then nodded, silent.

"I was working the medical ward when Anna was admitted. She was dying of complications from HIV."

"AIDS."

"Yes."

"How did she…?" Pete shook his head. "Never mind. I can figure that one out. She was in Potsdam?"

Kayla nodded. "We were both alone. We bonded."

Pete watched her. His hand plucked the comforter's edge, restive.

"She taught me about faith. About forgiveness. She'd found her road back to God, but said it was too late for anything else."

Sadness darkened Pete's features. "It was never too late."

"I see that now," Kayla replied. "She said she left her family because she feared she'd hurt them."

"Ari wouldn't hurt anyone."

Kayla couldn't agree. "There was a new baby in the house."

Pete acknowledged that. "Jess scared her."

"Perhaps."

"I'm sure she did," he continued. "Jess wasn't a rough baby, but she was a reminder of things Ari couldn't face." He pressed his lips in consternation. "My wife couldn't forgive herself. Because of that, she decided I couldn't forgive her, either." He lifted anguished eyes to Kayla. "But I did. I saw her behavior for what it was, a few weeks that meant nothing once she was back on her meds. But there was Jess to consider."

Pressure rose in Kayla's chest. "What do you mean, Mr. D.?"

"She didn't tell you?" He glanced around to be sure Marc hadn't come in. "That Jess isn't my biological child?"

Kayla shook her head. "I just realized who Anna was last week. The picture," she explained, waving her hand across the bed. "She never mentioned names and she looked…different."

Pete mulled that, then nodded acceptance. "After Marc was born, Ari never got pregnant, but the problem was mine, not hers. We decided not to push things because she had enough on her plate. They'd straightened out her meds, she was doing a great job with Marc…" He shrugged. "Why rock the boat?"

"But that changed?"

"She got restless. Two or three times a year she'd stop taking her meds and then I'd have a rough time straightening things out. As time went on, it was more often. She stopped going to church, stopped practicing her faith and then dumped the meds altogether."

"I'm sorry."

He shrugged. "Me, too. I knew I should have gone to church with her, but I was too busy making the farm a success. For what?" He eyed Kayla. "The farm was fine. We had everything we needed. I always wondered if I'd just gone to church with her, been her husband seven days a week instead of six, if we'd have ended up the same way."

"You think it could have made that much difference?"

"I'll never know, will I? But yeah, I think so."

Kayla glanced at the family picture. Arianna was beautiful, her smile wild and free. Kayla nodded. "Does Jess's father know about her?"

"I made sure of it. I also made sure he understood he had no rights whatsoever." Pete's face darkened. "I let him know what his life would be like if I went public since he was Ari's therapist. The only reason I didn't was to protect my wife and daughter. Oh, yeah, he knew." Pete's breath came out in a rush. "And he knew better than to come around looking for what was mine. He left a short while after and we haven't heard from him since."

"Mr. D." Kayla placed a hand over his. His agitation pushed his heart rate up. His skin had warmed, tingeing color beneath the waxy surface. "I didn't mean to upset you. I just wanted you to know that Arianna was surrounded with loving care when she died. She'd accepted Christ and was looking forward to heaven. Her deep faith inspired mine." Kayla pressed his hand. "Her only regret was she didn't have the forgiveness of her family."

"She had mine."

Kayla leaned forward. "You tell her that when you see her, all right?"

Pete looked suddenly drained. Defeated. "I will. Won't be long now."

"No. But you've got someone waiting for you."

His expression softened. "You think it's me she's waiting for?"

Memories of Anna's sorrow plucked at Kayla. "You were her only love. She told me so."

His eyes misted. "Well, then." He sniffed. Kayla handed him a clump of tissues. He nodded, abrupt, his eyes less troubled. "Well, then."

The sound of the back door ended their discussion. Jess burst in. She pulled off her coat as she walked, dropping it on a small bench. "Daddy. How are you? You look better."

Pete smiled. "I was debating with Miss Kayla. She got me riled up. Gave me some color."

Kayla flashed him a look of understanding. "It was a fine line." She turned a soft smile to Jess. "I didn't want to push him into overdrive, but a little gumption is never a bad thing."

"I've got gumption." Jess grinned at her father. "Dad says so all the time. 'A chip off the old block,' right, Dad?"

Pete didn't miss a beat. "The good looks came from your mother, but the gumption was all me, kid."

Kayla stood.

"Are you going?" Jess looked up, surprised and disappointed.

"No." Kayla reached for her bag. "Your dad and I had such a nice talk that I didn't get his vitals."

"Not much different, there," he retorted. "Bad and growing worse."

"Dad."

"Jess." He smiled up at his daughter. Kayla saw a look of love pass between them. Biology disregarded, Jess and Pete DeHollander were father and daughter. "We can't skate around the truth, Jess. No matter how much we might want to."

"I know." The girl didn't cry. She gave her father a dazzling smile instead. "I keep talking to God about how to handle this, what to do."

"The best place to turn." Pete nodded agreement.

"Then I wonder if God is doing this so Marc *has* to take me to church," Jess continued with wisdom beyond her years. "Maybe He's calling you home so Marc has a chance to find his way."

Pete reached a hand to Jess's cheek. "Sometimes I wonder which one of you will be in charge."

Jess laughed. "Me, too." She gave her dad a gentle hug. "We'll take turns."

"I think that's a good idea." Pete leaned back while Kayla checked his blood pressure. "I love you, Jess."

Jess hugged him again. "I love you, too, Dad."

Their embrace grew lengthy. Kayla refused to cry even though her throat tightened and her cheeks ached. Without a word she headed to the kitchen and started a pot of coffee. No doubt Marc would want some when he came in from the barn and she could do with some herself.

The image of father and daughter imprinted itself on her brain. Jess DeHollander was Pete's child, regardless of biology. It was there in every word, every action the man took.

But Pete would be gone soon. He was moving to his heavenly

reward, and that left the secret in Kayla's hands. Would it do any good for Marc and Jess to know the truth before Pete died?

None she could see. But how could she tell them afterward, in their time of grief? Was not telling them an option? What if Jess's father showed up, making demands?

Kayla pressed the heel of her hand to her brow.

"You okay?"

Marc's voice startled her. She swung and faced him.

Worry creased his brow. "I'll get you some ibuprofen." He headed to the cupboard, pulled out a container and shook two pills into his hand. "You might be coming down with something."

He poured a glass of water and handed everything to Kayla, then watched as she downed the pills. "Sit."

She forced a smile. "I'm fine, really. A lot going on today and I did too much thinking. You know how dangerous that can be for a blonde."

His lips quirked. He gave a one-shoulder shrug of agreement. "For this one, anyway. Sit."

He pulled out a chair. The look on his face suggested she follow directions. She sat.

His hands dropped to her shoulders. She straightened, then relaxed as his fingers kneaded. "Are you always this tight?"

"Hmm? I— No. I don't think so."

Think? How could she think when the gentle pressure of his hands soothed the aches of a long day, the stress of intimate knowledge of interfamily relationships?

"Right here." The heel of Marc's hand pressed a point between her neck and her right shoulder. Kayla jerked. Marc steadied her with his other hand. "This is where you tense under pressure. You carry your anxiety along the top of your back."

The movement of his hands indicated the muscles in question. Kayla dropped her head forward, allowing him better access. "I tense them when I'm anxious or flustered."

"Or mad."

Kayla sighed, resigned. "Yes."

"No argument? You flatter me." He eased his hands from her shoulders and moved to the coffeepot.

Kayla flexed her neck and rolled her shoulders. Better. Much better. She eyed his back. "Where do you carry your stress, Marc?"

He didn't turn. Deliberate, he fixed his coffee, then stood quiet, staring at fields of snow through the window beyond.

Kayla rose and moved to his side. "I didn't mean to upset you."

He turned then. One arm slipped around her shoulders as if it belonged there, his hand grasping her upper arm in a half hug. He dropped his mouth to her hair and pressed a kiss to her temple. "I'm not upset. Just thinking. Planning. Hoping."

He gave her shoulder a second squeeze before releasing her. He nodded to the mug. "Good coffee. That northeast wind sucked through every layer I had."

"Really?" Kayla looked up, smiling. "You always seem impervious to the cold."

"Used to it," he affirmed. "But I'd rather have the cold, dry winds of winter than the wet, cutting winds of spring."

"Does it bother the cattle?"

"Naw. They're hearty. I breed to maintain that vigor. When you live up here, it's important to have stock that can withstand whatever winter has to offer."

Kayla understood that firsthand. She'd faced the winters head-on, challenging the cold, and she'd won. She'd made it through five years and hadn't caved. So why was there little joy in the knowledge? She took a deep breath and charged in. "I've been offered a job in Virginia."

She wasn't sure why she blurted it out. When Marc's hand clenched the mug tighter, she wished she'd waited.

"You have a job here."

"That I'm leaving in June."

"Well." He took a long draw on his coffee and set down the cup. "That gives me three months."

"For?"

This time he met her eye. "To convince you to stay."

Her heart constricted under his gaze, strong and unflinching. There was no doubting his intentions if that look was any indication. Kayla gulped.

He brushed the curve of her cheek with one hand and smiled. "How's Dad?"

Those simple words brought her back to reality. She stepped back, away from his touch, away from his warmth. "I've got to get his vitals."

Marc glanced at his watch. "You've been here an hour."

She glanced away. "We…talked. Then Jess got home and I wanted them to have time together while your dad was awake."

Marc nodded. "Less often now."

"Yes."

He moved to the door, then paused, waiting. Passing him, she felt the strength in his presence, the solidity of the man who beckoned her with word and deed.

A man who kept a careful distance from faith and would most likely hate her for knowing family secrets that could tear his life apart.

She couldn't meet Marc's gaze, not now. She wasn't as practiced as Pete at hiding the truth. No wonder her shoulders had tightened. She was carrying the weight of the DeHollander family and had no clue how to unburden herself.

Trust.

The word filled her consciousness like a stream-filled mountain bed, smooth and flowing.

I have seen his ways, but I will heal him; I will lead him and restore comfort to him.

Isaiah's words echoed within her. As Kayla stepped into Pete's room, she felt Marc's supportive presence behind her. Jess looked at them, her face a mix of emotions, her eyes wet with unshed tears. She clasped one of Pete's hands between both of hers, a sandwich of warmth around his cooling skin.

"Here she is Dad, and she's brought reinforcements."

Pete smiled, his face drawn with fatigue. Kayla nodded, brisk. "I'll be quick and get out of here so you can rest."

"I've got supper in the slow cooker."

Kayla didn't dare turn. "Thanks, but I'll leave you guys to family stuff tonight. I'm going to catch up on some sleep."

"At five o'clock?"

Marc moved alongside her. From Pete's quick, tired smile, she was pretty sure he'd just given his father a wink. "Bread from Main Street Bakery."

"Fresh butter," chimed Jess. She seemed to enjoy the game. "And I thought I saw blueberry pie, too."

Kayla noted the look in Pete's eye. She heard a like note in Jess's entreaty.

Marc? She had no trouble reading his intent, but a huge problem resisting the deep timbre of his voice, the solid masculine presence over her shoulder. "You won't be hurt if I eat and run?"

"No."

The word was close enough to be whispered, but wasn't. As Marc clasped his father's other hand, his shoulder pressed Kayla's. "You set the time frame, Kayla."

She read the double entendre as she eased back. Marc followed suit.

"Dad? Can I bring you soup or bread?"

"No." Pete's smile dimmed. "Not so hungry."

Marc nodded. "Would you like us to eat in here?"

"If it's all the same, I'm ready for a nap."

Marc leaned down. "Then I'll be back in a little while."

"For?"

"To watch you nap."

"Not much fun there."

Marc didn't agree. "We'll be the judge of that, won't we, Jess?"

"Mmm-hmm." Jess stood, as well. "Love you, Daddy."

Pete mumbled a reply. His breathing evened out as he slipped into slumber.

Kayla looked up at Marc as they walked through the dining room. "You haven't had trouble washing him?"

"No. He's frail, but he doesn't weigh a lot."

He hesitated. Kayla sharpened her gaze. "What?"

"There's been almost nothing to empty from his bag."

No urinary output. Kayla nodded. "That's normal. As his body gives out, the systems shut down."

"If we hydrated him, would that help?"

Kayla laid a hand on his arm. "Help what?"

Marc scrubbed a hand of frustration across his face, then dragged it across the back of his neck. "It just seems like I should be doing something."

"You are."

Marc looked down.

"You're letting go. That's something."

He grunted. Kayla squeezed his arm. "Letting go is often harder than intervention that means nothing in the end."

He was silent a long moment, then covered her hand with his. "Thanks for staying."

What could she say to that? That she loved being here, loved the homey feel of the toasty old house, the smell of good food wafting from the kitchen?

"Marc, I—"

"No pressure, Kayla. It's just nice having you here."

Reasons to leave fled with the touch of his hand. She leaned her head against his shoulder. "Thanks."

He paused. Jess had gone on ahead. The clatter of ironstone told them she was setting the table. Marc eyed Kayla. His look said more than words ever could. For a brief moment she let herself drown in that look, those gray-green eyes.

He smiled and propelled her into the kitchen with gentle ease. "I thought you were in a hurry. Let's eat."

I am in a hurry, she thought as she took the seat he held out. For long seconds he rested his hands atop her shoulders, the touch reassuring.

His warmth was hard to resist. She wished it weren't so easy to envision a life here with Marc and Jess, and babies underfoot. The spacious old house was meant for family.

But Marc had two big issues he refused to deal with, his faith and his mother. Neither were open for discussion, and that spelled danger. She had promised herself fullness of life. She'd known the lack firsthand and refused to contemplate that choice again.

"Shall we say grace?" Jess reached for Marc's hand on one side and Kayla's on the other.

Head bowed, Jess offered a sweet prayer of thanksgiving. At the end she pressed Kayla's hand in a communal spirit.

Not Marc. He buttered a piece of bread and asked Jess how her day went.

Kayla pushed aside foolish hopes and dreams. A girl didn't make it through life on fantasies. She made it on good hard work, simple faith and well-laid plans.

Hello, Virginia.

Chapter Fifteen

The home health aide yelled Marc's name as he scrawled his signature across an invoice later that week. "Mr. DeHollander?"

Her tone brought him across the drive at a run, the new delivery forgotten. "What's wrong?"

"Your dad's breathing's gone funny. This could be it."

Marc's heart squeezed. Here? Now? In the middle of the day, with no one about? Jess was in school, Kayla was…somewhere else.

He hurried to the bedroom as he barked quick commands. "Call the school, ask them to get Jess, then call Miss Doherty and ask if she can get over here."

"But—"

"Now."

Kayla cued into the aide's anxiety right off. "Is the family there, Ardith?"

"The son is. The daughter's in school."

Kayla glanced at the clock. "Tell the school I'll pick up Jess. We'll be there in half an hour, give or take."

"I don't know that he's got that long," the woman warned.

Kayla blew out a breath. "Then it's in God's hands, isn't it?"

* * *

"Dad?" Marc knelt next to the bed. "It's me, Dad. How're you doing?"

His father's chest groaned on each light exhale. Marc closed his eyes and sandwiched his father's hands. "I'm here, Dad. Right here."

The noise diminished as Pete struggled to wakefulness. "Marc."

"I'm here."

"We have to talk."

"Dad, I—"

"Not much time."

Marc swallowed the objection. "No."

"Your mother."

Marc glanced at the picture alongside the bed.

"She loved you, son."

Right then Marc would have agreed to anything to ease Pete's mind. "I know."

His father shook his head. "You don't. I'm trying to tell you."

Marc's chest constricted. "I'm listening."

"She had to go, Marc."

Marc kept his silence.

"She was afraid she'd hurt Jess."

Marc frowned. "No one's going to hurt Jess, Dad. I'll see to it."

Pete frowned, impatient. His hand moved within Marc's. "Not now. Then. She felt guilty. She didn't trust herself around the baby."

None of this made any sense. "Why would Mom hurt Jess? She was a baby."

"Because she wasn't my child."

The words hit Marc like the kick of an angry bull. He pulled back. "She what?"

"Jess wasn't my child." Pete squeezed his son's hand with a vigor that surprised the young farmer. "Your mother didn't think I could forgive that."

"Who could?" Marc's anger rose at the thought of another impropriety added to an already-lengthy list.

"You've got to protect her, son." The effort to confess deflated Pete's air. His words slowed, softened.

"I will." Marc felt the strength ebb from his father's hands and clung tighter.

"I wanted to tell you before…"

Pete paused, dragging for breaths that refused to come. Marc pressed his hand in a tug of love. "It's okay, Dad. It's all okay."

"It's not." His father's voice thinned, a faint reminder of his true self. "But it can be. Ask Kayla…"

"Kayla?" Marc loosened one hand and smoothed his father's hair away from his forehead. His thoughts jumbled at this left turn. "What about Kayla?"

"She knows."

Like that was a surprise. "I'll talk to her."

"Take care of her."

"Jess will be fine, Dad. I promise."

"Not just Jess." His father's chest convulsed. "Kayla, too."

"Kayla? But, how…? Never mind." Why was Marc surprised that his father sensed his growing feelings for Kayla? Hadn't they always been in tune with one another?

A light squeeze pressed the back of his hand. "Be gentle, son."

"I will."

His father shook his head, each word punctuated by a tiny gasp. "You take better care of the cows than you do a woman's feelings. You might want to…" the words came with no small effort now "…adjust your strategies."

Marc thought of the times he'd hurt Jess with insensitive remarks. "I'll try harder."

His father's face relaxed. "That's all I ask."

Long moments of silence ensued. Marc leaned down. "Dad?"

Pete's eyes opened. He smiled, his gaze locked on something beyond Marc, beyond Earth. He sighed one last, long breath and sank deeper into the pillow.

Silence filled the room. Marc dropped his head to his father's chest and let the tears come. Warmth ebbed from his grasp of his father's hand, the heart beneath his ear silent and still.

Take me for a ride, Daddy!

Pete turned his gaze to Marc's mother. "Ari? We got time for a ride?"

"Supper's ready in an hour." She swung across the fence and landed with a small thud at his father's side. "Take good care of our boy, Pete."

His dad nodded, smiling. "I will. Just like I do of his mother." He'd leaned down and kissed her until Marc offered protest. "Okay, okay, we won't waste time on kisses." His dad doffed an imaginary cap to Marc's mom. "I'll catch up on those later. Back in an hour."

Ari's voice followed them. "Forty-five minutes, Pete. Save fifteen for cooldown or it'll be your supper that's cold."

Father and son laughed as they took off cross-pasture. The day rose sweet and pure, the sun high, the breeze cool. Marc sighed against his father's chest. He could have ridden like this forever. Way too soon his father reined in the horse, urging him back to the farm.

Dusk settled as they approached the house, the horse cooled, brushed, blanketed and fed.

An empty kitchen greeted them. There was no supper waiting. No smiles from Mama. His father read the note on the table, crumpled it, then tossed it into the garbage can. "Let's ride into town, get a bite to eat."

"But Mama made chicken and biscuits." Marc stared at his father, not understanding.

Marc loved chicken and biscuits. Chunks of chicken in hot, steamy gravy. Biscuits that soaked up the puddles.

His father laid a hand on the boy's shoulder. "We rode longer than we should have. Let's head into town."

Marc stared around the kitchen with maturing eyes. There was no sign of the good-smelling supper. Not a dish, not a plate. "Where did it go?"

Pete sighed. "To the pig, I expect."

"My chicken and biscuits? She fed it to the pig?"

Pete crouched down and met Marc's gaze. "We promised her we'd be back and we weren't. We broke our word."

"But—"

Pete straightened and clasped his hand. "There are no buts. We messed up and Mama dumped our dinner."

As his empty stomach gurgled and growled in protest, Marc didn't fight the anger that rose inside him. He reached up and clasped his father's big, strong hand. "I love you, Dad."

His father led him to the door. "I love you, too. We'll have to write your mom a note, tell her we're sorry."

Sorry? Marc wasn't a bit sorry. He was mad, through and through, but he wouldn't argue with his father. Heading to the truck, he glanced back at the house, wishing Mom would appear, flap a towel and say, "Come back, boys! Supper's still here."

Cool, dark windows stared back at him. No warm yellow light, no cheerful voice.

"Where do you think she went?"

Pete heaved a sigh as he climbed into the front seat of the truck. "No idea, son."

With all his might Marc wished that she'd stay wherever she was, and never come back. Then he and his dad could do whatever they wanted, whenever they wanted.

That would be perfect.

"Hey, Donny! Give me a hand, will ya?" Marc's voice pulled the attention of the lanky farmhand late the next day.

The younger man drew alongside Marc and worked to keep a frantic mother at bay while Marc castrated her newborn son. Her bawls blended with the high-throated cries of her baby. Hands sure, Marc ear-tagged the calf and administered a shot of Ral-Gro. "Done."

In a quick move, Marc hoisted the calf from the back of the truck and deposited him onto the ground. "There you go, fella."

Donny sidestepped as the calf careened toward his mother. The cow welcomed him with reassuring licks of her tongue. The baby's cries went from fear to hunger. He zeroed in on the full udder and comforted himself with a nice, long brunch.

"That the last one?"

Marc gave a quick nod. "So far. That's twenty-six, right? Plus the extra we've got at the barn."

One of the cows had dropped twins, a rarity in Herefords. Once the mother recognized her first calf, she shunned the other, despite Marc's diligence in presenting the baby back to her. Marc tagged them both, but ended up taking the rejected female to the barn for bottle-feeding.

She'd become one of Jess's jobs. As calves dropped, Jess was pressed into action despite the push of schoolwork. For these weeks, Jess was as much farmhand as student.

In one way the intensity was good. It didn't leave either of them a lot of time to think about what had happened yesterday.

On the other hand, grief was important. Marc knew that. He knew when the rush of spring calving lay behind them, they'd still return, night after night, to a house that echoed around them, Pete's quiet presence a thing of the past.

He didn't know when he'd be able to make stew again. Just the thought of it made him want to cry. The simmering pot brought back too many memories.

Getting through the funeral wouldn't be easy. Having to put off Dad's burial until the ground softened wasn't easy, either. Maybe by then he and Jess would have reconciled themselves to a life without a parent. A life bereft of Pete's common-sense directives.

Maybe.

"You okay?"

Marc blinked. Donny's look was sympathetic and a little uncomfortable. Marc nodded. "Fine. Can you do a fence check while I work on the engine of the big Deere?"

"I'm on it. Then I'll unload that feed order."

Marc swung up into the truck. "I'd appreciate it."

"They're both doing okay," Jess reported when Marc got back to the barn.

His answering smile felt more like a grimace. "And you?"

Jess paid close attention to cleaning a stall. "I'm fine. I'll be glad when tomorrow's over."

Marc frowned. Calling hours were tomorrow, followed by a funeral the next day. Then…

Nothing. Farmwork. School. Riding contests for Jess. Long days. Dark nights.

Marc clapped a hand to Jess's shoulder. She didn't look up. He dropped a kiss to her hair. "I'll be glad when tomorrow's over, too. I'm not big on public spectacles."

Jess leaned against him. "But the funeral will be nice. The pastor planned it just the way Dad wanted. It'll be like having him with me in church again. All his favorites."

Marc knew he was a meager replacement for his father in that regard. He gave her shoulder a gentle squeeze. "I'm going up for coffee. Want some hot chocolate?"

Jess shook her head. "Kayla brought me some cappuccino mix from the market. I had some of that. It was really good."

Cappuccino mix? What was the matter with a fourteen-year-old drinking hot chocolate? Why did Kayla insist on thrusting her into a grown-up world?

Marc swallowed the retort. Jess *was* growing up. He needed to understand that. She needed his love and support, not his criticism. On that matter, Kayla saw things clearer than he did. He headed to the house, thoughts jumbled.

Jess had yet to cry. He'd expected her to fall apart at their father's bedside, but she hadn't. She'd knelt, prayed and held Pete's cool hand until the undertaker arrived. Then she bent and kissed her father goodbye.

That worried Marc. Girls cried all the time, didn't they?

Not Jess. And not Kayla, either. What was up with that?

He had no clue, but he'd mention Jess's stoicism to Kayla when he saw her next. He wasn't sure if he should delve, ignore or commiserate, but Kayla might have advice. He didn't want Jess hiding her feelings out of concern for him, trying to protect him. She'd always had a soothing nature. She must have gotten that from his father, because it didn't come from his mother.

That thought stopped Marc.

Jess *didn't* get her nature from his father. Or anything else. She wasn't Pete DeHollander's child except in name.

Marc fought an urge to track down his mother and give her the tongue-lashing she deserved. Then he'd find the man she cheated with and...

And...

Marc dropped his chin. He flexed his hands.

If there hadn't been a man, there wouldn't be a Jess. Of that he was certain. Out of horrible circumstance came wondrous good.

Jess was wondrous. She was his sister, the kid he'd helped raise. The girl he'd schooled in principles of horse husbandry from the time she could walk. Strong, faithful, beautiful Jess was a DeHollander, regardless of blood, and he'd take on anyone who tried to prove otherwise.

His father told him to talk to Kayla.

He would, once the visiting hours and funeral were behind him. He'd sort things out, ferret out details his father may have shared.

He couldn't hate her for being attentive to his father's confession. Hadn't he deliberately steered clear of that?

But his father persisted, even to the point of death. He'd needed Marc's understanding and wanted Marc's forgiveness of his mother's wrongdoing.

One out of two he could grant his father. He'd give his understanding, but the revelation about his mother's impropriety just made her easier to resent.

She'd used his father from the beginning. That didn't win her sympathy points in Marc's book. She was cool and callous, self-absorbed. Those were the facts and nothing would change them.

The back door opened. Jess stepped in, her hair damp.

"The rain started?"

She nodded. "Like melted ice pellets."

"Two months of this and we might see spring."

She crossed the room to lay her head against his chest. "I love you, Marc. I'm so glad I have you for a brother."

He held her tight, refusing to weigh the portent of her words. "Me, too, kid."

A sigh grew within him, threatening to swallow him. He was her brother, regardless of birth. She was his baby sister, his to cherish and care for, bonded by all that was good and wholesome in this crazy, mixed-up world.

He'd defy anyone who tried to change that.

Chapter Sixteen

Kayla carried her hat and scarf to the Saturday morning funeral. The weather proved softer, no rain or snow, and a hint of spring freshened the air.

Fool's spring, the locals called it. Anyone with North Country experience knew the real thing didn't hit until May, if then. The late-day forecast called for rain out of the northeast and that generally meant a good soaking, plenty cold.

Kayla slipped into a back pew. She spied Sarah and Craig on the front left, with Craig's family.

People stood shoulder to shoulder in the small church. The DeHollanders touched a lot of lives. Between the farm and the feed store, there were few locals who didn't cross paths with Pete or Marc several times a month.

Kayla bowed her head and prayed that this show of love and support would bolster Marc and Jess. She prayed for Marc's strength and an easing of his bitterness and anger toward his mother.

A gentle touch brought her head up.

Marc leaned down. "Sit with us. Please?"

He looked burdened and weary. Kayla stood. "Of course."

He held her hand as they made their way forward. For just a moment Kayla imagined herself a bride, her white dress soft and flowing. Flowers in her hair. A veil trailing against scattered petals.

Jess hugged her as they reached the front pew. "Thanks for sitting with us. I miss you already."

Kayla hugged her back. "I'm always here, honey." Guilt nudged her. She wouldn't always be there. She was leaving soon, pursuing different challenges, new horizons.

Jess could call her. They'd have gabfests on the phone. Laugh about fashions, cry over boys. It wasn't the same as comforting the girl in person, but it was the best Kayla could offer.

With the interment postponed, everyone gathered at the farm to celebrate Pete's life once the service concluded. Friends and family laughed and cried together, their kinship born of hard work and shared times, good and bad.

Hours later, the last guest left. The Macklin women cleaned up, refusing to budge until the last pan was put away. Once everyone had gone, Kayla got the full import of how empty the house seemed.

"Too quiet." Marc's gaze wandered the kitchen. Jess had gone to bed despite the early hour.

"Yes." The rain came, wind-driven and hard, a bone-chilling nor'easter. It beat against the still-hard ground, vengeful, gathering in swift-moving rivulets, the ice-packed soil unreceptive.

"Thanks for coming."

"I wanted to be there. And here." Kayla swept the house a look. "For a quiet man, he certainly had a presence."

"Yes." Marc drained his mug and looked at her. "Can I talk to you about something?"

Kayla looked up at him, unsure what to expect. "Sure."

"Come in here." Marc led the way to the darkened living room. Dappled firelight played a game of shadows as flames licked clean-split logs. He flicked on a lamp. "Have a seat."

His voice was serious. Kayla sat and watched him pace before he drew up a chair. "Dad talked to me before he died."

He glanced over his shoulder. Seeing the clear stairway, he turned back. "I don't want Jess to hear this."

Kayla exhaled. "Okay."

"He talked about my mother. He said…" Marc hesitated, his

look questioning, his voice low. "Things. He wasn't real clear, but he made two statements I need to share with you."

"Why me?" Kayla sank as deep into the cushion as she could without disappearing altogether.

"He said you knew about them."

Drat. "Marc, I—"

"Let me finish. He said Mom left because she feared she'd hurt Jess." Marc shook his head. "The idea that anyone could hurt a baby is beyond me, but that's what he said."

Kayla nodded.

"And that Jess wasn't his child."

Dear God. Kayla dropped her head. How did she get herself into the middle of this? Why was she involved at all?

Blessed are the peacemakers, for they shall be called the children of God.

She didn't feel like a peacemaker. She felt like an interfering know-it-all who managed to plunk herself into the middle of an already-convoluted family dynamic.

"Kayla? I need help understanding this, and I don't know who else to ask. Did Dad talk to you?"

Kayla gnawed her lower lip, awkward. "Yes."

Marc regarded her, his look inscrutable. "I need you to be honest with me."

Now was the time to explain her relationship with Arianna. For a long moment Kayla stared at the floor. The whorls in the aged-sculpted carpet blurred, then cleared. She gritted her teeth, sought Marc's gaze and began her story. She hadn't gotten very far when Marc grabbed her hands.

"She came back?"

"Yes." Kayla sighed and met his look. "I took care of her in the hospital. She's the reason I went into hospice care. Anna, Arianna," she corrected herself, "was also the reason I started going to church."

Marc stared at her. "Go on."

Kayla stood and paced. "She was ill. I didn't know who she was because she used her maiden name."

"Hernandez."

"Yes. She was so warm, so kind." Kayla paused at the window, scowling at the dark skies, the driving rain. "Nothing like the woman you remember."

"How'd she die?"

"HIV."

"Sex and needles. That's my mom." Disgust colored Marc's voice.

"She was different when I knew her," Kayla insisted. She crossed back to Marc. "She was sorry for what she'd done."

"Too little, too late."

"She wanted forgiveness."

"Fat chance."

"Marc."

He looked up, his expression flat.

"Your father forgave her."

"I'll never understand why." Marc's face hardened as she watched. "Especially if what he said about Jess was true."

"It's true. He told me last week," she revealed. She put her hands out, palms up. "He knew all along and forgave her anyway."

"He was always weak where she was concerned."

"Weak or in love?"

"Is there a difference?" Marc clenched his hands. The veins on the back bulged. "He coddled her."

"He understood she was sick."

Marc's laugh bore no amusement. "Sick? Spoiled, maybe. Conceited. Full of herself." He shook his head. "That's not sick, it's selfish."

"She was bipolar," Kayla began.

"And didn't like her meds. Yeah, I've heard the excuses," Marc retorted. "It doesn't wash, Kayla. She was selfish and egocentric. She made choices, day by day. If the meds helped and she truly loved us, she would have taken them." His jaw went rigid. His eyes narrowed. "But she didn't and used every excuse in the book to gain my father's sympathy."

"He loved her."

"She cheated on him, made our lives a living hell and bore

another man's child, then abandoned that child so that Dad and I raised her. What kind of love is that?"

Kayla folded her arms to ward off the chill of his words. A high-pitched cry from the stairs grabbed their attention.

"Jess." Marc crossed the room, his hands out. "Did we wake you?"

She stared at him, mouth open. "I'm not Daddy's little girl?"

Kayla moved forward.

Marc reached out a hand. "Jess, come here. I don't know what you heard, but—"

Jess looked from Marc to Kayla and back. "I'm not your sister?" She descended the last stairs, her hand pressed against her mouth. "Then who am I?"

"You're my sister." He reached the stairs and tugged Jess into his arms. "You've always been my sister. You're all I've got, Jess."

She pulled away, her face wreathed in grief and disbelief. "Whose child am I?"

Marc shook his head.

Jess turned to Kayla. "Do you know?"

Kayla reached out a hand that Jess shrugged off. "Don't ask me that, Jess. I've seen you with your father. You're his child in every way that counts."

"Except biology." Jess's expression broke Kayla's heart.

Marc stepped forward. "Jess, let's sit down and talk about this." He ran a hand through his hair. The anguish on his face reflected his sister's pain.

"No." Jess grabbed her coat and headed to the door. "Just leave me alone. I don't want to hear any more lies from either of you." At the door she whirled about. "I trusted you. Both of you." Her torment encompassed Kayla and Marc. "Look what's come of it."

"Jess."

Jess leveled a heated stare at her big brother. "Right now I hate you, Marc. All I ever wanted was what you took for granted. A mother and a father who loved me. You had that, and didn't appreciate it. Now I realize I never had either."

The door slammed in her wake.

Marc grabbed a flannel. "I've got to go after her."

"Of course. Take a light. And your cell phone. It's getting dark."

Marc strode to the kitchen and came back carrying a long-handled flashlight. The phone was tucked in the pack on his waist. He didn't waste time on goodbyes. At the door, he turned. "Kayla—"

"Go."

He nodded and disappeared through the door. Kayla moved to the window and watched him turn toward the barn. "Watch over them, Father. Help them cling to one another."

Jess's expression came back to her. The girl's existence had just been jerked out from under her. That was catastrophic at any age. Fourteen? Riddled with hormones and unanswered questions? Kayla prayed for a good outcome.

The phone rang an hour later. "I can't find her." Marc sounded frantic. "I've checked everywhere. I'm in the Jeep and the trails are bad."

"Would she have gone that far?" Kayla tried to think like a fourteen-year-old. She came up short.

"I checked the barns and the store before I took off," Marc explained. There was a short pause. "I'll keep looking. Call me if she shows up."

"I will."

Kayla eyed the dark, the storm. Would Jess have willingly stayed out in the growing torrent?

No.

Kayla tugged on one of Marc's hooded flannels. She stepped off the porch and ran for the barn, her feet slapping droplets of cold water against her legs.

She was thankful that Marc left a constant light on in the barn. A gust of wind jerked the heavy door from her hands as she stumbled in, sending it into the wall. The quick bang startled some stock. Thuds of shifting hooves and bulky bodies sent adrenaline through Kayla's veins. Tugging, she pulled the door shut and worked to calm her heart.

The wet night held the smell of old straw and fresh urine. She wrinkled her nose and edged forward.

Something skittered.

Kayla wavered, staring in the direction of the disturbance, then moved her eyes away. She wasn't sure she wanted to see the responsible party.

"Jess?" Kayla edged forward, then tried again, louder. "Jess?"

A bawl resounded near her right ear. Kayla turned and stared into the eyes of a big red cow sporting a shaggy white mullet, very "eighties." The cow bawled again and reached a damp snout toward Kayla.

"Back, you."

A wall ladder led to the upper reaches of the barn. Kayla headed that way, eyes darting.

Another cow wailed. Hooves shifted just before a second cow peered at Kayla over a wooden divider. "Nice cow. You're locked in there, right?"

The cow declined comment. She stared at Kayla, wondering...what? What did cows think? Kayla had no clue.

"Okay, then." Swiping damp palms against her pants, she grasped the ladder. Surely Jess would be here, snug in the haystacks. She wouldn't stay out in the rain, soaked and sodden, when there was a warmer alternative? "Jess? I'm coming up."

Rung by rung she climbed the ladder, despairing her slick-bottomed clogs. More than once they slipped, causing her to hold tight with her hands while she worked to regain her footing. On rung three that wasn't so bad. By rung fourteen, she was more concerned about the drop to the concrete floor. Reaching the top rung, she stared into the shadows. "Jess? It's Kayla. Are you up here?"

A slight sound came from the piled straw. Kayla nodded. "I'm coming."

Grasping the bar, Kayla pulled herself through the entry. Her left foot scrabbled, but the bar provided balance. She pushed forward, eyeing the upper reaches of the gambrel roofline.

The loft lay before her, large and airy. Stacks of straw stood sentinel around the open middle. At the far end stood a basketball hoop, key lines painted on the floor below. Marc, no doubt. Sarah had said he was a teenage jock. Kayla pictured him here, practicing his shots, banking the balls. Another sound interrupted her thoughts. She moved forward. "Jess?"

She half expected to see the teen curled into the loose straw, but no. No Jess.

A light shone from the right. Kayla moved that way

A small room stood there. There was nothing aesthetic about the enclosure, thrown together with aged two-by-fours and barn siding. Kayla moved to the front of the room. The door stood ajar. The door, like the walls, was a patched job of crossed wood and planking. She nudged it open. "Jess?"

A tiny sound came from within. Stifling a thankful sigh, Kayla pushed through the door. Her action set the door in motion. As she stepped into the room, grateful to have found Jess warm and dry, the door swung shut with a gentle click.

Kayla turned at the sound, then swung back, eyeing the room.

Jess was nowhere to be seen. The room was small, maybe ten feet square. Harnesses hung on the walls. A couple of old saddles sat in a corner, near a wooden stand. Bleached-yellow loose straw littered much of the floor.

No Jess.

Kayla didn't want to think about what she'd heard, the tiny cry. On a need-to-know basis of barn sounds, she wanted to be out of the loop. Decisive, she crossed to the door and pulled.

It didn't budge.

She gave the knob another hard twist and yanked.

The mechanism came away in her hand. As her predicament registered, she heard the other half of the rusted handle clatter to the floor beyond the door.

Kayla stared at the broken lever in disbelief. A chill raced down her spine. Fighting panic, she pushed the doorknob into the hole and wiggled it.

Nothing. Stripped clean.

A skittering beyond the door made her step back. She'd heard that sound before. Oh, yeah. Some sounds you never forget. Looking for something to use as a weapon, her eyes traveled up.

The window. The one she'd noticed on an early visit to the farm. Small, high and dirty.

The square casement was unreachable. The way the light bounced off the glass revealed its grimy state.

Another shiver climbed. The hairs on her neck stood out in protest.

"I've got to get out of here." As the sense of urgency rose, Kayla plied the door handle repeatedly.

Nothing.

She eyed the room. The noises on the far side of the door grew bolder with her absence, as if the rats could tell she posed no real threat.

"Mama."

Kayla sank to her knees, remembering.

A little girl, ordered to silence, locked away in a narrow attic room with only one small, out-of-reach window. "Mama, let me out. Please."

No answer.

Kayla felt the chill of the floor against her knocking knees. "Please, Mama. I'm hungry."

She'd watched the sun come up in the little window. Long hours later it went down. Then up, again. Then down.

Still her mama didn't come for her, didn't unlock the door and send her off to school.

"Mama."

Kayla fought the rising panic. No use. Trapped in the little room, lit with a lone, dusty bulb, she studied the window.

There was no reaching the smudged pane. She'd known it then, when she was just a girl. She knew it now.

She shrank to the floor, hugging herself, trying to block the invading thoughts, but the effort proved impossible. She could control the impulses most of the time, pushing the memories away, but not when so many buttons were pushed at once.

How hard she'd tried to get to that childhood window. She saw herself, a girl of eleven, trying to find a way out of that dark, dusty attic, scrabbling for anything to put her in reach of that glass. The door was immovable, and the silence below lay frightening in its completeness.

Another skitter in the present made Kayla hug herself more tightly.

There'd been rats in the attic, too. Nasty ones. She didn't dare sleep, not on purpose anyway, and especially not at night.

"Mama, there's rats up there."

"Not as big as the ones down here," her mother scolded. "You don't make a sound up there, no matter what you hear, Kayla." Her mother gripped her shoulders. "You understand?"

"Yes, Mama."

"Now, go. I'm expecting company. Get up there, do your homework and don't make a sound."

God, help me.

Kayla put her head to the floor of the barn room and prayed. *I can't do this, can't handle it. I need to get out of here. Help me, God. Please.*

The skittering pattered across the outer floor, then paused at the door.

There couldn't be a way in, could there? Kayla's senses went to full alert. "Get away from here! Shoo!" Panicked, she hurled a clog at the door. The shoe hit square and clattered to the floor.

For a short moment, she thought she'd scared them. Then the skitters grew louder, racing back and forth across the outer floor.

Help me. Please, help me.

She wasn't sure if she thought the phrase or said it, then realized her voice was the only useful tool she had. Her cell phone lay in her purse on the DeHollanders' back porch.

If Jess was in the barn, she'd hear Kayla's cries. She rose and pounded on the door. "Help! Help me! I'm trapped up here! Marc! Jess! Please!"

She pressed her ear to the wood and listened.

Nothing.

She tried again. "Marc, help me! I'm locked in! Marc! Jess! Someone help me!"

The little girl Kayla wasn't allowed to scream for help. That might have brought the interest of men up those stairs, to the adolescent girl above. How hard the little Kayla worked to block out the sounds from below, the words, the noises that meant Mama would have money come morning.

She didn't ask what went on at night. She didn't want to know. When she was older and figured it out, she didn't care to remember, so she didn't.

But there was no help for it now, locked in the small room with the sound of tiny feet sniffing the perimeter, hunting for a way in.

The rats in the apartment had been sizable. She remembered the policeman's surprise as he wrapped her in a blanket and carried her down three long flights of stairs. "Mind the rats," he told a uniformed woman they passed. He'd nodded to the third floor. "Big ones. I'm getting this little one out to the ambulance."

He'd kept the quilt up, over her eyes. She'd burrowed into his shoulder, feeling safe for the first time in days.

The feeling lasted short seconds. As the burly policeman rounded the first corner, the quilt shifted.

A sea of uniformed figures obscured her vision, but she saw enough to understand why Mama hadn't unlocked the door.

"Mama!"

The policeman redrew the blanket around her. "Hush, now. Let's get you some help."

There'd be no help for Mama. Not anymore. Kayla understood that.

"Marc! Please!" Kayla pounded fists against the door, praying it would open, set her free.

She couldn't keep the memories at bay up here. They flooded her brain, overtaking her. The sounds she'd been trained to ignore, the cries for help, her mother's final screams—

It came flooding back, torturing her.

And there was nothing she could do. Again.

Chapter Seventeen

"Thank God." Marc crossed Nan's riding ring and embraced his little sister. "Thank God I found you."

"You don't believe in God," Jess retorted. She tried to pull away. Marc wouldn't let her. "Or anything else."

"Jess." Marc pulled her closer, his arm firm around her shoulders. "Do you have any idea how much you mean to me? How much I love being your brother?"

Jess's face crumpled. Her lower lip stuck out, petulant.

"Jess." Marc turned her face to his. "I love you, kid. Having you around was what made everything bearable when Mom left."

"Right."

"It was," Marc insisted. He tweaked her nose. "You were so cute, so funny. And Dad and I were absolutely inept. We had no clue what to do with you."

"Still don't."

"No argument there. But I'm learning. I don't have lots of experience raising teenage girls."

"Lucky me."

"Jess." Marc held her gaze. "About what you heard—"

"That someone else is my father? That you and Kayla knew, but no one bothered to tell me? What did you want to explain, Marc?"

His father's words came back. *Be gentle.* He took a breath and calmed his heart, choosing words with care. "You never knew Mom."

Jess snorted.

"She was beautiful, like you," Marc continued. "Same hair, same eyes, same skin. I think that's why Dad and I went overboard with denim and flannel, because you were so pretty and feminine."

Jess leaned back. "Really?"

"Yup." Her look of surprise told him she didn't see herself as either pretty or feminine. He sighed. "Jess, Mom had her problems. I'm only now beginning to figure them out, so I'm not much help there, but Dad loved her."

"She slept with someone else and had his child. That would be me."

Marc tugged her closer. "I guess she did, but is that the end of the world?"

"Yes."

"No." Marc pressed a kiss to her hair, still damp from the rain. "I don't know what I would have done all these years without you. Dad and I, both. We loved you. We doted on you. It was like you were the hope for the future. If Mom hadn't had you—"

"Then she probably wouldn't have run away," Jess interrupted.

Vehement, Marc shook his head. "It would have happened anyway, Jess. It had nothing to do with you. She wasn't happy inside. She didn't laugh, she didn't pray." Marc shrugged. "She stopped caring. She'd pretend to take her meds to fool Dad, but he knew."

"How could he love her, Marc?" Jess looked up, confused. "How could he care, knowing what she did?"

"Love's a funny thing, Jess."

Jess sat silent, eyes down. Grimacing, she turned. "He loved me, didn't he?"

Marc gathered her into his arms. He felt her body shudder and knew she was finally crying the tears she'd held back. "With all his heart. He showed that every day, didn't he?"

"Yes." The reply was muffled against his shirt. He held tight, letting her cry, hoping tears might begin the healing.

His phone jabbed his side. Holding Jess, he reached around her to pull the phone out. "Gotta call Kayla and tell her you're all right. She was worried."

Jess nodded as he pushed buttons.

No answer.

Marc frowned, stared at the number, then shrugged.

"She didn't pick up?"

"No." Marc studied the phone once more, wondering.

"Maybe she got an emergency call."

Without telling him? Or leaving a message? Marc stood and hauled Jess up with him. "Let's say good-night to Rooster and head home, kid. I'm wet and tired."

"Me, too."

"We'll get you warmed up in no time."

"How'd you know to look here?"

"Because I always head to the barn when I need time," Marc acknowledged. "When you weren't in ours, I figured Nan's was the next best thing."

"Pretty smart for a boy."

"That was after I spent an hour making mud tracks with the Jeep."

"Okay. Not so smart."

"But trainable."

Jess leaned her head against Marc's chest. "Will we be okay?"

"Yes." He pressed a kiss to her forehead. "We'll be fine."

On the way out the door he tried their home number again, just in case. "She might have been in the bathroom or something," he explained to Jess.

Still no answer. Marc hid his disappointment. Tonight he needed to concentrate on Jess, make sure she understood her place in the family.

Tomorrow he'd track down Kayla and finish the conversation he wished he'd never begun.

The ringing phone jarred Marc out of his sleep over two hours later. He stumbled in the hall, nearly knocked over a table and got to the phone just before the answering machine picked up. "Hello."

"Marc, it's Beth Pickering. Bill just nicked a car parked on the roadside a bit south of your place. The road was icing and he slid into the back of it."

"A car?" Marc thought hard. "Why would there be a car parked on the road? Anyone in it?"

Jess came out of her room, her pajamas rumpled, eyes squinting.

"No." Beth's voice sounded as confused as he felt. "Bill said it's a red car, one of those snazzy ones."

Marc's chest tightened. "A Grand Am?"

Jess touched his arm. "Kayla parked down the road," she whispered. "She wanted to leave parking spaces near the house for guests."

Then that meant... "Beth, I think it's a friend's car. I'll check it out."

"Tell them Bill's really sorry. It wasn't a bad bang-up, but still. Nothing he could do under the circumstances."

"Of course."

Marc disconnected and hurried to his bedroom. He threw on pants and a shirt in quick order.

"Where is she, Marc?"

He shook his head. Jess moved closer. "Did she go out looking for me?"

Marc grabbed her shoulders. "I don't know, Jess, but maybe."

"If her car's here..." Her look of fear mirrored what he didn't want to acknowledge.

"I'll find her."

He had to. There were no other options. Jess ran back to her bedroom. "I'm coming, too."

"No."

She turned.

Marc jerked his head. "Stoke up the fire. Make some coffee. Get things comfortable."

She thought, then nodded, agreeing. "Okay."

Downstairs, he reached to the pegs for his other lined flannel. It wasn't there. With a frown he stepped out to the back porch and flicked the switch.

Kayla's coat and purse lay tucked neatly on the back counter. Jess rounded the corner and stopped dead. "She's not wearing her coat?"

The thought of hypothermia chilled Marc's blood. "I think she's got my flannel. It's not on the peg."

Jess pretended comfort. "It's lined and has a hood. She'll be fine."

Dear God, please let her be fine. For the second time tonight, he put someone he loved in God's hands. He could only pray it was trust well spent.

The flashlight beam helped Marc pick his way across the iced drive. The falling temperatures had turned the rain to sheeted ice. The coated drive made for treacherous walking.

He entered the barn through the side door and noticed the back lights were on. Why hadn't he realized that before?

Because the front light's always on. Sure, if he'd looked carefully, he'd have noticed the brighter glow, but he was tired and wet when he came home. All he'd wanted was a bed and a pillow, both dry and warm.

"Kayla?" He set the flashlight on a shelf. "Kayla? Where are you?"

The lights meant she'd been there. Marc hunted the lower level, calling her name. He tried not to envision the things that could happen to a tenderfoot in a barn filled with huge animals and heavy equipment. Did she stumble into a stall and get trampled? Fall and impale herself on a piece of equipment?

In the far reaches he reprimanded himself for not replacing the bulbs in an overhead light. It was dim in that corner, and he picked his way with care.

Nothing.

He swallowed the curse he wanted to say and moved to the barn's center.

The loft ladder was directly to his right. Would Kayla have ventured up there in those ridiculous shoes?

No.

Reality smacked him.

Sure she would, if she thought Jess was there. He climbed the roughed-in ladder and swung into the loft.

Tiny kittens raced across the floor, disappearing into a pile of oat straw, a sure sign of spring.

"Kayla?" Marc crossed the floor, hunting the shadows. "Kayla? Where are you?"

She had to be here. The thought of her alone in the elements scared him. She wouldn't have ventured into the fields, with no light and only a flannel shirt, would she?

"No." He comforted himself out loud. "She's here, I know she is." He moved to the front of the barn, calling her name. "Kayla! Where are you? Are you asleep? Wake up, honey."

"Mama?"

Marc stopped dead. Iced fingers raced down his spine. "Kayla? Keep talking, honey, I'll find you."

"Mama?"

Marc turned toward the sound. The harness room. He stared at the closed door and the knob lying on the floor. He crossed the short distance in a heartbeat and snatched up the handle. "Kayla? You in there?"

A childlike sob answered him. Muttering, he thrust the knob into the notch and turned.

The door opened.

He wasn't sure how to approach the terrified woman burrowed in the corner, head down, arms folded around shaking legs. Marc took two quiet steps and crouched. "Kayla?"

Kayla swayed back and forth, gaze down. "Mama. Come get me. Mama. Come get me. Mama…"

He crept forward. "It's Marc, Kayla. It's okay. Everything's all right. You got locked in, but the door's open now. See?" Every male instinct pushed him to speed, but her posture slowed him. He got close enough to touch her. "Kayla?"

She shrank away.

"Come here, honey." Setting his arms around her, Marc gathered her in. "I've got you, now. I've got you."

"I didn't make a sound."

The childlike whisper raised goose bumps on Marc's arms.

He felt the chill of her hands, her cheeks, and knew he had to get her to the house, but there was no moving her like this.

"You did good, Kayla."

"I tried my best."

His heart broke to hear the little girl tones. "I know you did, honey."

A skittering noise yanked her attention. The crown of her head caught his chin. He arched back, holding her with one hand and his throbbing chin with the other. "What the—"

A smoke-gray kitten careened to the now-open door. It danced sideways, a caricature cat, before disappearing into the straw.

"Don't let them get me."

"Kayla." Marc gave one last rub to his chin and tipped her head back. "It's a kitten, Kayla. A tiny, gray kitten. Just a baby."

He saw the moment his words registered. She straightened. Her eyes darted, then calmed. She made a move to rise, as if that one moment of lucidity erased the terror. "A kitten? How silly of me."

Marc held tight. "Where are you going?"

He saw a flash of insecure girl, followed by a glimpse of self-assured woman. "Home."

"Right." He tugged her head back to his shoulder. "Where are you, Kayla?"

She didn't hesitate. "With you."

"No." Marc pressed his lips to her cold forehead. "I mean, where are you? When I walked in, you weren't here, in this barn."

"Barns smell."

"Sometimes. Don't change the subject."

"I've got to go."

"I'm taking you back to the house to warm up. You can bunk with Jess tonight and go home in the morning."

"Okay."

No argument. A rare blessing. He stretched his legs, already cramped on the cold, hard floor. "Can you stand?"

"Of course."

Her legs buckled the moment she tried.

Marc scooped her up. "Thought as much. What in the world were you doing in here?" He grabbed up her loose shoe and pushed through the doorway as he headed toward the ladder. Two kittens pranced after him, then stutter-stepped away. "Looking for Jess?"

She nodded. "I thought I heard her crying."

"The kittens. They yowl like a babe sometimes." Marc eyed the ladder, then Kayla. "How're we going to get you down?"

She swung a leg. "I can feel my feet now."

"Great." He set her down. "I'll go first. If you have to let go, I'll be right under you. I'll catch you." He reached a finger to the curve of her cheek. "I promise."

He descended and watched from below. "Swing your hand over, now your foot. Good. Now the other. Okay. Come on down."

"You sound like a game show host."

Sparring with him. That was good, but he intended to find out what turned her into the terrorized child he'd found upstairs. He grabbed her shoulders as she stepped off the ladder. "Good job." He kissed her forehead and led her to the door, one arm around her shoulders, caring for her. She seemed wobbly, but better. "It's icy. We've got to go slow."

"Okay."

Way too agreeable. Probably hoping to throw him off track, make him forget what he saw and heard. Not likely.

The storm hit them with ferocity that defined March in the North Country. He gave her the flashlight and sheltered her as they picked their way across the drive. The stoked fire provided a warm, soothing welcome. Marc breathed a sigh of relief. "Jess! I've got her."

Jess appeared from the kitchen. "Kayla. Are you frozen?" She grabbed Kayla in a hug, then pulled her toward the wood stove while Marc shed his outerwear. "Come here. Warm up."

Marc tugged off Kayla's shoes and socks, then chafed her feet while Jess fixed Kayla a steaming mug of coffee. "Not bad," he noted, assessing the chill.

"Good socks."

Marc smiled. Her color heightened. He hoped it was him and not the heat of the fire that brought the warmth to her cheeks. "I'm glad you had them on."

"The barn stays pretty warm, actually," Jess offered, puzzled.

"Not the loft."

Jess swung back to Kayla. "You were in the loft?"

"Locked in the harness room," Marc explained. "The handle fell off the door."

"Kayla, really?" asked Jess, distressed. "I'm so sorry. You were looking for me?"

Kayla sipped the coffee, nodding. "Yes, but don't get all upset and run off again. I've had enough for one night."

Marc agreed. "Yes."

Kayla shot him a look that begged no questions. He rubbed her feet and acquiesced for the moment. He'd have his answers eventually, but tonight she needed warmth and rest.

"Want a warm shower?"

She shook her head. Her eyes looked sleepy as heat crept into her bones. "No. Too tired."

"I've got pajamas for you." Jess nodded to a pair of green plaid flannels. "They're not stylish, but they're comfy."

"Comfy's good." Kayla sat up. "Listen, guys, I'm sorry I caused so much trouble. I didn't mean to make things worse."

"You didn't." Jess leaned forward and gave Kayla another hug. "I'm just so glad you're all right. If anything had happened to you—"

Kayla flashed a worried glance to Marc. He met it with a solid one in return.

"I don't know what I'd do," Jess finished. "I would never forgive myself, Kayla."

"But nothing did." Marc stood and held a hand out. "Come on, let's get you to bed. I'm ready for sleep. Again."

"Marc…"

Her voice trailed. Marc looked down at her, then shrugged his arm around her. "What?"

"Nothing."

He nodded. "We'll talk soon."

She didn't look reassured. "All right."

He walked her upstairs. Jess had the second bed in her room folded down. He heard Kayla's sigh of gratitude and kissed her temple. "I'll see you in the morning. And not real early, either."

"Church is at ten," Jess reminded him.

Ah, yes. Church. For once Marc didn't think he'd have a real hard time praying. He nodded. "I'll have the chores done." Then, after glancing at his watch, he added, "Most of them." He hugged Jess. "Night, kid."

Kayla gave him a half smile. "Good night, Farmer Boy."

He met her gaze. "Sleep well, Kayla."

Chapter Eighteen

Kayla made a beeline for her car while Marc did morning chores. He caught up with her in the driveway.

"Heading out?"

She kept her gaze fixed beyond his shoulder, but not toward the barn with the too-high-to-reach window. "Heading home."

He moved closer, cautious. "Okay. I brought your car up to the house." He stepped toward the rear of the Grand Am. "Bill Pickering slid into the back of it last night when the roads got icy. That's how I knew you were still here. I'm sure he'll call it in to the insurance company today."

At the moment Kayla could have cared less about the smashed left taillight. All she wanted was to escape Marc's penetrating look and his inevitable questions. "All right."

Marc bent, searching her face. "You're okay to drive?"

"I'm fine." Her tone was clipped. She didn't care. Every instinct pushed her to run from this man who'd seen her with her defenses down.

He moved closer, invading her space. "You could stay. Go to church with Jess and me."

For a fleeting moment the idea of walking into the church as a unit appealed. Right until she remembered Marc's attitude. His presence in church answered an obligation, not a need.

No. She'd lived without grace too long. She knew how easy

it was to shrug her shoulders and go her own way. She'd done just that until Anna broke through with words of love and forgiveness.

The man in front of her hated Anna and didn't believe in God. Insurmountable obstacles from her vantage point. "I've got to go."

Marc followed her around the car. He leaned down after she slipped into the seat. "I'll come by later."

"Sorry." Kayla worked her keys, willing her fingers not to shake. "I'm busy."

His jaw hardened. She saw him work to relax the clench. "With?"

"Things I can't do when I'm working. Unlike you, I don't work at home."

He showed no reaction to the jab, just nodded, slow. "Soon, then."

Not if she had a choice. Backing away, she realized the unlikelihood of that. She had three months to go. Marc was a determined man. No way could she keep him at bay until she'd moved south.

At the moment she'd settle for time to regroup, away from the DeHollanders. Away from their needs, their problems.

She hated to walk out on Jess, but the idea of Marc questioning her put her into a cold sweat. She'd spent a lifetime filtering what she could handle from what needed to be set aside.

Right now, Marc DeHollander needed to be set aside. As she glanced at his diminishing reflection through her rearview mirror, she recognized the difficulty of the task.

Marc wasn't the type to be shrugged off easily. He was solid and sure, a man of promise and worth. That knowledge warmed her from within.

It scared her even more.

"Hi! You've reached five-five-five, four-one-two-seven. We're not in right now, but leave a message at the tone."

Knuckles braced, Marc gripped the phone. "Pick up, Kayla. Please."

Silence answered him. Stifling a growl, he disconnected and studied the hydraulics of his seeder, restless. The necessary parts had been back-ordered. Now they had arrived, but the store was hopping with spring business and Joan Mettleman's chicks and bunnies. His clerk was down with the flu and cows were dropping calves in the field daily.

Why he'd said yes to the neighboring farmer's marketing ploy of live critters in the store's sales room, he had no idea, because the rustling sounds of baby animals, even penned, had him gritting his teeth.

But Easter was coming and Joan made a valid point. Chicks and bunnies were hot items, and country folk seldom minded an extra mouth to feed around the barn. Today's Rhode Island Red chick could be this fall's 4-H project in the right child's hands.

He pushed aside thoughts of children. Anyone's children.

He didn't want to think of relationships gone bad and buried dreams.

The silence greeting his phone calls and trips to Kayla's door sent their own message. *Unwelcome.*

The situation grated, but he wasn't a begging man.

Sure you are. You'd beg in a heartbeat if you thought it would do any good.

No way, no how.

Right. Keep telling yourself that, DeHollander.

Marc flinched.

He knew she was scared. Frankly, he was more than a little intimidated himself. The Kayla he'd found in the barn was a fear-filled woman whose neediness unnerved him. Her instability touched too many childhood memories.

Your father loved your mother, Kayla insisted. *He stood by her through thick and thin.*

Considering the outcome, Marc was pretty sure his father made the wrong choice, unknowing. The difference was, Marc saw the quandary. He lived it firsthand. Was he willing to step into the same lion's den that caused his family sorrow and heart-break?

No.

Kayla's lapse into childhood scared him. He didn't have the wherewithal to deal with an unstable woman, regardless of his feelings. Forewarned was forearmed. Sure he'd seen flashes of insecurity from her. He'd written them off as normal baggage.

What he read in her face on the night of Pete's funeral was nothing he considered normal.

He should run screaming. Back away as far as possible. He didn't need a woman toting an emotional load. He didn't need a relationship with someone who had an ongoing love affair with trendsetting looks and spiked heels.

Although her legs looked nice in those. Real nice.

Marc pinched the bridge of his nose, then climbed beneath the PTO connection and focused on the mechanics of well-manufactured hydraulics.

"We need to talk."

The voice surprised Kayla as she approached her apartment, mid-April. She sucked air, startled, as a hand steadied her arm.

Marc's hand.

"There's nothing to say." She shrugged and looked anywhere but at him. "Go away."

"No." His grip tightened. "Just talk, Kayla. Talk can't hurt you."

But it could. He didn't know the half of it. She glanced up.

Those eyes. Gray-green, warm and cool, blended with pointed sparks of amber. He held her gaze, his look firm, his jaw tight. He nodded to the outside stairway. "Can I come up?"

She'd hoped he'd given up. His phone calls had dwindled the past two weeks. She thought she was ready to put him behind her, but his proximity made her want to ease the narrow distance between them. How easy it would be to move into the curve of his arm, feel him rest his chin on her hair.

A gust of wind broke her chain of thought. She stepped back. "I don't think so."

He stepped forward. His left hand touched her chin, her cheek. "Please?"

He didn't look angry. He didn't look perturbed. He looked…

Concerned.

That realization almost undid her. No one got past her line of defense. No one broke through to the needy soul residing within.

"No, Marc." Stepping back, she tried to slip away.

He didn't let go. "You're afraid."

Because she was, his assessment made her angry. "You don't know what you're talking about."

"Only because you won't tell me."

"There's nothing to tell."

"Sure there is. And it scares you."

Indignation spiraled up. "Nothing scares me. Not anymore."

"Oh, no?" Deliberate, he let his gaze encompass their situation. Her stance, his distance, the stairs to her apartment. "Then let me up. That's what friends do."

Friends.

She wanted to cry and scream, but she'd held those emotions in check for a long, long time. She did neither.

"If nothing else, I'd like to be your friend. I think we could both use one."

"I have friends."

"Then one more couldn't hurt." His look slid to the stairway again. "Coffee. Some conversation to right my brain about all this stuff with my father and mother and Jess. Then…"

"Then, what?"

He regarded her, his look unreadable. "Then I go home and try to run two businesses that need me night and day, raise a motherless sister who's lost her father and a good chunk of her faith in mankind, deal with my grief at losing a man who meant the world to me and maybe go slowly crazy trying to keep all the plates spinning."

His openness shamed her. She'd been so worried about herself, her needs, protecting her fragile ego, that she'd conveniently pushed aside his dilemma. She drew a breath and exhaled, long and slow, then acquiesced. "Okay."

His presence behind her on the stairway unnerved her. The sight of him, his scent, so masculine, so…

Marc.

She'd let him in and hope he'd gulp his coffee. Then she'd ease him out the door and lay plans for the next segment of her life. Virginia should be beautiful this time of year. Cherry blossoms, spring blooms, grass-lined trails, gracious homes.

Potsdam blustered, despite the April date. A Canadian clipper sent a late surge of snow. The melting remains left everything sodden and dirty. Nothing pretty about it.

Inside, she moved to start coffee. Would he notice her hand tremors, the rise in breathing?

She didn't want this confrontation, but saw no way out. He'd been through a lot and she'd left him high and dry. Jess, too. She wasn't that kind of person, and didn't want him to remember her that way.

What do you care how he sees you? This guy doesn't share your beliefs, makes a show of tolerating faith and hates his mother. Not exactly pick-of-the-litter.

"Coffee's—"

She turned into his chest, a very nice chest, broad and thick.

"I smelled it." He leaned back to ease their sudden proximity. "I switched the space heater on. Take the chill off."

She filled two mugs and nodded. "Then we'll have it in there, okay?"

He roamed the other room, mug in hand, before pausing in front of a framed print. "I like this."

Kayla smiled, agreeing. "Me, too. The little bungalow, the flowers, the waving grasses. The ever-present source of light. That's my dream home."

Marc turned. "Small."

She shrugged. "I don't need much. A good roof, warm floors and lots of flowers."

"With plenty of closet space."

She wrinkled her nose. "Yeah."

Marc sank onto the small sofa. "Did you have gardens when you were little?"

Red alert. She struggled to maintain a calm expression. "I've always appreciated them."

He angled his head, eyes narrowed. "Nice dodge. Where did you grow up, Kayla?"

Her heart buzzed danger. Her fingers tingled. "How's Jess?"

"Where, Kayla?"

She stood. "Listen, I thought you wanted to talk about your dad and Anna. I'm not willing to—"

"Talk about yourself? That's not fair."

"Fair's got nothing to do with this."

"You're my friend. I worry about my friends when they're having problems."

"I'm fine."

"Good. Where'd you grow up?"

Hot tears startled her. Her throat tightened. Her hands clenched. A full-frontal emotional overload took charge. For the life of her, she wouldn't move forward and couldn't step back. "You need to leave."

"Come here."

"Now."

"Right here." He patted the spot beside him. "Tell me about Kayla. About the little girl inside the woman's body."

Her jaw slackened. Tears slipped down her cheeks. "I can't do this. Please, Marc."

He nodded, encouraging her. "Sure you can. Come here, Kayla." He stretched out an arm and stood. "Talk to me."

She stood silent, rooted.

Unfair tactics. He'd gotten there under the guise of needing to talk, then turned the tables once he got in the door.

He stretched out his second arm. "Come here, honey."

Was it the endearment that spurred her faltering shift forward, or was it the expression offering help and acceptance?

She had no idea, but his face softened as she moved. He nodded, confident. "I'm right here."

He enveloped her when she reached him, his cheek pressed against her hair. He held her, swaying gently. Her tears wet his shirt, his chest. Strong arms sheltered her from the onslaught of emotional baggage. He drew her into the loveseat, cradling her. "Shh… It's all right. It's all right. I've got you, girl. I've got you."

He did. She felt the strength of his embrace, the shelter of his arms, the softness of ribbed cotton, scented with spice. She sighed and relaxed into a warmth she'd never known and would most likely never know again. Taking a deep breath, she sighed once more and began. "My mother was a prostitute."

Chapter Nineteen

Marc listened, unmoving, wishing he could help. He kept his arms snugged and held tight, hoping to share his warmth and strength, knowing she needed both.

"I didn't know that when I was little. What it meant."

Marc nodded, his chin to her hair.

"We moved often. All over Ohio, a little in Pennsylvania." Kayla paused. Her shoulders relaxed. "When I was small, she waitressed in a Greek diner. I remember a big dining room. The curtains were covered with flags and wheels. I don't know how old I was then," Kayla continued, steadier. "Five, maybe? I went to school, so I would have been five or six."

"Did you stay there long?"

"I don't think so. My next memories are of traveling from place to place with whatever guy my mom was seeing at the time."

Marc fought the clench of anger, understanding what Kayla didn't say.

"They'd stay for a bit, then move on. We ended up in Cleveland when I was almost eight."

"Whereabouts?"

"Off Detroit Ave. I walked by lots of railroad tracks."

She went silent. Marc didn't intrude. Already she'd opened up a carefully screened chapter of her life. He had no right to push for speed.

The fingers of her left hand plucked his sleeve. Her breathing pattern changed. The rate of respirations climbed. "We had an upper apartment in an old, drafty house."

Marc swept the third-story walk-up a look as another puzzle piece clicked into place. "Yes?"

"I'd get so tired climbing those steps every day. I carried every book I had so no one would take them."

"Cautious," he observed.

"Smart," she corrected. "Everything we had got hocked or stolen. My third-grade teacher told me I was smart, that I could be anything I wanted if I worked hard, so I did."

That he could believe. The image of a tiny Kayla, clutching her books as a ticket to well-being wasn't a long stretch. Feisty, even then. "Cleveland's got some long, cold winters."

"Not as bad as here," she argued. "But cold wet springs. Lots of rain and snow off the lake."

"I bet." He wasn't sure how to lead her, or even if he should, but his pragmatic side told him it was now or never. He pressed his lips to her hair. "You lived with your mom there?"

Silence. He couldn't see her face, had no way to read her expression, but felt the heightened tension. "The guy-of-the-hour dumped us about a month after he got Mom hooked on crack."

Marc tightened his hold.

"She used to say that waitresses and hookers always had change in their pockets."

He cringed.

"I think the prostitution started in Cleveland." Kayla's voice assumed a detached air. "I don't remember the stream of men before that. Oh, there were guys," she acknowledged. "Left and right. A week here, two there. But not customers."

"You were eight?"

She nodded. The scent of her hair invaded his senses with her movement. Sassy. Sprightly. Nothing soft and floral for Kayla. Her scent reminded him of summers at the beach, sun and sand.

"There was a room."

Her fingers clenched, one hand on his sleeve, one tucked beneath her chin.

"An attic, actually."

"Big?"

"No."

The word came too sharp. He sensed her move toward dark water, untamed, uncharted. Once again, her breathing hitched upward.

"It was a small room, filled with stuff. Dusty. Smelly. I cleaned off an old piece of furniture and pretended it was a desk. There was a light that hung from the ceiling with a chain you pulled."

"Sounds like an attic."

"Rats."

His stomach surged. He restrained it with a firm swallow. "In the attic?"

"Everywhere."

Marc wondered if he should be doing this. Shouldn't Kayla be pouring her heart out to someone who understood childhood dilemmas, someone skilled in psychotherapy? Someone who knew how far to push?

He leaned to catch a glimpse of her face. "Do you want to stop talking about this?"

She scowled. "I thought you wanted details. They too much for you to handle?"

He wanted to know her, to understand what drove her. What he didn't want was to push her over some undefined ledge he couldn't see. "I want you to trust me, Kayla."

"A precious commodity not easily given."

"Then even more worthwhile."

She went silent, eyes down.

No pushing this time. He'd offered her a way out. It was up to her to decide how far to go, what to reveal.

"I thought the kittens in the barn were rats."

Marc eased back, still holding her. "I realized that." He shrugged. "I wondered why."

"I used to have to stay awake to keep them away from me. Only I couldn't stay awake forever, you know?"

"Yes."

"I told my mother about them and she just shook her head. 'Kayla,' she told me, 'there's nothin' in that attic as scary as what could happen if one of my callers finds you. You study, you turn out the light, you don't make a sound. No matter what you hear, you keep yourself quiet. You got that?'

"I said, 'Yes, Mama.'" Her hands tensed. Her body tightened. "'Don't make a sound no matter what you hear.'"

"And you didn't."

Her chin quivered. Her mouth softened, but she stiffened it. "I didn't. Through all the nights and all the sounds, I stayed up there and clamped my lips together, trying to ignore what went on. Sometimes she would cry, sometimes she would scream, sometimes…"

She stopped. A tear slipped down her cheek. He caught it with his thumb. "I've got you." The slight ease of her limbs told him his words meant something.

"She'd unlock the door in the morning and then go to bed. I always thought that was weird because she'd been in bed all night. How stupid I was."

"You were a child. A little girl," he reminded her, gently. "Why should you have any idea what was going on?" Anger at the thought of Kayla being privy to her mother's illicit habits pushed him more upright. "No one should raise a kid in an environment like that."

"Well, she did," Kayla asserted. "For three years. She worked her night job between the sheets, fed her habit and life slid downhill. I protected her from social workers and the police. No easy task as time went on."

He'd wondered why she was so strong, so tough. It was a miracle she wasn't hopelessly jaded, considering.

"Did they eventually take you away?"

Her hands stopped. Her breath stilled. She went motionless in his arms.

"Kayla?"

"One night the noises got real loud. Different. I understood it later, but right then I just knew that the man's voice was angry and mean. I climbed under the big comforter we'd gotten from the thrift store and buried my head in the pillow, but it didn't do any good."

Marc's heart went quiet. He waited, not breathing.

"Then Mama screamed. Again and again, she screamed."

Her hands grew clammy. Sweat appeared on her upper lip.

"She'd screamed before, but not like this. Nothing like this. I heard him yell and she'd scream, then he'd yell some more. There was all this banging around. Thumps and bumps. So much noise. So many different sounds."

Marc's insides spasmed, pushing his stomach toward his throat.

"I knew something was wrong, but I couldn't tell what. I thought of going down and pounding on the door, hoping he'd stop, but then he'd know I was in the attic and Mama always said, 'No matter what, you do not come down those stairs, young lady. You do not let these men know you're in the house.'"

"It got real quiet."

No.

"I think I fell asleep," she admitted. "I must have, because when I woke up there was a rat staring at me. I jumped up and saw it was light outside."

"Through the windows?"

"One window," she explained. "Small and dirty, too high for me to reach, even with stuff to climb on."

The resemblance to the harness room came clear.

"I went downstairs and tried to open the door."

"And?"

"I couldn't. It was still locked."

Dread filled Marc. "So you…?"

"I waited, then I called for help. I called and called. No one came."

Why, God? If you're up there, or wherever it is you claim to be, why would you put a little kid through this?

"It got cold."

"I bet."

"Real cold. I could see snowflakes during the day. Even then the attic wasn't very bright. It was cloudy and snowy, with just that one dirty window." Her face tightened as remembrances spilled forth.

"I got so hungry. And I was anxious because I was missing school. I kept calling my mom, telling her to wake up, telling her I'd be late. The teachers don't like it if you're late, I said."

Silence ensued. Marc hung tight, wondering why he'd started this. What was the matter with him? Couldn't he leave well enough alone? She'd been doing all right, forging along—

"It got dark. I must have slept some, because I remember the streetlight coming through the window that night. I chased the rats off a couple of times, and I was glad I'd slept during the day so they couldn't get me in the dark.

"When she didn't unlock the door the next morning, I tried not to think of what might have happened. I kept telling myself she must have needed something at the store. Every little while I would yell for her." She paused and shrugged. "After a while, I yelled for anyone to hear me. By then I didn't care who, as long as someone came to let me out."

"They did."

"Two days later. I watched the sky get light and dark two more times before I heard people. I hollered for help and a policeman broke down the attic door. He came upstairs and found me.

"I was never so happy to see anybody in my life." Relief softened her expression. "He tugged the blanket around me. He even covered my head. He kept saying, 'We're gonna get you warm, honey, don't you worry.'

"I thought he was wrapping me up because of the cold, but the blanket slipped when he got to the second floor."

Another silence lengthened as she dealt with memories he'd pushed her to face. Marc felt like a heel. He rubbed a hand up and down her arm, sharing the present.

"There were people moving around. Some wore uniforms, some didn't. One lady was taking pictures and she looked startled to see me. Almost scared to see me watching her."

Her lower lip shuddered as she stared at a memory long consigned to the far reaches of her mind, a child's reckoning with death.

Marc knew what she was about to say, he understood what Kayla, the child, saw at the bottom of those stairs.

"The photographer called the policeman's name, then pointed to me. He grabbed the quilt back up, but not before I realized why Mama never opened the door."

"Kayla." He held tight, rocking her, soothing her. "Kayla, I'm so sorry."

She wasn't crying now. She'd spent her tears. Eyes dry, she stared at nothing special. Her hands lay limp, her lips parted, her brow pensive. "I laid on that floor above, listening to her beg for her life, plead for another chance, all the while that monster cut her up.

"And I never made a sound."

Kayla thought she'd be more emotional at the end.

She wasn't.

She'd hated her part in that whole thing for so long that it was second nature to accept the guilt now. If she could have gotten some kind of help, her mother might not have died at the hands of a murdering savage.

That night, anyway.

Marc held her. His lips pressed gentle kisses to her hair, her cheek.

What a pair. The two of them were a high school chemistry class run amuck, waiting for the inevitable explosion.

He'd wanted the story, he got the story. Now he could run with a clear conscience. Who in their right mind longed to be saddled with that kind of baggage?

Not her, but her options were limited. She'd lived the experience. It was hers, like it or not. She'd spared Marc the sordid details of her mother's activities, the pieces of the puzzle she understood as she matured.

Marc was a smart guy. He understood what she left unsaid. Life with her mother wasn't Walton's Mountain. More like an Oprah Book Club entry.

His arms felt good around her. His breath against her hair felt natural and right.

But she refused to fool herself. Neither of them was strong enough to partner the other through life's ups and downs. She had faith but serious issues of control and forgiveness.

He had no faith and a serious problem with women in crisis.

Their relationship had code blue stamped across the cover. No way could they breathe life into a viable future. Shaky, at best.

Disastrous, at worst, and Kayla'd become good at avoiding disasters. She'd learned to examine and evaluate whatever came her way.

Marc DeHollander didn't even make the "high risk" category of potential prospects. He was firmly in the "out of bounds" classification, and now he understood why. She was a woman with grave issues.

Marc wanted Betty Crocker. Nothing more serious than what to cook for supper. At least now he would understand why she'd avoided him, what she'd been afraid to say for so long.

Goodbye.

Chapter Twenty

Marc wanted to help Kayla. Hold her. Soothe her the rest of her days.

Mission: Impossible.

He recognized the fact and still cradled her, letting his arms provide sanctuary.

More like a temporary haven, right, Bucko?

For the first time he saw what she'd recognized. They had too many issues to be good for one another. A relationship between them was a broken home, waiting to happen.

He had no clue how to deal with the guilt she carried and she had no use for an agnostic husband who couldn't come to terms with his mother's self-absorbedness.

What a pair. They could go down in history like Romeo and Juliet. Sam and Diane. Tristan and what's-her-name. He shifted slightly. "Sorry. My arm is going to sleep."

She edged away. "Of course. I didn't mean to lean so hard."

"That's what friends are for."

Her clenched jaw said she read his meaning. She flashed a smile, bittersweet. "Right."

Marc leaned forward. "I'm glad you told me."

"Not much choice. You caught me at a bad time."

He frowned. "Why?"

"Lost a patient today."

Marc lifted a brow. "I'm missing something. That's what you do, right? Work with the dying?"

She flushed. "This one wasn't supposed to go so soon. The family wasn't ready, they hadn't said their goodbyes and the paperwork wasn't processed."

"Rough time line."

"Story of my life." She stood and faced him. "I'm tired, Marc. I need to get to bed."

He rose. "Kayla—"

She shook her head. "Really tired. Crying jags do that to me."

He had a hard time believing she indulged often but accepted that. "When will I see you again?"

"I'll send you a Christmas card from Virginia."

"About that…"

She stepped to the door. "Good night, Marc. Give my best to Jess."

He gripped the door knob before he opened it. After a moment's hesitation, he turned back.

She hugged herself to ward off the cold. Marc felt guilty holding the door ajar. "I'll call you."

Kayla shook her head, resigned. "Don't. Please. Have a good life, Marc."

The door swung softly shut. He heard the lock engage and stood silent while her footsteps padded across the living room. A moment later, the light winked out.

She'd bared her soul, then pulled back as far as she could.

Which was good, right? He'd learned a sage lesson by watching his dysfunctional family. Marrying a woman with a scant hold on reality was akin to life imprisonment. He'd seen the act firsthand. Not pretty.

The walk to his truck seemed especially cold. Gusts soaked him with ice-flecked rain, the dampness bone-chilling.

Life would go on. He knew that. He was in the thick of spring busyness, fields needed to be primed for seeding once the weather broke and the feed store was full of activity.

Jess's riding circuit would begin in earnest and how he was going to fit it all in and paint the house was beyond him.

But he'd manage, like always. Oh, yeah. He'd do just fine. Right.

"You don't look so hot." Craig observed as he approached Marc, ready to perform cattle testing in early summer.

Marc grunted, hoping that would thwart Craig's questioning. Wrong.

"You could use a barber, a shave and a bath."

Marc kept his eyes trained ahead as they rounded the barn.

"How's Jess doing?"

"Fine."

"And you?"

"Same."

"Right." Craig set up his testing kit on the off side of the fence. Marc moved to the metal crush he'd put in place. Jerry Broom, a summer hand, stood at the end of the crush, waiting to load the first young steer.

Usually he'd chat with Craig during testing. Sarah was due in six weeks and McKenna was a precocious toddler now.

He tried not to care that Craig was happier than he'd ever seen him. He pushed aside thoughts of how nice it would be to come home to a wife after a long day's work. Someone beside you through thick and thin, curled next to you in bed each and every morning.

He wouldn't think of what he might have had if circumstances had been different.

It wasn't his fault. He felt like a rejected insurance applicant, tossed out of the risk pool by a preexisting condition he didn't cause, didn't want and had no control over.

She'd left nearly five weeks before. He knew because he drove by her apartment on every trip to Potsdam. The For Rent sign stabbed his heart the first time he saw it. The second time, too.

His gut twisted, remembering.

Almost heaven, Virginia. Wasn't that the phrase in some old song? West Virginia, Marc corrected himself, recalling the ad campaign Virginia launched on Sports Center. Sprawling paddocks, gracious plantations, happy couples strolling hand-in-hand in front of restored village homes.

The North Country had a beauty all its own, not designed for the faint of heart. Sure it got cold, but that's what coats were for, right? Boots. Scarves. Hoods.

Unless you were too foolish to wear proper footwear. Then of course you'd get uncomfortable. It all came down to choices, good and bad.

Craig finished drawing blood and turned Marc's way. "I don't know what you're thinking about, but you're scary. Should I run?"

"Shut up."

"I could, I suppose." Craig stowed the labeled vials into their proper slots. "I could pretend that my best friend wasn't going through a rough time, but I've been doing that for a while and don't see any improvement. Want to talk?"

Marc tightened his jaw. His left eye twitched. "Talking won't bring Dad back. Talking doesn't get the farm work done, or the house painted, or get Jess where she needs to be each night, or the feed store up and running every single morning."

"And it doesn't bring Kayla back."

"That's got nothing to do with anything."

Craig packed his kit into an insulated bag. "Sarah heard from her last week."

Marc wanted to ask how she was doing. Was the trip down okay? Was she safe, was she sound?

He stayed silent, his eyes trained on the distant woods.

"She said it's funny, but she misses the north. Said Virginia's beautiful, but she feels out of place. Like she doesn't belong."

"She belongs wherever she wants to be. She's beautiful and smart, a trained professional. She can make a go of it anywhere."

Craig flicked Marc a look. "Still, she says she misses everything she left up here."

A tiny spark leaped in Marc's chest, then ebbed.

Her missing the North Country meant little when they were still the same two people with the same issues. Marc turned Craig's way. "Jess misses her."

"Kayla's a special lady," Craig noted.

"With baggage."

"Everyone's got baggage. Checked the mirror lately?"

"I deal with my past each and every day. I have to. There's Jess to consider."

"So you've forgiven your mother? You understand she made a foolish choice and compounded it?"

Marc grabbed Craig's sleeve. "Kayla told you that Dad wasn't Jess's father? She broke the rules of confidentiality?"

Craig's expression told him he was way off base. "I don't know what you're talking about. I meant your mother left a wonderful family because she didn't like the compromises she had to make. What do you mean about Jess's father?"

Marc groaned. Why didn't he learn to shut his stupid mouth? Why couldn't he—

"Forget I said anything." Marc scrubbed a hand across his face. "It's complicated."

"I guess."

"Don't mention this, please. Not even to Sarah."

"You have my word. But Kayla knows?"

"Yes."

"Does Jess know?"

"She overheard me yelling at Kayla about it."

Craig frowned. "You really need to stop doing that, man. Get a clue."

Marc twisted his face in regret. "She's gone. Not much to worry about there."

"The road travels both ways."

Marc scowled.

Craig stepped closer. "She wants a man of faith, someone to love her, to worship with her. Someone to stand by her side through thick and thin. Kayla's never had that privilege."

Marc mentally replayed her history. "True."

"Then get your sorry backside into church, beg God's forgiveness and see if you can't change the direction your life's taken."

"Quick turnaround?"

Craig shook his head. "Maybe not so quick, but you've got nothing to lose. You and I did youth group together, back in the day."

A smile tugged Marc's right cheek. "Truthfully, I was more interested in Mary Sue Thompson than the Bible."

Craig grinned. "You were fourteen. Mary Sue was a sight for sore eyes, wasn't she?"

"And then some." Marc scrubbed a hand across his neck again. "I can't deny I've spent time praying these last months, taking Jess to church and all. I hear the words, but they don't touch me."

"Kind of rough with that cement wall you've erected."

"I've got a lot on my plate."

"All the more reason to share." Craig jerked his head west. "Come to Trinity with Sarah and me. Maybe it's not the words but the location. The delivery. Maybe you need something new."

The offer was tempting, but unrealistic. A change of venue couldn't lighten his burden.

Still…

Jess could use some different exposure. Hadn't he been saying that for months? Maybe driving to Grasse Bend for church would be a good start.

"What time is the service?"

"Ten. We can meet you there."

Marc stared at the summer sky, considering.

Craig waited, silent.

"Okay. Sunday, it is." He reached out a hand to shake Craig's. "Don't expect miracles."

Craig grinned. "I not only expect them, I see them. Every day."

Marc considered Craig's position. A devoted wife, a beautiful daughter, a second child on the way. "I guess you do."

"Sunday." Craig reiterated as he climbed into his SUV. "And take a bath, would ya?"

Marc grinned and realized something.

It felt good to smile. To relax with a friend. He angled his chin and ran a thoughtful hand over his scruffy face. "I might even shave."

Craig laughed. "God won't care one way or the other, but the rest of the congregation might appreciate it. At least when Kayla was around, you smelled half human."

You smell good, she'd told him. *Like winter nights and sweet hay.* His chest tightened at the memory.

He missed her so much he hurt inside. He had trouble separating his losses. His father. Kayla. The look in Jess's eyes that told him she couldn't forget the revelation she'd heard on a cold, dreary night.

So much, grouped together. He breathed deep and backed away from Craig's car. "I'll see you Sunday morning."

As Craig pulled away, Marc strode toward the house. He needed to check Jess's schedule. If she and Rooster made it to the finals, those would be Sunday afternoon.

And church Sunday morning?

He tried not to think of what needed to be done, the work waiting for him at every turn. A swan's call pulled his attention.

The graceful birds swam, necks arched, ever-calm. Well, except if something threatened their nest. Same with the geese. They knew, intrinsically, that things would work out. Day would follow day.

He swung back, toward the house, and saw it, really saw it.

The old place looked bleak. Unloved. None of the subtle touches that made a house a home were evidenced outside.

Where the pond lay lush with peaceful life, the house reflected Marc's inner turmoil. Peeling paint peppered the sun-scarred surface. The shutters still sat in the basement from two years back when he'd intended to get the whole thing scraped, primed and painted.

Then his dad's illness flared and everything went on hold. Suddenly there was one set of hands where there had been two. Priorities insisted that farm work take precedence, but at what cost to their home?

Eyeing it, he tried to see the house through Kayla's eyes.

She'd always seemed comfortable there. She liked the warmth of the wood stove, the luster of the old oak moldings, but the exterior stood stark and spare. It looked sad. Uncared for.

He and the house had a lot in common.

Chapter Twenty-One

Marc straightened his tie for the tenth time as he and Jess approached the white clapboard church.

At the moment, he had no idea what he hoped to gain. He'd tried to listen to their heartfelt minister the past few months. He'd made an effort to be a good brother, a churchgoing man, for Jess's sake. He'd sat and stood shoulder to shoulder with a roomful of Christians, and felt nothing.

Maybe nothing was better than downright hypocritical like he'd been six months ago. Who would have thought of "nothing" as a step up?

Pathetic, DeHollander.

That was him, all right.

"Marc."

Marc swung around. Sarah gave him a big hug. Her rounded belly made it awkward. He set her back and laughed. "You've blossomed."

"Oh, yes." Sarah's quiet, deep tones were half joy, half lament. "I'm a whale."

"You're beautiful," Jess proclaimed. She hugged Sarah, then looked around. "Where's Craig?"

"Behind you." Sarah motioned to the garden surrounding the church's gazebo. "McKenna likes to 'mell da fowers.'"

"That's so sweet!" Jess laughed. "I love baby talk."

Marc felt the familiar clench, half loss, half envy. "She loves flowers, huh?"

"She does." Sarah confirmed. "Kayla walked her in the flowers from the time she was a newborn. She'd show McKenna the different leaves, the colors. McKenna sucked it up like a sponge."

Kayla. Babies. Gardens. Marc swallowed a lump of self-pity the size of a small town.

It was easy to picture her among the blooms. Her eyes so blue, her cheeks fair. The narrow jaw, the quick smile. *My dream home,* she'd said, eyeing the picture of a small, thatched cottage.

It wasn't the house she envisioned. He realized that now.

It was the tranquil setting, surrounded by faith, adorned with flowers, flooded with light.

Something tweaked inside him. Something warm and flowing.

Church bells pealed their call to worship. This time Marc went willingly.

"The wise woman builds her house, but with her own hands the foolish one tears hers down."

The pastor regarded the congregation. "Proverbs is filled with abbreviated wisdoms. Ben Franklin used Proverbs as a basis for his early work."

Marc's heart quickened. He stared at the graying man.

"God grants us choices. We choose what food to eat, what deodorant to use, the toothpaste we apply to our brush.

"We choose whom to see and what to do. Where to dine, what to say.

"Free will allows us more than mundane choices," the pastor continued. He paused, contemplative, his gaze gentle. "Free will allows us to accept God's word or reject Him. To embrace His ways, or disparage them. To come to the altar, or sit in our seats, hating those who wronged us."

His words seared Marc's soul.

Was it that easy? Was it all about choices, his choices? Not those of the parents, but those of the son?

McKenna reached for Marc. She flashed him a dimpled grin

as he gathered her in. He held her, her softness warm against his chest, his cheek.

He wanted the peace he saw in Craig and Sarah. He wanted Jess's simple conviction, the faith of a child. He began to understand Kayla's withdrawal from a man who bore no belief system.

A candle flickered, its flame bright, inviting.

He wanted to be a better man than he'd been. Could he do it?

He wasn't a man accustomed to failure. How much stronger could he be with faith to uphold him?

Come unto me, all who are burdened...

Could it be that easy? Could he lay down his burdens to God, to Christ Jesus?

A glow flickered within him.

Come unto me, all who are burdened...

Light flooded his soul. It started from the edges and worked its way inward, teasing and bright.

McKenna burbled in his arms, her baby voice bright and funny. "Wuv ooo, Unca Marc."

His heart filled. He put his lips to her forehead, while a goofy grin spread across his face. "I love you, too. Shh..." He laid a finger to his mouth. "We've got to be good," he whispered. "We're in church."

The toddler nodded sagely. "I be good."

Jess fought a giggle. The baby's antics were pure, a source of light.

I see miracles every day, Craig had declared.

Marc wanted to recognize them. He wanted the assurance of his father, the faith of a child.

I'm yours, God. Give it your best shot. I'm stupid and stubborn, but I'm good with cattle.

His prayer might seem lame, but God understood cattlemen. Wasn't he the original sower, the first farmer of all? God knew a farmer's heart. He created a farmer's soul. He'd understand the intent behind the words.

"Hey, Jess, can you load the dishwasher before we head out?"

"Sure. We have to leave in an hour, okay?"

"I'll be ready."

She'd made it into the finals the previous day. Luckily, this show was close enough to avoid an overnight stay. Heading toward the barn, Marc added, "I'll talk to Jerry, make sure he knows what needs to be done."

After locating the hand, Marc headed back to the house, whistling.

He felt rejuvenated. Like he'd finally made a step toward the future meant for him.

In a house that looked bedraggled.

Marc frowned. He scrubbed a hand across his jaw and furrowed his brow deeper.

Time to paint escaped him, no matter how hard he tried to fit it in. Painting a big, old farmhouse was no easy task. Nothing to be undertaken lightly. The prep work alone was monumental. Scraping. Stripping. Caulking. Bleaching the two shaded sides that leaned toward mold.

But it was past time to prioritize the work. Marc tightened his jaw, considering.

He recalled the picture in Kayla's living room. He drew a deep breath and angled his look.

The picture had been a garden print with light pouring from the front window, bathing flowers below. Her dream home, she said.

Marc narrowed his gaze, eyeing the walk, the grass, already scruffy from heat and sun.

An idea took shape in an ill-used corner of his brain. A ghost of an idea, a hint of what could be with a little time, a little care, some cold, hard cash and a bottle of Roundup.

"Hey, Marc? You want to wait until tomorrow to cull the herd since you'll be gone today?" Jerry approached him from the far side of the barn.

"Yes."

Jerry turned. Marc stopped his progress with a question. "Jer, is your brother still looking for work?"

"Yup. He's got a spot at the market, but he's looking for extra jobs. College tuition's a killer."

Marc understood that. His father had worked hard to pay his

way. He wondered now if he appreciated the sacrifices Pete made without a word of regret. Probably not. "Tell him to come around. I need to get the house painted and I'm running out of time. I'd like to get started on it ASAP."

"I'll call him right now." Jerry grabbed his cell phone. "He's good at that kind of stuff, too. Almost girly, he's so fussy."

"I won't mention you said that."

Jerry shrugged. "Nothin' I don't tell him every day. I'll get those young ones moved back up the hill."

"Thanks, Jer."

Fresh paint. Hung shutters. Maybe a new porch light, one that bathed the front of the house at night. The kind that welcomed someone home after a long day at work. A light that beckoned.

And a garden. It was late to start a garden, but he had a hose. He could water things through the heat of summer. Lay down a thick bed of mulch. Come fall, the new plants would welcome the cooler days with strong root growth.

By next spring, this sweep of land could be lush.

Jess would help. She loved to get dirty. She'd help him pick plants that meshed shades of green with a host of color.

And those wavy grass things. There were lots of those in Kayla's picture. He had no clue what they were, but he'd find them, one way or another.

He approached the steps, wrestling misgiving.

It could be for nothing. He knew that. He understood she hadn't left a scarred-up house and a scrabbled yard. She'd left him, because he wasn't what she needed.

Could he be?

He didn't have that answer yet. But he knew one thing. A farm wasn't built in a day. It took years of painstaking planning, stage-by-stage growth, a focus on tomorrow.

Why hadn't he realized that life and love required that much time and respect?

Step by step. If nothing else, he'd have a farmhouse that looked good and a yard that said "welcome." And maybe, just maybe, another chance at the gold ring he'd missed so completely that winter.

Chapter Twenty-Two

Kayla waited for Sarah to pick up the phone, her toe tapping impatiently against the ceramic tile.

Didn't happen. The Macklins' answering machine greeted her in Sarah's soothing tones.

Kayla headed outside, disgruntled. She strode into town, her soft-soled shoes no distraction in the Sunday afternoon quiet.

She didn't want to spend another Sunday doing nothing. She wanted to visit friends, play with babies, romp through gardens.

She'd loved taking McKenna through the flowers. The baby's eyes widened at the sight and scent of fragrant blooms. Kayla saw the wonders of the universe reflected in that childlike innocence.

She missed Sarah and Craig. She missed the baby. She missed her job in the North Country, the comfortable routine, the established trust relationships she'd earned.

She refused to dwell on Marc and Jess. Some chapters were meant to close. That didn't keep her from missing the give-and-take at the diner when she'd grab her coffee. Or the tête-à-têtes with the nursing staff, the daily commiseration.

Why hadn't she realized how different it would be to start anew?

Beautiful Virginia, green and majestic, the hills awesome in verdant splendor.

But it wasn't home. Not hers, anyway.

That thought halted her progress. When had the North Country become home? Her plan had always been to leave at the end of her contract. When had her feelings turned around?

Marc's face sprang to mind, the touch of field-roughened hands against her cheek, her jaw. Hands that tussled full-grown cattle grew tender around her.

She wondered how Jess was faring, but didn't call. That would reopen a door best left closed, despite her affection for the teen. Jess didn't need an occasional friend. She needed someone willing to go the distance.

A soft gust shifted Kayla's hair as she surveyed the small town nestled in the mountain's crook. She turned into the breeze, basking in the cooler air.

She knew why she had to leave Potsdam. Avoiding Marc had been next to impossible those last weeks, but she'd done what she needed to do.

Marc DeHollander knew more about her than any other person on the planet. She didn't like that, but accepted it. At least he'd come to understand what had been clear to her. Two people harboring their problems should never consider happily ever after. Life wasn't a Disney presentation, and she had no interest in becoming a statistic in the column of broken homes. She'd do it once, she'd do it right, no qualifiers allowed.

Kayla sighed, dejected. The hills rose in pictorial splendor, green and lush, their shadows cooling the streets of the quaint town.

She didn't care for that. She liked hills well enough, but she liked sunshine more. Even in the dead of winter, the sun was a regular visitor to St. Lawrence County, its rays bright and slanted.

Cold, Kayla, she reminded herself. *Bitter cold, windswept tundra-land. Have you forgotten?*

She scrunched her face, then relaxed her jaw.

She hadn't forgotten. She just hadn't minded the cold as much this past winter. Caring for Pete, letting the warmth of the DeHollander house seep into her bones...

Nope, the winter hadn't seemed all that bad.

* * *

"Looks good, Mike." Appreciation tinged Marc's voice as he surveyed the paint job. "Real good."

Mike Broom grinned from the scaffold. "What color did you pick for the shutters?"

"Dark green," Marc answered. He looked to Jess for confirmation.

"I should have them done by the weekend," Jess replied. She turned to Marc, her eyes bright. "And the new front door looks great. I love the side windows."

"Sidelights."

"Oh." Jess grinned. Her expression sized him up. "Sidelights, huh?"

Marc headed inside. He had no intention of explaining himself. It was time to spend a little money on this old place, give the worn surfaces a more inviting look.

What did it matter that the new door and its flanking windows resembled the cottage in Kayla's print? Pure coincidence.

Part of Pete's insurance money was invested to ensure Jess's future. College didn't come cheap, and Marc had every intention of making sure Jess could concentrate on her studies. Paying the shot out of Dad's insurance fund would help.

But there was enough to help upgrade the house, maybe redo the kitchen and spiff up the floors.

Winter stuff, Marc decided. He refused to dangle hope that he might have a vocal second opinion as to what should be done. Women were particular about their kitchens, and he wanted this to be just right.

If the woman was interested.

He poured coffee despite the heat and surveyed the entry from the kitchen. The look fit his vision of fresh paint, evergreen shutters and the sweep of a garden he had yet to create.

He'd treated the grass to kill the roots, but he wouldn't be able to till the soil until Mike finished the front of the house. He felt pushed to hurry, but held himself in check.

Barely.

Jess came through the front and headed for the living room.

Marc poked his head in. "I've got some work to do upstairs. Can you make sandwiches?"

"Work? Upstairs?"

"On the computer."

"Sure. Tuna good?"

"Fine."

Once upstairs, he stared at the computer, thoughts jumbled.

Maybe he should handwrite his letter to Kayla. Or call her. Would she pick up the phone, seeing his number? Maybe. Maybe not.

Stop shilly-shallying and just do it, moron.

Marc sank into the chair, worrying he'd say too much, too fast.

Or too little and she'd brush him off.

Should he pour out his heart, lay it all on the line, or just tell her of his growing faith and let her fill in the blanks?

"Marc? Sandwiches are ready."

So soon? Marc stared at the computer screen, its blank image a taunt. He sighed and backed away.

He hated writing. Always had. Hadn't he picked some of his university courses because they didn't have much written content?

Pretty much. And there was too much riding on this letter to mess it up.

He gave a reluctant last look to the computer screen, his Hereford desktop picture a reminder of farm life.

Would she be happy here? Could she be happy here? The fear of a solid "no" pushed him toward the stairs, unsure what to say. What to do.

He was better. Stronger. Definitely more faithful than the jerk who met her at the door seven months ago.

But not strong enough to handle the possibility of rejection. Not yet.

"You sound lonely, Kayla."

Kayla fought the emotion Sarah's words evoked. "A little. Things are different here."

"Sure they are," Sarah agreed. "And you don't have friends like you did up here. Are you sure this is what you really want?"

Kayla swallowed hard. "What other choice is there? I loved what I was doing in Potsdam, and how everything progressed, but after last winter…" She paused and tried not to envision what she left. The offer from a man of honor but no faith. "I couldn't stay."

"I understand." Sarah's voice had its usual calming effect. Kayla felt cared for when she talked to her friend. Loved. "And of course, change begets change."

Kayla paused, hearing a hidden message. "Such as?"

"The domino theory. Ripple effect. Remove one cog from the wheel and others bear the strain."

"Quit the riddles and tell me what's going on."

Sarah laughed. "Marc and Jess are coming to church with us. He answered the altar call last week."

"Really?" Warmth spread through Kayla. "Oh, Sarah, I'm so glad."

"Us, too. He went through a tough time, but I think he's crested the hill."

"Good." Relief swept Kayla. "It's not good to hold that bitterness in check so long."

"Words of wisdom, my friend."

Kayla bit her lip. "I don't cling to old things, Sarah. It's just not possible to really forget them. They creep up, unexpectedly."

"Give them to God, Kayla. What's done is done and He's opened a future for you. Don't blow it off because you think you're undeserving."

Kayla's heart crunched.

That was exactly how she saw herself. Despite all she'd done to make herself whole, she was still the little girl who listened to her mother's screams and did nothing. "I've got to go, Sarah."

"We love you, Kayla. We miss you. Hang on a minute, would you? McKenna wants to talk."

"Wuv oo, Kawa."

Kayla's throat constricted. "I love you, too, baby girl. I'll come see you soon, okay?"

"'Kay. Wuv oo."

Kayla hung up and stared at the wall.

She was a centrifuge, spinning her way through life, not stopping long enough to let the contents sort themselves.

Why was that? Why was she more concerned with where she was going than where she'd been?

Marc had made a serious step toward peace. She was happy for him. Happy for Jess.

But he hadn't called. That omission said she didn't make the short list. Why should that surprise her?

She sucked in a knowing breath. She'd dumped her life in his lap that cold April evening. Knowing what he did, no wonder he chose to avoid her. Despite his newfound peace, Marc was still a man whose emotional mother left after bearing someone else's child. Women with issues weren't high on his priority list.

Still, she was happy for him. She'd prayed for his peace, his salvation. She would focus on the joy of that and not on how much she missed the man. She turned and walked back to the waiting basket of laundry.

That's it?

Kayla dropped the cotton T-shirt.

You dip your chin and fold some clothes? Haven't I taught you better than that?

The nudge of conscience made Kayla look around. With a sigh, she reached into the basket of pastels once more.

What more do you want from him?

Once again Kayla's hands quieted.

He's embracing his faith, caring for his sister, working two jobs and living life to the full. What are you waiting for?

His call, she realized. A letter. A message. Something that said he cared despite what he knew.

What he knows? The voice within flooded Kayla with knowledge. *He knows a young girl forged a life of worth after many false starts. He knows you're willing to meet him on even ground, regardless. He knows you've blessed the poor and the lame, the sick and dying. What more do you think he wants, my child?*

That answer was simple. Marc wanted someone normal, someone who didn't weigh him down.

Define "normal."

That nudge inspired a grin. Normal *was* pretty subjective these days.

"See! The winter is past; the rains are over and gone. Flowers appear on the earth; the season of singing has come..."

The verse from Songs brought heat to her cheeks. She pressed cool palms against her face, remembering the chapter, its song of ardent love.

"...Arise, come, my darling; my beautiful one, come with me."

No way. It would be foolish to head back north. Hadn't she promised herself a respite from winter? A haven from hurt, promises that couldn't be kept. Marc DeHollander couldn't possibly want her as his life mate, his helpmate.

Could he?

A little tough to answer that one from here. You sent him packing pretty firm, remember?

Oh, she remembered. She'd told him to have a nice life and shut the door in his face.

Heat suffused her. She'd hurt him, but he'd stepped back, as well. Hadn't he?

She knew where Marc was, where he always would be. He was a North Country man. Strong. Vibrant. Sturdy. A man among men, solid and sure.

And now a man of faith.

Kayla contemplated her choices. She hated rejection. Feared it more. But the words of Scripture offered hope.

What could she possibly lose that she hadn't lost already?

Not a thing.

What could she gain?

Acceptance. Love. A chance for the home and family she longed for, the chance to do it right. Hands trembling, she picked up the phone and set new wheels in motion.

Chapter Twenty-Three

Marc shifted his gaze to the large pond.

Three swans rippled the surface, the arc of their necks majestic. Pigeons roosted on the boathouse, enjoying an afternoon siesta. Ducks foraged, flapping their wings to gain advantage.

The outline of the new garden lay evident along the walk. He'd swept the curve of the garden up and away, keeping the line unstructured and free. He and Jess had purchased plants suitable for part sun, part shade. Some small bushes, some perennials, and a bunch of that grassy stuff.

At least, that's what the nursery lady said. They'd grabbed breakfast at Hosler's and drove the truck full of potted wonders home at gentle speeds. Now the pots stood under the tree to avoid the crush of summer sun. He'd ordered mulch to top dress the site, and slow-release fertilizer spikes for the evergreens.

A fool's dream, he told himself as he set pots around. His big hands were cumbersome clutching the small, plastic vessels. The silly things kept tipping, messing with his visual.

Jess would have helped, but she was working at Nan's, preparing for a regional show, late summer.

He refused to interrupt her focus. He'd noticed an equestrian coach from St. Lawrence University at their last contest. That had been a firm heads-up. The possibility of an equestrian career for Jess wouldn't surprise him. And scholarship money was never a bad thing. With her grades and proficiency, collegiate equestrian programs would vie for her.

He refused to think of how alone he'd be with her gone. The house had seemed quiet after Pete's death. How much more would it be with Jess away?

The house doesn't have to be quiet, an inner voice chastised. *Just go call the girl. Write the letter you've been whining about. Do something!*

He was doing something. He was working night and day, running both businesses, making significant improvements on the house, taking care of Jess the best way he knew how and sleeping here and there.

And he liked himself, finally. He liked the person he was becoming. The man who didn't try to handle it alone, unafraid to lean. He felt richer, and the feeling had nothing to do with a bank account.

Call her. Go to her. You could fly there and back in a day, have your say and see what happens. Get a move on, Farmer Boy.

The crunch of wheels against stone sounded behind him.

Pensive, he didn't look up. The feed store was staffed and he had a garden to plant.

He eyed the rich soil, assessing. Laying a flower garden was nothing like planting vegetables with their straight rows. This was...

Disordered. If he worked his way in, he'd kneel on baby plants. If he went the opposite way, he'd compact the soil. Sitting back, he surveyed the path of least destruction and frowned.

"Need help, Farmer Boy?"

His heart leaped. A smile stuck square in his throat. He swallowed hard. "It appears I do."

Light footsteps sounded along the drive. She squatted next to him, her gaze forward, smelling of flowers and spice, of yesterday and tomorrow. He breathed deep, her scent spinning him back to a winter of growth, death and hope. He waved a hand and tried to hide the slight tremble of his fingers. "I'm kind of big to carry this off without crushing things."

"I see that. Whereas I'm lighter."

He swallowed again and nodded. "You are."

"And my hands are smaller. See?"

Oh, he saw. Long, slim fingers tipped with bright pink polish. "You might chip a nail."

"We're in a new millennium, Farmer Boy. They're replaceable. In fact there's a great nail place in Malone, this side of the Market Barn."

"Yeah?" He turned now.

She was so beautiful. So perfectly wonderful. Her eyes searched his, her head angled as she tried to read his face, his expression. He cleared his throat, searching for his voice. "How about if I offer to pay for damage incurred by my soil?"

She considered that, then nodded. "Deal."

He eyed her outfit. "You're not going to plant in that, are you?"

She stood and brushed off her knees. "Jess will have some overalls I can wear, right?"

"Right."

He stood, as well, facing her. "You're back."

She nodded again.

He wanted to touch her. It was all he could do to hold himself back, keep his hands at his sides. "To visit?"

"To stay."

His heart soared, but he couldn't take credit for her decision. He hadn't called, hadn't written, hadn't taken the slightest step forward. "Why?"

Marc wasn't sure he wanted to know the answer to that question, but knew he had to ask.

Kayla eyed the improvements to the house. She noted the scaffolding alongside the barn. Mike stood atop the piped supports, busily working for more college money now that the house was complete. She shrugged. "I missed the North Country."

"Yeah?" He stepped closer. He hoped his proximity was having the same effect on her that hers was having on him. "Just the North Country?"

She edged back. "And my friends." She turned slightly. When she did, one strap of her tank top slipped, leaving her throat delightfully bare. She shoved it into place and looked beyond him. In an unusually perceptive moment, Marc realized she was nervous.

He put a gentle hand to her shoulder. "Come inside."

She glanced up, then away, as if weighing choices, then let out a breath. "Okay."

He took her hand once they crossed the new threshold and led her up the stairs. He drew her into the back bedroom that doubled as his office area. The computer's blinking light winked green.

She turned, puzzled.

Marc leaned over the desk and drew up a Word document. "There."

She leaned down. A smile curved her lips as she surveyed the long column of half-finished letters. She turned and met his eye, her gaze teasing. "Writing isn't exactly your forte?"

"No. Which is why they're still sitting in my computer." He reached out a hand and drew her away from the humming PC. "I'm better in person."

Those words made her draw a breath. Or maybe it was the look he gave her, the one that said he'd missed her. He loved her.

"I wanted the house to be right."

She did the face crunch he remembered so well. "It's beautiful, Marc. It always was. You guys filled it with love and that's what's important."

He nodded and looped his hands around her back. "I agree. But a girl needs a place that welcomes her home. That reaches out to her. A place flooded with light."

She blinked back tears. "You remembered."

"Oh, yeah." He dropped his mouth to hers and gave her a kiss, reveling in the feel of her in his arms. "How could I possibly forget?"

"Marc—"

"Will you marry me, Kayla?"

"What?"

He leaned back and brought her chin up with his thumb, stroking, caressing. "Will you marry me? Be my wife? Live on a crazy North Country farm? Break some nails? Have my babies? Grow old with me?"

She smiled. "You're right. You're way better with words in person."

"Is that a yes?"

She tilted her chin, teasing, contemplating. "It is."

"Really?"

She waved a hand toward the window. "You did get the garden ready."

He nodded.

"And painted the house."

He sighed. He couldn't lie. "I hired it done."

"But signed the check, so it's the same thing," she assured him. "And you put in a beautiful new door."

"With sidelights. And a front porch light."

"Well, then." She stretched up and drew him down. "That seals the deal."

"I love you, Kayla."

The simple declaration overwhelmed her.

He sandwiched her hands between his and dropped to one knee. "I love you, Kayla," he repeated. "Everything about you. Marry me. Please?"

She slid a soft hand across his cheek, his jaw, then tugged him upright. "I will always love you, Marc."

His heart sang, but he gave her a little grin. "Then say yes and get to work. That garden's waiting and we don't have all day."

She laughed and hugged him. He spun her gently, then set her back on the floor. She arched a brow in wonder. "We don't? How come?"

"Because we need to go ring shopping." He grazed his hand along the curve of her cheek, then cupped her chin. "And set a date. Call the pastor. So many things, Kayla." He dropped his mouth to hers once more.

She answered his kiss with one of her own, then pressed her

cheek to his chest. "Then by all means, let's plant. We both know how I love to shop."

Marc groaned. "So true." He gave her one last kiss before he turned. "But this will be the only time you get to shop for an engagement ring. Make it count."

She preened and grinned. "Oh, I will. Now head downstairs so I can get changed. I've got a garden to tend."

He laughed and moved toward the stairs, his step light, his heart full.

"Marc?"

"Yeah?" He turned, half expecting another teasing jab. The look on her face wasn't teasing. He frowned and took a step back. "What, honey?"

"It's my first garden."

Four little words that said so much. His heart stretched further in his chest. "I know. But it won't be your last."

Her smile made him feel like the greatest man alive. A superhero. All because of a little plot of land, newly turned.

And a leap of faith.

He started fresh coffee and eyed the kitchen. He'd tell her about that later, let her shop and pick whatever she wanted to accomplish that upgrade. For right now he had every intention of getting a ring and a license, the sooner the better.

The midsummer sun angled through the right sidelight. The glass prismed the ray into a rainbow across the faded carpet.

A covenant. The promise of a new tomorrow.

Overhead, gentle thumps meant shoes were hitting the floor as Kayla changed outfits. They might need to add a closet or at least a shoe rack.

Maybe two.

He shrugged and stepped onto the porch. He'd build her a room for shoes, if necessary, but he'd rather design a nursery.

That thought pumped his chest. Kayla swung out the door behind him, her step light and hurried. "Okay, let's get to it. Are you going to help or do you have chores you should be doing?"

He did, as a matter of fact. There was a list of things tacked to the barn wall to keep him and Jerry on their toes.

He dropped a kiss to her forehead and snaked a lazy arm around her shoulders. "Nothing that can't wait until tomorrow. Let's plant some flowers. And grassy things."

"Ornamental grasses," she corrected him. "And I think they'd look best over here, don't you?"

He grinned at the sight of her in the dirt, the first pot of grass gripped in her left hand. "Whatever you want, honey."

She smiled up at him. Her face bore no shadows, no sadness, no reminders of the cold, dark nights of her childhood. She glanced around the farmyard, the maze of buildings, the gray-stoned drive. She tipped her chin to the side and blinked, long and slow. "I want you, Marc. I want you."

* * * * *

Dear Reader,

Like many of you, I'm part of the sandwich generation, caught between aging parents and growing children. For most of us these worlds intersect like a Venn diagram, overlapping and overshadowing from time to time.

A long-term smoker, my Irish mother's lung cancer wasn't a huge surprise at age seventy-eight, but difficult nonetheless. Her ensuing home hospice allowed weeks of family hurting and healing, a time where nine children, countless grandchildren and great-grandchildren, old friends and family stopped by with food, hugs, sympathy and empathy. I hope the beauty of that experience is caught in this book, a story of bad choices and good decisions, of personal responsibility and human frailty. God allows choice and free will. Perfection isn't part of the deal and accepting one another's flaws and failings is just part of being a family.

It is what it is.

I welcome letters and e-mails sharing your thoughts and experiences. Come visit me at www.ruthloganherne.com, e-mail me at loganherne@gmail.com or mail me c/o Steeple Hill Books, 233 Broadway, Suite 1001 New York, NY 10279.

Ruthy

QUESTIONS FOR DISCUSSION

1. A former hospital nurse, Kayla altered her professional life after meeting an indigent woman whose simple faith inspired Kayla's change of heart. Are coincidences something that happen, or does God offer us opportunities when we least expect it?

2. Pete DeHollander's choices aren't all perfect. His cancer is probably evidence of that. Does God forgive our human weaknesses?

3. Marc is caught between old anger and new responsibilities thrust on him by circumstances beyond his control. While the man shoulders the burdens, the boy inside resents the bad choices surrounding him but has no clue how to handle his anger. Is it harder for strong, self-made adults to humble themselves and ask God's help?

4. Marc's animosity makes Kayla's job harder initially, but she doesn't give up or give in to the impulse to smack him like she might have a few years back. How does faith help us to be less impetuous and more understanding?

5. Kayla remembers feeling safe in a church as a young foster child. Do you think those early memories helped firm her later faith options?

6. Arianna recognizes she had choices all along and ignored them. It isn't until she's dying and alone that she identifies all she gave up. Why do we so often wait until we hit rock bottom to change our ways?

7. Jess's simple faith is nurtured by her father's constant presence on the farm and in church. Do you think this faith base helped her find closure after realizing Pete wasn't her biological father?

8. Sarah and Kayla have a deep, abiding friendship. They recognize each other's wounds and share a mutual "survivor" respect. Why do the bonds of friendship sometimes come harder to people who've suffered?

9. Jess's strong faith shames her brother and gives him cause to second-guess his anger and antipathy toward their mother. Eventually Marc realizes that the only choices he's responsible for are the ones he makes for himself. How does this realization help him to forgive his mother's problems and desertion?

10. Kayla's constant battle with cold underscores the emotional development of the story. Her need to conquer keeps her from seeking a warmer, more comfortable setting, as if doing penance will make her stronger. What helps her to realize that punishing herself was never necessary?

11. Marc is taken aback by Kayla's state in the harness room. Her emotional instability reminds him of his mother, and yet he needs to find out what pushed her to that state of mind. When she reveals her story he believes there is no hope for a future with her. They have too many strikes against them. How does time and space help Marc to readjust his strategies?

12. Kayla's departure leaves a void in Marc's life that's revealed in his physical, emotional and mental appearance. When Craig and Jess both point this out to him, Marc gets angry but realizes they're right. He's got nothing to lose by trying something new. A new church, a new chance. How does little McKenna's presence affect his first visit to Craig and Sarah's church?

13. Kayla thinks that the warmer climate of Virginia will help ease the chill in her soul, but it doesn't happen. When she learns Marc has had a change in heart, she's hurt that he

hasn't contacted her. Her conscience prods her to see things through his eyes. How does stepping into someone else's shoes help us to do what Jesus would do, to see things more clearly?

14. Marc's home makeover is analogical to his mental, spiritual, physical and emotional makeover. The physical attributes of his home reflect his overall personal improvements. Don't most of us feel heartened when we make positive choices that thrust us forward?

15. Kayla's return is scary for both Marc and Kayla. He fears she'll reject him and she's afraid she ran him off for good, yet both are willing to finally take that chance. How do faith and time lend us strength to meet life's challenges and take chances?

*When his niece unexpectedly arrives at his
Montana ranch, Jules Parrish has no idea
what to do with her—or with Olivia Rose,
the pretty teacher who brought her.
Will they be able to build a life—
and family—together?*

*Here's a sneak peek of "Montana Rose"
by Cheryl St.John, one of the
touching stories in the new collection,
TO BE A MOTHER,
available April 2010
from Love Inspired Historical.*

Jules Parrish squinted from beneath his hat brim, certain the
waves of heat were playing with his eyes. Two females—one a
woman, the other a child—stood as he approached.

The woman walked toward him. Jules dismounted and
approached her. "What are you doing here?"

The woman stopped several feet away. "Mr. Parrish?"

"Yeah, who are you?"

"I'm Olivia Rose. I was an instructor at the Hedward Girls
Academy." She glanced back over her shoulder at the girl who
watched them. "My young charge is Emily Sadler, the daughter
of Meriel Sadler."

She had his attention now. He hadn't heard his sister's name
in years. *Meriel.*

"The academy was forced to close. I thought Emily should
be with family. You're the only family she has, so I brought her to
you."

He took off his hat and raked his fingers through dark, wavy
hair. "Lady, I spend every waking hour working horses and

cows. I sleep in a one-room cabin. I don't know anything about kids—and especially not girls."

"What do you suggest?"

"I don't know. All I know is, she can't stay here."

Will Olivia be able to change Jules's mind
and find a home for Emily—and herself?

Find out in
TO BE A MOTHER,
the heartwarming anthology from
Cheryl St.John and Ruth Axtell Morren,
available April 2010
only from Love Inspired Historical.

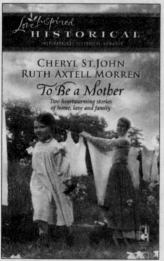

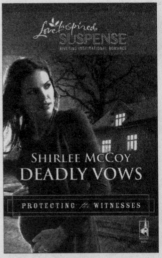

LARGER-PRINT BOOKS!

GET 2 FREE
LARGER-PRINT NOVELS
PLUS 2 FREE
MYSTERY GIFTS

Love Inspired®

Larger-print novels are now available...

LILP10

EMILY
& the INTERGALACTIC
LEMONADE STAND

a story of ponies, robots....
and world domination

writte

illustrati

Published by Amazeink, a division of SLG Publishing
PO Box 26427
San Jose. CA 95159-6427
www.slavelabor.com

SLG President & Publisher: Dan Vado
Editor-In Chief: Jennifer de Guzman
Director of Sales: Deb Moskyok

ISBN 0-943151-96-1

First Printing. June 2004
Printed in China
10 9 8 7 6 5 4 3 2 1

5

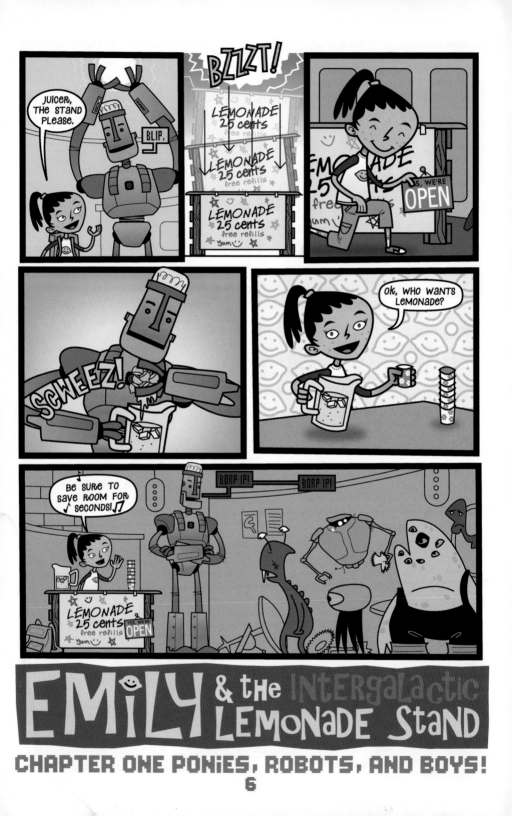

EMILY & the INTERGALACTIC LEMONADE STAND
CHAPTER ONE PONIES, ROBOTS, AND BOYS!

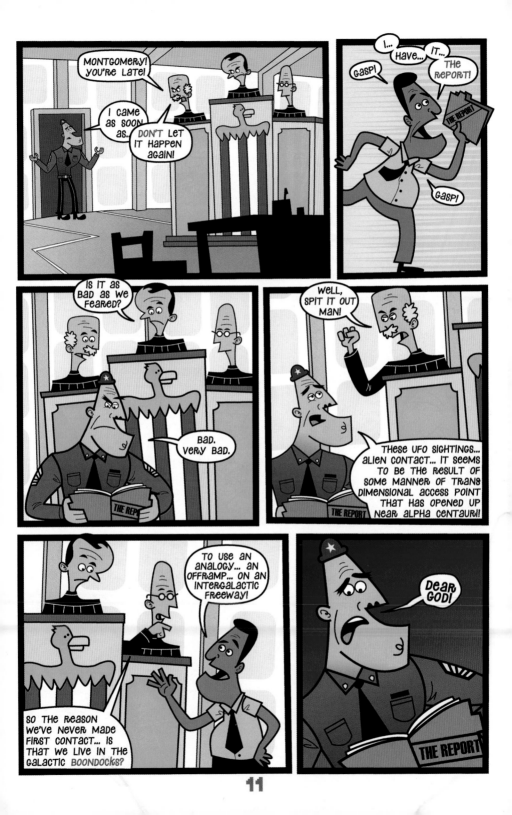

11

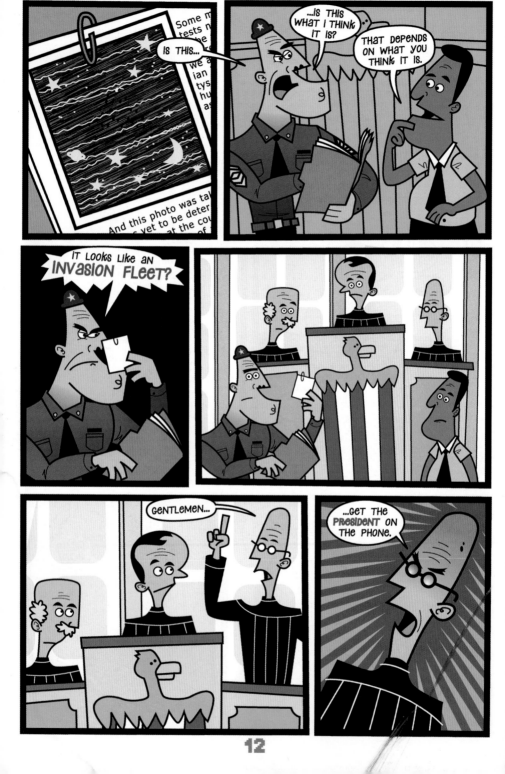

12

13

14

15

16

20

21

22

24 end... chapter one

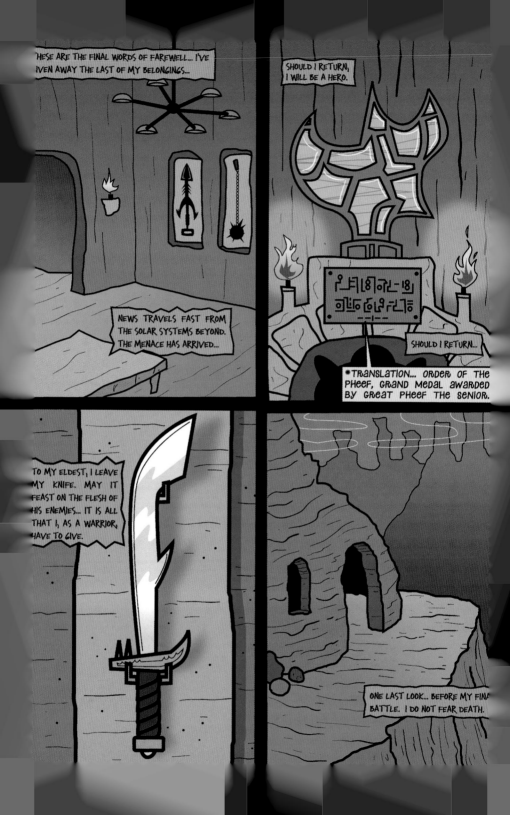

CHAPTER TWO: ENGAGING THE ENEMY

27

29

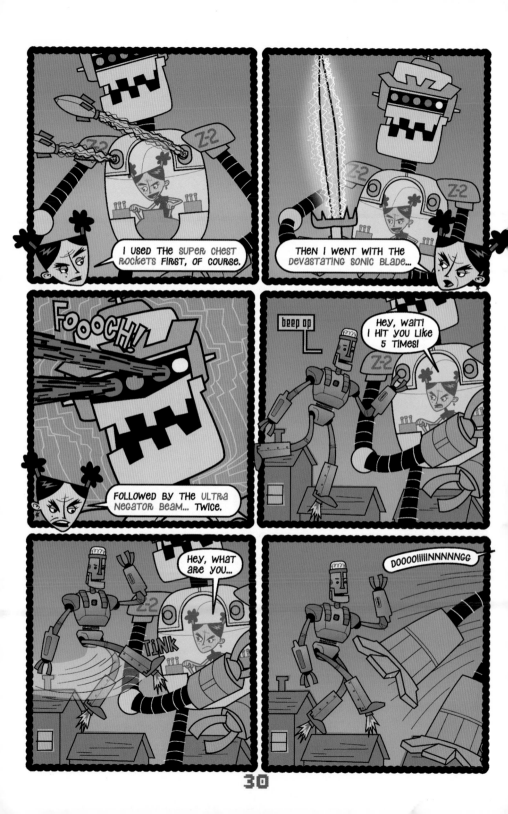

30

31

32

34

35

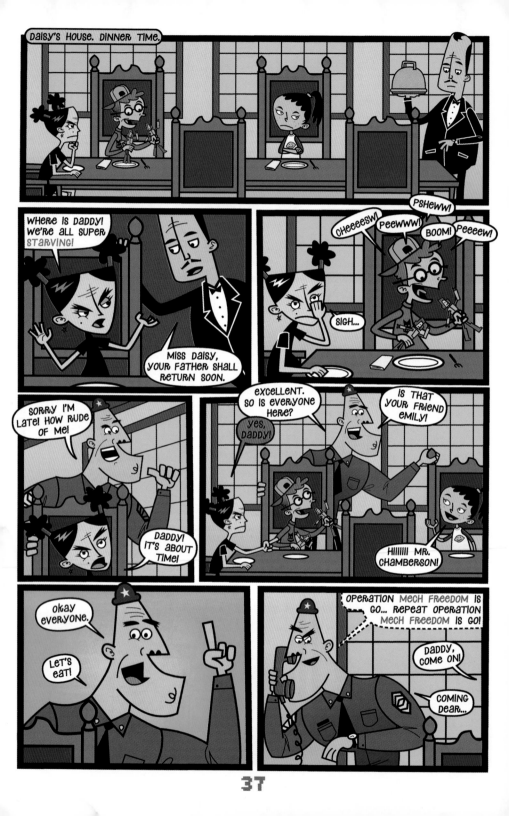

38

42

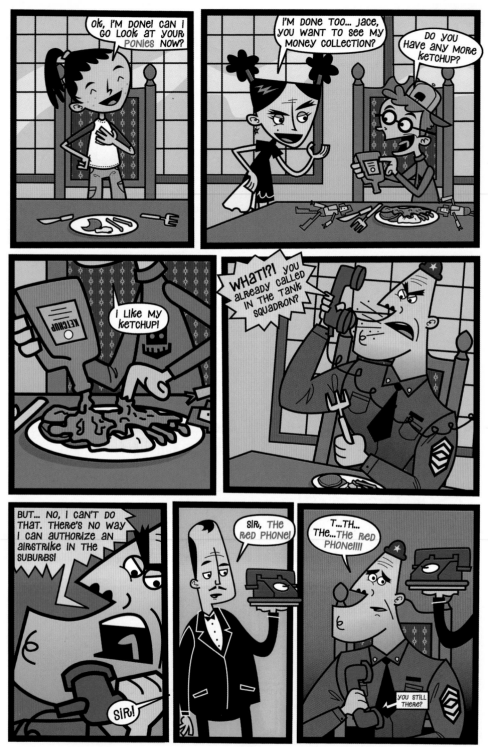

43

44

45

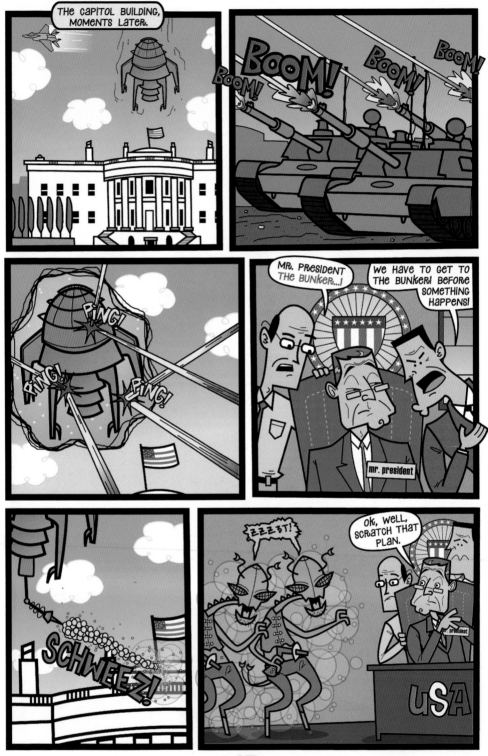

47

48 END CHAPTER TWO...

49

CHAPTER THREE: A WARRIOR'S LAMENT

53

54

58

59

60

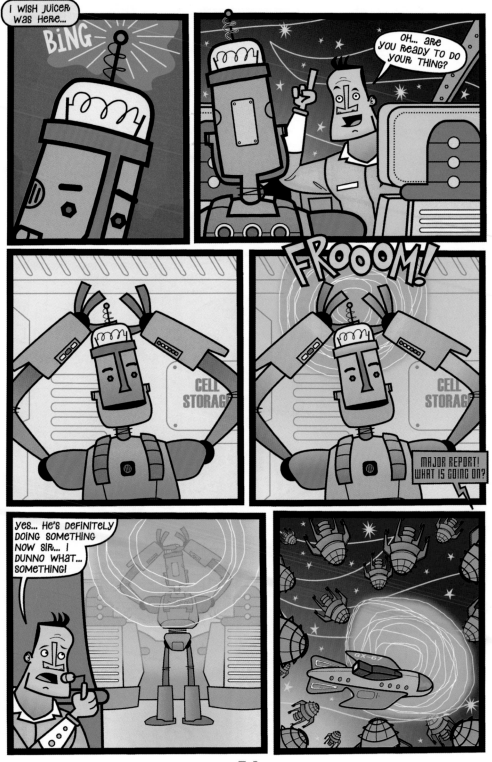

61

62

63

65

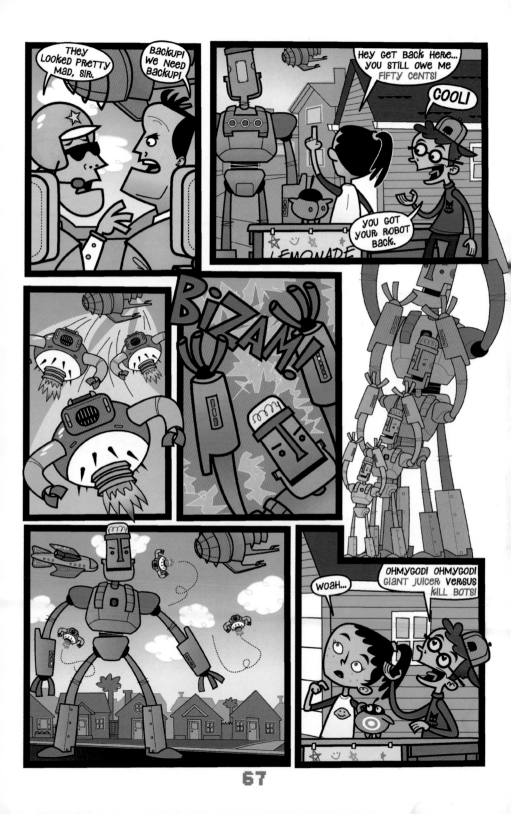

67

68

ZAM!

BEWOOOP!

WOW, THAT WAS THE COOLEST...

JUICER!

PHEEF?

PHEEF!

IT HAS COME DOWN TO THIS. MY WARRIOR'S BLOOD BOILS, AND I CANNOT STAND IDLE!

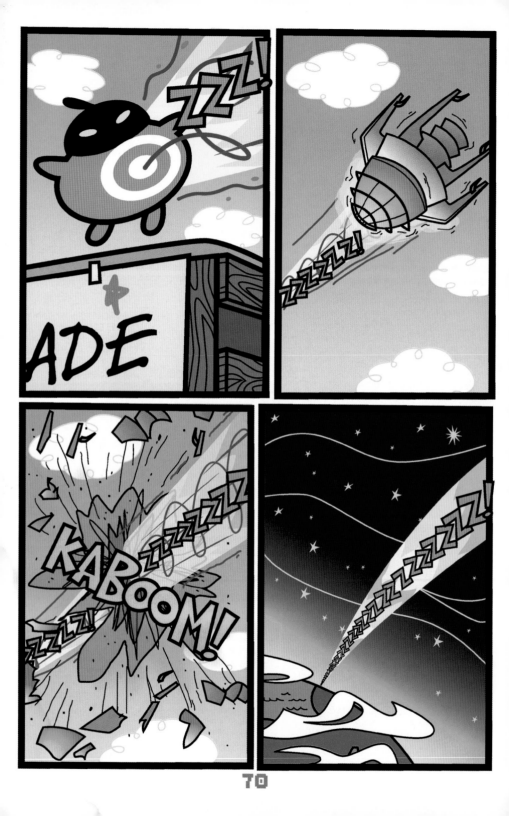

71

72 END CHAPTER THREE...

74

75

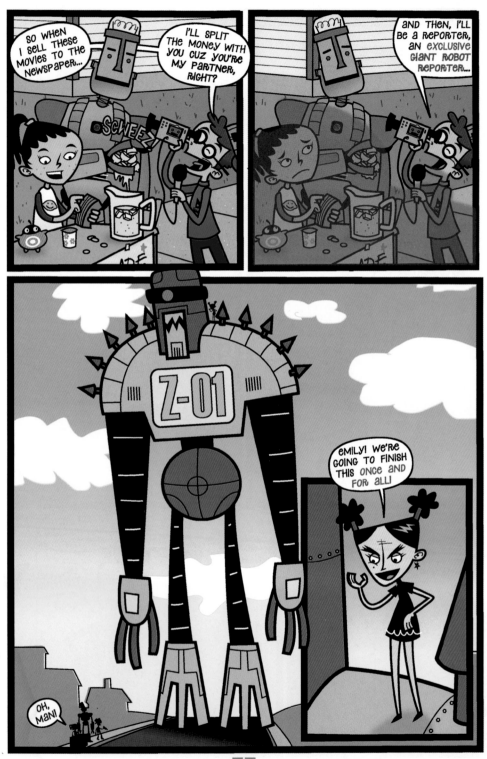

78

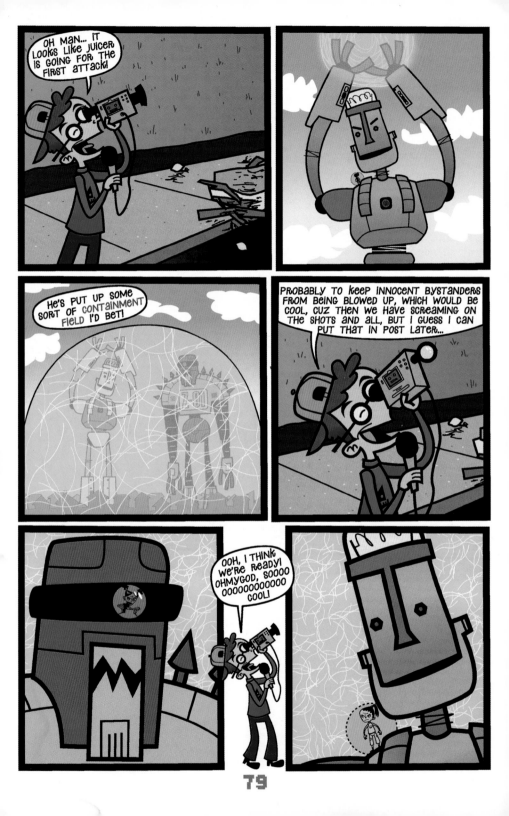

79

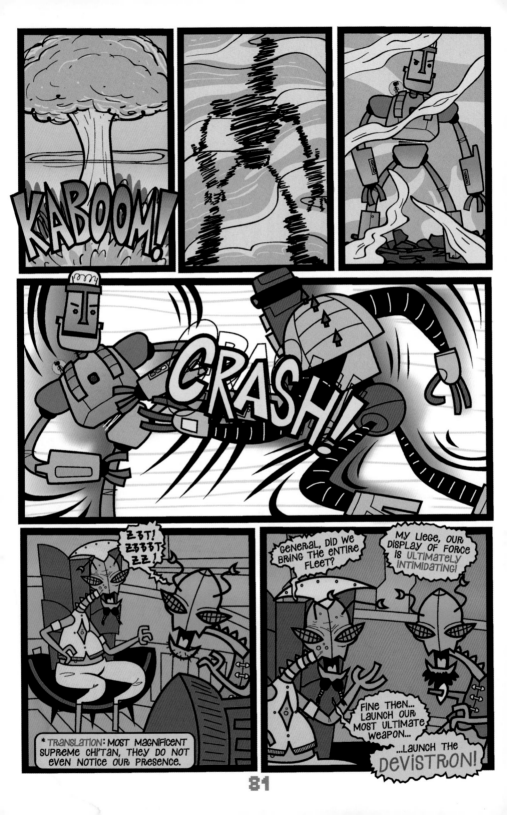

82

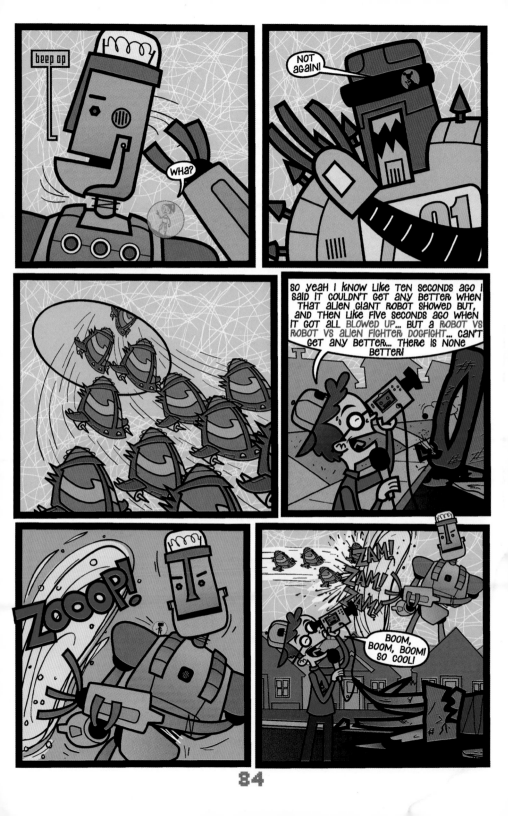

85

87

88

89

90

95   the end...

the end...

ACKNOWLEDGMENTS

The creators would like to thank the kind reader for giving our humble robot/ girl/pheef tale at least a decent thumb-through. We hope you enjoyed it!

Of course, none of this would be possible without the support of Dan, Jennifer, and SLG. There's no cooler, or tougher, publisher around.

Nothing is created in a vacuum. Friends and family are both our inspiration and motivation. I'd list you all, but I know I'd miss someone and then get smacked upside the head. You know who you are!

Thankyou to Eric Kilkenny for this fabulous pin-up! Check out his work at www.erickilkenny.com

onesmithtwosmith

Ian Smith

Writer half of Smith Brothers duo. Notable comic writing began in college with mini-comics, zines, and drummer wanted flyers. Self published The Odd Adventure-Zine for 4 issues, which became the critically acclaimed Oddjob series for SLG publishing. Jumped to moving sequential art upon completing The Sexy Chef, a feature length low budget comedy. Currently resides in Portland OR, sharing a house with like minded artist malcontents, working on new scripts for both comic and film, and recording music with studio band Somerset Meadows.

Tyson Smith

Artist half of Smith Brothers duo. Switched from hand-drawn art in the early Odd Adventure-zines to computer work in OAZ #4, opening a number of eyes. Fine-tuned his computer illustration skills over the run of Oddjob for SLG. Produced and directed The Sexy Chef, and is currently in pre-production for the next film. Currently resides in Portland OR with his wife, and Quimby the dog, and works as a freelance illustrator. A partial list of clients include the Wall Street Journal, New York Daily News, Nike, Utne Magazine, HP, Nickelodeon, Golf Digest, and many other magazines and newspapers.

Related Reading/Viewing/Listening:

*Odd Adventure-zine – Original, self published 4 issue run.
*Oddjob: The Collected Stories – the entire run of 8 issues in one trade from SLG publishing
*The Sexy Chef – Feature film now available on DVD
*Somerset Meadows – now on CD

keep up to date with what the Smith Brothers are working on...

www.onesmithtwosmith.com

DATE DUE			
MAR 2 9 2005			
OCT 3 1 2006			
FEB 1 4 2007			
GAYLORD No. 2333			PRINTED IN U.S.A.